2

'I must find a new position.'

William Stanton didn't seem to be anticipating that. He leaned back into the sofa and crossed one leg over his knee. 'May I ask why?'

Because she was already thinking about kissing him again and finding it hard not to stare at his lips. Because she didn't think she'd ever be able to look at him the same way again.

'Well, I…I should do so, since you'll return Mary to school soon.'

'I've made no plans yet.' He rose and walked close, stopping just a few feet from her, his gaze wandering across her face. 'I've no intention of kissing you again, if that's what you're worried about.'

She took a rallying breath. 'I still think I should find another position.'

'But I quite like you here.'

His voice was soft, seductive, and she finally met his gaze—a mistake, because she became trapped by his hypnotic eyes. Eyes that had gone dark, that travelled down her freckled nose to settle on her lips. He was leaning in— or was she imagining it? She felt her eyelids begin to droop. There'd be little harm in one more kiss if she planned to leave anyway. Just one, and then she'd pack her belongings.

Sarah Elliott grew up in Pennsylvania and studied English at Smith College. She moved to London in 2003 and lives there still. In addition to writing, Sarah enjoys cooking, art, antiques and classic films. She loves to hear from readers and can be contacted at sarah@sarahelliott.net

Previous novels by this author:

REFORMING THE RAKE
THE RAKE'S PROPOSAL

THE EARL AND THE GOVERNESS

Sarah Elliott

First published in Great Britain 2009
Harlequin Mills & Boon Limited,
Eton House, 18-24 Paradise Road, Richmond, Surrey TW9 1SR

© Sarah Lindsey 2009

ISBN: 978 0 263 20983 9

Set in Times Roman
08-0909-78201

Harlequin Mills & Boon policy is to use papers that are natural, renewable and recyclable products and made from wood grown in sustainable forests. The logging and manufacturing process conform to the legal environmental regulations of the country of origin.

Printed and bound in Great Britain
by CPI Antony Rowe, Chippenham, Wiltshire

THE EARL AND
THE GOVERNESS

Chapter One

17 May 1822

*O*uch.

William Stanton frowned and sat up, rubbing his injured head. He'd been sleeping peacefully until his driver had reined the carriage to an abrupt standstill, causing him to hit his head on the brass hook that held the velvet curtains back. He glowered at the front wall of his carriage, in the general direction of his driver's back, but McGrath was already remonstrating loudly with some obstacle in the street.

'Wot th' bloody 'ell you doing?'

Will stuck his head out of the window and craned his neck to see what was blocking their passage. A vegetable-laden cart had apparently pulled out in front of them, and as it swerved to avoid them, it nearly overturned, losing half its load. The rotund greengrocer who'd been driving it was now collecting his belongings with deliberate slowness, picking up each cabbage head and carrot one at a time while smirking at McGrath.

Will sighed and sank back into his seat, regarding the scenery outside his window and wondering how long this would take. He'd been away for four days and was eager to get home. He'd neither planned nor desired to leave London in the first place; the event had been thrust upon him by one Miss Matilda Hume, headmistress of Miss

Hume's School for Girls. His goddaughter, Mary Weston-Burke, was a student there. She'd become his ward three months ago, when her father died—meaning, apparently, that whenever she decided to put a newt in her French tutor's teacup it was now Will's responsibility to sort things out.

Frankly, he thought Miss Hume had made rather too much of what seemed to be nothing more than a childish prank. There was, he'd pointed out during their meeting, no actual tea in the cup, and therefore the newt had not been in peril. Miss Hume was more concerned about Monsieur Lavelle, who'd nearly suffered *une crise cardiaque*.

He hoped he'd managed to smooth things over. Apparently young Mary was a bit of a hellion, although he'd not have known it from the sallow, quiet creature he'd treated to tea.

McGrath had chosen a direct, but not picturesque, route through east London. Shabby buildings, many with boarded-up windows, lined the pockmarked road, and the only businesses that seemed to thrive were public houses. The curious stopped what they were doing to stare at his gilded carriage with resentful eyes. Filthy dogs with protruding ribs sprawled on the pavement unattended, while a group of ragged children entertained themselves by rolling a hoop.

And then he noticed a rather pretty girl, walking briskly not far from his carriage.

Will had known enough beautiful women that most did not turn his head, but he made an exception this time, perhaps only because she looked so entirely out of place. She was taller than most of the people who surrounded her, including the men. He'd caught just a glimpse of her face, but he'd noticed high cheekbones and full lips. Her skin was fair, in keeping with her unruly chignon of red hair. He wondered if she had freckles, and he wondered where she was going and what she was doing there to begin with. She was nicely, although not fashionably, dressed. Her high-waisted muslin gown followed the lines of the current style, but made no other concessions to trends. She appeared modest, respectable and perhaps even rather severe. And that just didn't make sense.

For a woman with a face like hers, in a neighborhood like this, the only money to be made was on her back. But she definitely wasn't a doxy.

He realised he wasn't the only one watching her. Two men, sitting lazily on a wall in patched trousers and heavy labourer's boots, allowed their heads to rotate as she passed them. She seemed to be oblivious to the attention and walked on, head held high.

'Bloody 'ell, 'urry up!'

Will turned his head to see what his driver was shouting at now. The greengrocer was moving even slower, in apparent protest at this derisive treatment. Will lost interest and turned his attention back to the girl.

She was easy enough to locate, since she hadn't gone far. She'd stopped walking, in fact, and seemed to be scanning the crowd rather nervously as if looking for someone or something. The leather bag sat unattended at her feet, and Will felt his body tense. Even from a distance he could sense several pairs of eyes regarding it with speculative interest. He opened the carriage door and stepped out, waving to his disgruntled driver as he crossed the street.

He walked quickly. He didn't really know what he was going to do—offer his assistance, perhaps, although there was a good chance she wouldn't welcome it. Utterly foolhardy for her to be walking there, whoever she was. But he wasn't fast enough to offer anything. When he was still about ten paces away, a lanky youth hurtled into her, sending her off balance. She was quick enough to grab the bag's handle, but the boy latched on, as well, and he was stronger. The tug of war lasted about three seconds before he yanked the bag from her hands, sending her flying backwards on to the pavement. She started to scramble up, but the boy had already turned on his heel to flee.

Unfortunately for him, he wasn't looking where he was going. Two long strides and he'd collided with a very large and solid human form.

Will didn't do anything more than grab the boy by the shoulder, but the pressure was so strong he winced and instantly dropped the bag, spilling its contents on to the street.

Will was a full head taller than him, and as he looked down at the boy's face he saw fear. Real fear, that he would be arrested and hanged for attacking a lady.

He released the pressure.

'Run along.'

The boy did as instructed and immediately disappeared down an alley. Will watched him go, wondering how his thus far pleasant day had ended up like this. The girl was at his feet, hurriedly trying to collect her belongings. He couldn't see her face. Just the back of her head and her slender neck. Her hair had become loose in the struggle, and a long curl was now tumbling about her shoulders. He realised he was staring and knelt to help her.

'Here, let me…'

She didn't acknowledge his presence, just started pushing things into her bag faster. Will's eye was drawn to one item in particular. A smart red morocco case, half-opened to reveal what appeared to be a pearl necklace. He reached out to retrieve it for her, but her hand darted out to grab it first.

'I don't need assistance, thank you,' she said, not even bothering to look at him. She hastily shoved the case back into her bag and closed it, carefully buckling it this time to prevent further accidents. Her voice sounded soft and rich…if rather hostile. She obviously thought he was as much of a threat as the boy had been.

She rose stiffly.

Will rose, too, proffering his hand in assistance as he did so. She ignored it, but finally looked up. He was struck once more by her beauty. It was an odd sort of beauty, and her features might have looked misplaced on any other face. Her lips, slightly parted in surprise, were luscious and temptingly kissable. Her nose was small, pert and sprinkled with freckles. His gaze wanted to travel down her neck, looking for more freckles, but with great willpower he managed to direct his attention elsewhere. He looked at her eyes instead—a disconcerting violet blue, very surprised and staring back at him.

* * *

Isabelle Thomas looked at the ground the second her gaze met his, but she couldn't conceal the blush that started at her neck and bloomed all the way to the roots of her red hair. She'd expected him to look like every other disreputable man she'd seen on the street; at worst, she'd expected him to look exactly like the man who—if she wasn't mistaken—had been following her all morning. The man she thought she'd finally managed to elude.

She'd certainly no idea that her wary gaze would settle on a gentleman, and an impossibly handsome one, at that.

She hadn't meant to speak so sharply to him…it was just that her nerves were on edge and she'd fully anticipated that he'd carry on where the boy had left off. She silently cursed her overly active imagination, but when she looked up once more, he seemed oblivious to her rudeness—that, or completely unimpressed. She rather suspected the latter.

She'd hoped he'd be less attractive upon second viewing, but he was still downright devastating. Too perfect, if that were possible. Tall and broad shouldered, with slightly dishevelled blond hair and emerald green eyes. Dressed impeccably in buff breeches and a dark blue, woollen coat. And she…oh, she, like a bedraggled grey mouse who'd just lost a bout with an alley cat.

It didn't help that he was still staring at her, but she quickly realised that he'd asked her a question and was simply waiting for her answer.

'Hmm?'

He moved a step closer, possibly because he now thought she was hard of hearing. Yet his voice was quiet. 'I said I hope you're uninjured.'

'I…I am all right.' She hadn't even had time to consider if that was true. Was she? She felt well enough, except for her backside, which had managed to land in a puddle. She couldn't bear to think of the state of her dress.

'Do you have everything? Is that your paper?'

She looked down at her feet, where a slip of paper floated in a shallow puddle the colour of milky tea. It was hers, and the address she'd scrawled across it that morning in black ink was gradually dissolving.

'Oh!'

She moved quickly to grab it, but he leaned forwards at the same time. Their foreheads connected loudly. They both straightened immediately.

'I'm so sorry,' she said awkwardly.

He grinned ruefully, and she realised that in addition to golden hair and a chiselled jaw, he possessed dimples and straight, white teeth. 'That wasn't very coordinated of us. Shall I…?'

She was too embarrassed to protest, so she just stood there dumbly and allowed him to pick up the paper. He handed it to her. The writing was now barely legible, but she could just make out the words 16 Litch—luckily, she remembered the rest. Sixteen Litchfield Terrace. That was where she'd find one Josiah Fairly, surely an ironical name for a pawnbroker. She'd been given the address by Samuel, the boy who delivered coal to the boarding house where she'd taken a room. Fairly was his uncle and she'd been assured he'd offer an acceptable price for her possessions.

'Can you still read it?' the man asked.

'Read it? Oh, yes.' She stuffed the paper in her pocket. 'I must go. Thank you for helping me.' She turned to continue walking, but she felt his hand on her arm. Warm and firm—not hurting her, but not letting her go, either. She turned around slowly, looking down her nose at the offending object.

'You shouldn't be carrying that bag,' he chided. 'Not unless you want to be robbed again. I'll accompany you wherever you're going.'

She knew he was right. She'd known she was being foolish when she'd started out that morning. But she hadn't had much choice about it, and she didn't need him to tell her. 'Remove your hand, sir.'

He raised an eyebrow at her imperious tone, but did as bid. He also took a step closer. Although she was tall, she still found herself craning her neck to look up at him. She wasn't used to that. His voice remained reasonable, but she suspected he might be losing his patience. 'Half the street knows you're carrying something worth stealing. If you'd like to keep your possessions, I'd advise you to accept my offer.'

Her gaze darted quickly from left to right, assessing the risk. They made a conspicuous pair, to say the least, and several people were blatantly staring. If he walked away right now and left her there alone, then she'd no doubt that someone would soon relieve her of her belongings—in fact, her belongings were probably the least of her worries. She'd be lucky to make it home unharmed.

She returned her attention to his face. He was certainly big enough to make anyone think twice—and, if she really were being followed, that wasn't such a bad thing. And yet she didn't want him to come with her. It didn't matter that she'd no idea who he was and would never see him again. She was going to a pawnbroker's, and it was too humiliating.

Unconsciously, she bit her lower lip in indecision. She tried to sound confident, but she knew she didn't quite succeed. 'I'm going rather far. I imagine you have better things to do.'

He seemed to sense her uncertainty. His tone brooked no refusal. 'Actually, I have the afternoon free, and we could take my carriage. It's just across the road.'

She turned her head. His carriage gleamed with a fresh coat of glossy green paint, and two sleek bays waited impatiently to depart. His coachman, in green livery to match, had alighted in order to confront a cart driver over some infraction. A coat of arms surmounted by an earl's coronet decorated the carriage door.

Oh, God. He was not only handsome, but he was rich and probably titled, too.

'Your driver is making friends, I see,' she said drily. She was now more resolved than ever that he would not come with her. She'd some pride left—not much, maybe, but enough that she didn't want him to witness her sell the last of her valuable possessions.

He smiled again, and she wished she hadn't attempted humor. 'McGrath loves an argument. If we linger much longer, they'll be asking us to second them at dawn. Shall we go?' He held out his arm.

She stared at it for a second before simply starting to walk again, carrying on in the same direction. The pawnbroker's shouldn't be much further now, and she needed to get rid of him quickly. 'I think that would be unwise. I thank you for your help, but I no longer require it.'

He fell in beside her, easily keeping pace with her long strides. 'I can perfectly well understand your reluctance to ride in my carriage, but I assure you it would be wiser than wandering around here on foot. We'll probably both be robbed.'

'You needn't come with me,' she said stiffly.

He sighed. 'Much as I'm tempted to leave you here, I'm afraid my conscience won't allow it.'

She kept walking, looking straight ahead. She knew he was watching her face, probably hoping that his mild statement would elicit some reaction: eyes widened in shock, maybe even a verbal rebuke. She refused to indulge him.

'You're right to be suspicious, of course,' he continued after a few seconds of silence. 'I wouldn't trust anyone I met wandering around here.'

'So why are *you* wandering around here?' She knew she sounded accusatory, but, well, what *was* someone like him doing there, and why had he decided to take an interest in her? Her arm was starting to ache from the weight of her bag, and he'd made no sign of leaving. With an annoyed sigh, she placed the bag on the ground and then crossed her arms over her chest, waiting impatiently for his answer.

He looked as if he found her irritation comical. 'I assure you, I wasn't. I was just passing through on my way back from the country when I saw you about to be robbed. Could hardly just stand by and watch.'

'Oh.' She picked up the bag and started walking again, now feeling rather guilty for her curt behaviour. He was infuriating, but she'd be far worse off if not for his intervention. 'I…I am grateful that you stopped that man. I'm sorry if I've seemed rude, but I really will be all right on my own. I don't want to take up any more of your time.'

He nodded, but otherwise seemed to disregard her words. He walked along beside her quietly for a few seconds before offering, 'I'm William Stanton, by the by. Earl of Lennox, actually, but you needn't m'lord me.'

'I won't.'

She hoped she sounded as unimpressed as she'd intended, but her impertinence seemed only to amuse him. Until a few years ago, she wouldn't have felt so intimidated by his title. All right, so she'd never been nearly as grand as an earl—*quite* a few stations in life separated them. But she'd had a bit of money once, and what had seemed to be a respectable family, too. She'd grown up in a rambling brick house draped in wisteria and surrounded by neat gravel paths and herb gardens. She'd never been fashionable—the plain clothes she wore now represented the sort of sensible attire she'd worn her whole life. However, they were well made and reasonably expensive. She'd never had reason to be ashamed of her status.

Only things had changed. The gardens had been replaced by a squalid street, and her unfashionable dresses had become both unfashionable and worn. The one she wore now was several seasons old and many times mended.

'You might introduce yourself,' he said, his gaze wandering over her face. 'It's your turn.'

She stopped walking to answer him, feeling depressed and defeated. 'Isabelle Thomas.'

'How do you do, Miss Thomas. Let me carry your bag.'

'No, thank you.'

Finally, she'd managed to provoke him. He actually sounded offended. 'I assure you I've no interest in stealing from you. It's heavy.'

'No.' Her grip tightened.

He sighed loudly and then, after a moment's consideration, began fiddling with his waistcoat.

She turned her head to the side to stare at him, feeling mildly alarmed. 'What *are* you doing?'

He made a face at her. 'My, but you're suspicious. I'm removing my watch.'

'Why?'

'Because we're going to trade. I will carry your bag, Miss Thomas, and you will carry my watch. So you can rest assured I won't abscond with your possessions.' He held it out to her, but when she didn't immediately accept it he took her hand in his, placed the watch on her palm, and then closed her fist around it. 'Now, I'll have your bag.'

She saw no reasonable argument against accepting his offer, but she still didn't want him to come with her. 'You barely know me, sir,' she pointed out. 'I might run off with it.'

'Then I will catch you. I don't recommend you test my word.'

She didn't doubt him, and, seeing no alternative, handed him her bag. Her arm cried out in relief, and she tucked the watch into her pocket. She wouldn't have dreamed of running off with it anyway, not just because she believed his threat, but also because that would be stealing. She hadn't yet stooped to that level.

'I wouldn't take your watch, you know,' she said quietly as they started walking again. 'I'm not a thief.'

'I'm pleased to hear it. What's in this bag? Stones?'

She paled. 'If you're going to complain—'

'I'm not complaining.'

'Don't open it.'

'I *won't*,' he replied grumpily. 'Lead the way, Miss Thomas.'

She looked nervously up the street, hoping she remembered Samuel's directions. She'd written them down and had studied them that morning, but examining them in public would have made her look lost and vulnerable. She knew she had to turn somewhere…

'Um, left here.' *I think*. She started walking slowly, feeling less sure of herself. Left took them up an alley, intersected after about thirty paces by another road. The faded and flaking sign read Litchfield Terrace. She turned right.

'Where are you taking me, by the by?' he asked. It was a reasonable question, since Litchfield Terrace looked like a particularly unwelcoming street. It was narrow and unpaved, and the mean houses that lined it seemed to be deserted—or they would, anyway, if not for the high-pitched cry of a baby that carried from a broken window and the rat that skulked along the edge of the road, sniffing for scraps.

'I'm not taking you anywhere. You're following me, and I can go the rest of the way myself.'

'Out of the question.'

And she knew that he meant it. Her footsteps were already beginning to drag with apprehension. Josiah Fairly's disreputable premises would appear at any second and, oh, the embarrassment…

At the same time, though, she could admit to herself that she was glad William Stanton had insisted on coming. She'd be terrified right now if he hadn't.

'So…' he said, looking at her curiously, 'I've revealed that I was just passing through…what are you doing in this godforsaken area?'

'Picking daffodils, obviously.'

That comment got her a burst of laughter. Warm, genuine laughter, and she felt a smile tugging at her own lips, even though she really didn't want to start enjoying his company. But she managed to suppress it, which wasn't so hard because they'd reached her destination.

Number 16 waited for her at the end of the road, set apart from the terraced houses that lined the sides of the street. Like the dilapidated buildings around it, it had been built right up against the road, without a front garden to soften its appearance. The word *'Pawnbroker'* had been painted messily over the door, and two dusty bow windows advertised the faded delights inside: some battered books, a garish, plumed hat, old boots and a pair of candlesticks, their silver plating worn thin to reveal the base metal beneath.

Isabelle stopped walking and wondered if it wasn't too late to change her mind. Perhaps she could say she'd lost her way and that she'd decided to go home after all. She could come back tomorrow without him…

He noticed her hesitate and gently touched her arm. 'Miss Thomas, what's wrong?'

She ignored the unfamiliar shiver his touch produced. Red shame was creeping up her neck and her lip was threatening to tremble. But she wouldn't allow herself to be such a coward, so she forced herself to meet his gaze. 'I…I thank you again for your company. I will be all right from here.'

He looked dubiously at the shop. 'What—is *this* where we're going?'

She pretended she hadn't heard the note of disdain in his voice. 'My bag, please.'

There was understanding in his green eyes—sympathy, too—and that made it even worse. 'You've no need to feel embarrassed, you know. You're not the first person who's had to—'

'My bag, sir.' She held out her hand, waiting impatiently.

He seemed reluctant to give it to her. 'I doubt he'll give you an honest price.'

'Probably not, but that is my affair.'

Finally, he handed it to her. 'I'll wait for you.'

She'd expected him to say that, and frankly she didn't want him to leave. She just didn't want him to know how scared she was. 'I cannot stop you.'

And then she straightened her back like a fire poker and walked alone the rest of the way to the shop and up its crooked stone steps. She took a deep breath and opened the heavy, groaning door.

When she emerged four minutes later, her bag was no lighter. As feared, Josiah Fairly had offered insultingly low prices for her belongings, but she was too despondent to feel angry. She was tired and hungry, and she simply wanted to give up.

She immediately began searching the street, looking for him. She didn't see him anywhere, and it was clear to her that he'd abandoned her. She couldn't blame him, and she should have felt relieved, but instead she felt even worse. She sank down on to the steps, placing her bag beside her. Then she crossed her arms over her knees and buried her head inside them. She hadn't cried in years. She'd been through worse humiliations. But right now—

'Miss Thomas? What's wrong?'

She raised her head slowly. He'd returned, and he stood right in front of her, looking so handsome…and she knew her eyes were red and her lips swollen.

'Nothing,' she said quietly, wiping away a tear.

'Please don't cry.'

'I'm not.'

He mounted the steps and sat next to her. Not indecently close, but close enough that she forgot about the horrible man in the shop, and began to worry instead about his proximity.

'I'd just walked down the road a bit,' he said. 'I'm sorry—I expected you to be inside longer. He wasn't helpful?'

She shook her head, waiting to hear him say he told her so.

But he didn't. 'So what's it to be now? Would an ice cream cheer you up?'

She shook her head again.

'No? Um…some proper food, then? How about a very large glass of brandy?'

She looked at him sideways, but she couldn't help smiling this time. It had been so long since someone had been kind to her or cared if she was happy. 'You're absurd.'

The warmth in his green eyes made her catch her breath. 'If it makes you smile. May I look in your bag?'

'No.'

'Please? Perhaps I can suggest something.'

Why not? she thought. She didn't have the energy to argue any more. She shrugged. 'Very well.' She slid the bag across the step until it sat at his feet.

He opened it rather hesitantly, as if he expected it to contain snakes. 'Don't know why you've been so mysterious about it. I'm sure if you took your necklace to a respectable dealer...' But then he broke off, frowning into the bag's depths. 'Miss Thomas, you really are carrying stones.'

Chapter Two

She bit her lip, trying to control the smile that threatened to break through. But he sounded so nonplussed it really *was* comical. Finally, she gave up and grinned at him. 'They're marble, actually.'

He nodded slowly, allowing his gaze to drift over her face slightly longer than was proper. She flushed and looked away, wishing he didn't have such a disturbing effect on her—he, no doubt, thought her blushes were ridiculously missish. When she'd regained her composure and looked back, he'd removed one of the items in question. A fragment of a woman's face, small enough to fit in his hand, delicately carved in white marble. All that remained of it was an almond-shaped eye, an ear, and an elegant nose. Isabelle knew her bag contained two more like it.

'I take it she used to be a Roman goddess, or something like that,' he said slowly.

'Well…'

He didn't let her finish. 'And I was starting to think you were only a little bit eccentric. Why would you carry these things around?'

Her smile faded, and she replied coldly, 'I was trying to sell them, clearly.'

'Did the man offer you any money at all?'

She shook her head. 'He didn't quite know what to make of them.'

'I shouldn't think so. What do you think they're worth?'

'I don't know. Next to nothing.'

He returned the object to the bag. 'More than that, surely.'

She shrugged. 'I…I'm going home now.'

He didn't pass the bag back to her. 'But I thought I was going to help you.'

'How can you possibly help me?'

His answer didn't come readily, suggesting he had no more idea than she. 'Well…some advice, maybe. Perhaps you could sell these things to a collector? Someone with an interest in antiquities? You won't find anyone who wants to buy them around here.'

She sighed unhappily. 'A collector wouldn't want them, either, since they're not really old.'

'No? Then why are they broken?'

'They were broken to begin with, to make them look more, um…authentic.'

'I see.' He was looking at her curiously, and she suspected he didn't see at all. 'You mean they're forgeries.'

She didn't want to say the words. She just nodded.

'You told the man they weren't real, I trust?'

She frowned at him, not liking the implication. 'Of course. I'm not dishonest.'

He reached into the bag and removed the red morocco case. 'What about this necklace? Are the pearls real?'

She nodded. It was the last nice thing she owned, and it was more valuable than many of the things she'd already sold. She'd held on to it for personal reasons, but she could no longer afford to be sentimental.

'It *is* yours, I hope.'

'Are you suggesting I stole it?'

'Did you?' he asked.

She wanted to be angry, but it was a perfectly reasonable question. 'It was a gift. It is mine to do with as I like.'

He nodded. 'In that case I would be happy to buy it from you.'

She took the necklace from his hands and returned it to her bag. 'I do not think it will become you.'

'No?'

There was a lilting, teasing note to his voice, but she was entirely serious—serious and, now, getting angry. 'No. I will not accept your charity. You've just met me and you needn't feel you have to help me.'

'It isn't charity,' he protested.

'Oh? What use have you of my necklace?'

'You needn't sound so incredulous. I'm sure I can find someone to give it to.'

'Who?' she demanded, but then she immediately blushed, realising how naïve her question sounded. A man like him undoubtedly had about five mistresses, if not a wife.

'I wouldn't have to look that far. I could give it to you, for one.'

'To me?' She didn't quite understand what he was proposing, probably because all rational thought was quickly slipping from her mind. All she knew was that he suddenly seemed every bit as dangerous as the man who'd been following her that morning, and the boy who'd tried to rob her. More dangerous, in fact, at least to her sense of self-preservation.

'Yes,' he said softly. 'I'll buy it from you, and then I'll give it back. As a gift.'

'That's unnecessary. I…I must return now.' She rose and started walking back the way they had come.

He caught up a few seconds later, taking the bag from her when he reached her side. 'You're remarkably stubborn, you know.'

She didn't turn her head to look at him. 'If that bothers you, then you may leave. I know precisely where I'm going, so I can walk on my own.'

'I'm far too stubborn m'self.' He caught her hand, forcing her to stop. 'And I would like to buy your necklace. I don't see why you're denying me, since it's clearly for sale. And, if you promised not to be difficult about it, then I'd even be happy to allow you to keep it. Perhaps it has special meaning for you?'

It did. It had belonged to her mother. There was pity in his eyes, and she hated it. 'Then that would be charity, sir.'

He frowned. 'You needn't worry that I would expect anything in return.'

That just made her blush. She started walking again. 'It's very expensive.'

'How expensive?'

'Two hundred pounds,' she said, hoping the outrageous price would end the subject. She glanced at him sideways.

He raised an eyebrow, but otherwise showed little reaction. 'Yes, that does seem rather dear.'

'Well, I'm sorry—'

'Would you settle for fifty pounds…' he was patting his jacket's inner pocket as if looking for something '…and sixpence?' He extracted a coin.

She stopped to stare. 'You don't travel with that sort of money.'

He smiled. 'No, I tend to rely on credit. I think the sixpence would be about all I could manage at the moment.'

'You think I'd give you my necklace for sixpence?'

'A mere deposit. You can come to my house and I can give you the rest.'

Go to his house? No. 'Your offer is too high.' She resumed walking.

'It's considerably less than you requested.'

'I wasn't serious!'

He sighed. 'Yes, I rather realised that. But I thought the object was to sell everything in this bag, and you've so far failed miserably. You're clearly in need of money, or you wouldn't be here.'

Isabelle ignored his point. He was right: she really was a fool. He was offering her the money she needed—much more than she'd hoped for—and yet she was refusing. Why? 'I don't need money that badly…I'm looking for employment, you see, and I only need enough to tide myself over until then.'

'Oh? What sort of employment are you trained for?'

Another perceptive question. Drat. He asked it politely, as if he were merely curious, but she suspected he'd already guessed the answer. 'I'm not trained for anything, if you must know. A governess, I suppose. I am reasonably well educated.'

He looked so dubious she added defensively, 'Well, I am. You needn't make a face.'

'I'm not doubting your education, Miss Thomas. But somehow you don't seem to realise that few mothers would eagerly welcome someone like you into their homes.'

She flushed with anger. 'I don't know what you mean by that.'

'There's no need to get upset. All I mean is that women like their children's governesses to be stout and homely. Or skinny and homely. But…homely *is* important, I'm afraid.' His voice dropped an octave. 'You're…what I mean to say is you're *not* homely. The very opposite, in fact. It's a compliment.'

Her heart was beating like a hammer. She forced herself not to look at him and fixed her sights on a sleeping dog at the end of the road. But she knew he was looking at her. She could feel his gaze on the side of her face.

So she started to babble. 'I…I might also work in a shop. Or I…might take in sewing. I could do any—'

'Miss Thomas?'

'Yes?'

'I have no doubt you'll be successful in whatever you choose to do, but it might take a while. And you still haven't sold your necklace, so you haven't any money to tide you over. Just accept my offer, please. Don't think of it as charity, since I am getting something in return.'

Isabelle said nothing. She didn't want to take his money—she really didn't. But she also didn't know why it mattered, since she'd planned to sell her necklace anyway. And the money he offered would pay for her lodgings for several months. It would feed her. It might even cover some of her debt…

But taking money from him *was* different. It was more shaming. No matter what he said, it was charity.

In the end, though, necessity won out over pride, although she still couldn't meet his gaze. 'If you truly wish to buy it, then I won't argue. But I insist you keep it. I…I don't need your gift.'

He nodded, and they walked on in uncomfortable silence.

After another minute, they reached the crowded street where she'd first encountered him.

'My carriage is just over there.'

She looked in the direction he indicated. His carriage had pulled to the side in order not to obstruct traffic; his driver, who'd been arguing energetically when she'd last seen him, now glared sullenly at the greengrocer, who'd still not moved his cart.

'Your carriage?' she asked.

He was regarding the vehicle with mild displeasure, but he looked back at her to answer the question. 'Yes—you're coming to my house, remember?'

Ride in his carriage with him? It was far too intimate. She couldn't do it. 'Perhaps I might hire a hack?'

'Don't be silly. It could be an hour before you see a hack around here.'

'I could walk, then.'

'You expect me to trust you with my sixpence? How do I know you won't abscond with it?'

She frowned at him. 'You can have your sixpence back.'

He crossed his arms over his chest. 'Oh, for the…' He managed to catch himself before emitting an oath. 'You're being silly. I'll hire a hack for myself, so you won't be alone with me, if that's what's stopping you. You can have my carriage to yourself.'

No. 'As you pointed out, hacks rarely come to these parts. I cannot allow you to inconvenience—'

'It is not inconvenient,' he said tightly, patently already both annoyed and inconvenienced. 'You are *not* walking, but if you propose to stand here and debate it all day then I am willing to oblige you.'

She didn't want to debate all day, nor did she want to walk. Her stomach rumbled and her feet hurt. She looked away, wishing she hadn't argued with him. It *wasn't* proper for her to ride in his carriage, alone or otherwise, but she'd abandoned propriety many months ago. She was in no position to be so fastidious.

'You will at least let me pay your fare.'

'No, I won't,' he said irritably, his gentleman's honour obviously insulted that she would offer.

She blushed again, embarrassed by her gaucheness. But she had to acknowledge his generosity somehow.

'I really am grateful for your kindness. I'm sorry if I've seemed impolite. What I mean to say is, well, thank you, my lord.'

'You don't have to be so formal.'

But she did. Formality was all that was keeping her from melting on the spot. His eyes had warmed with her apology, and his tone had dropped subtly: deeper, richer, entreating. She couldn't look away, and in the heavy silence, he reached out to tuck a loose curl behind her ear. She found herself staring at his lips. She thought he was going to kiss her, and stopping him was far from her mind. He was so close, and all he'd have to do was tilt his head...

'Do you know what I think?'

'What?' she asked, feeling rather mesmerised.

'I think you need more help than you'll admit.'

She blinked and looked away, realising that any kissing was merely the product of her overheated imagination.

Will glanced in the direction of his carriage, where the argument had recommenced. 'You'd better wait here while I sort this out. I don't trust McGrath to mind his tongue when he's riled. And pay attention this time.'

He gave her a stern look and deposited the bag at her feet before walking purposely towards the carriage, just on the other side of the road. She watched him go, feeling rather dizzy. That morning she'd been penniless, friendless and scared. Through sheer happenstance she now had the promise of money and a most unlikely champion.

She allowed herself to look at him, safe in the knowledge that for the moment he wasn't paying attention to her. She liked the way his hair fell over his temples as he lowered his head to listen to the greengrocer. After a few seconds, he pushed it back, looking frustrated. He seemed—quite valiantly, she thought—to be holding his temper in check. He started patting his pockets, and she assumed the man was demanding money for his damaged potatoes. She couldn't suppress her smile. Pity she'd taken his last sixpence, but she was certain he'd think of something. What with all that credit. There'd be a small parade of beggars, all with hands held out, following him home before the day was through.

She looked at the sky, watching the clouds drift past and wondering how late it was. She'd been enjoying herself, in an odd sort of way, and she suspected more time had passed than she was aware of.

Mrs William Stanton. She rather liked the sound of that. No, no—Isabelle, Lady Lennox. Or the Countess of Lennox, perhaps. How terribly grand. If only her father'd been a duke instead of a criminal.

She rolled her eyes at her folly and returned her gaze to the street. Right, he'd instructed her to *pay attention…*

But then the second her mind drifted back to earth she saw the man again. The one who'd followed her. She blinked, not quite believing her eyes, but it was definitely him. Dark hair, medium height. He didn't seem to have seen her, but he appeared to be searching the crowd. She didn't know who he was, but she had an awful idea who might have sent him.

She immediately stooped to pick up her bag, gripping it tightly. She gave William Stanton one last glance, but he was still occupied with his driver. So much for riding in his carriage.

She turned her body slowly in the other direction, hoping not to attract any attention as she eased deeper into the crowd. She looked over her shoulder, hoping the man still hadn't noticed her.

But now he was heading in her direction.

She turned her head and started walking faster, not caring if it looked odd. He hadn't necessarily seen her; perhaps it was chance that he'd seemed to be closer. After a few long strides, she turned again. This time, there was no sign of the man. She hoped she'd lost him. Or, perhaps, he'd merely blended in with the crowd. He could be as close as ever.

She started to run.

* * *

Isabelle arrived at her boarding house an hour later with a swiftly beating heart. She'd taken a circuitous route, hoping the man wouldn't reappear. And, as far as she was aware, he hadn't. She'd run much of the way, stopping to catch her breath only a few times; after a mere ten minutes she'd abandoned the marble heads on the side of the road. Worthless anyway, and they slowed her down.

Now, she stood at the top of her front steps, facing a slightly shabby door. She wondered if the man knew where she lived, and she supposed he probably did.

She wouldn't think about it. She began fishing around her pocket, hoping that she hadn't lost her key in the rush. She'd already forgotten it once, and Miss Standish, the house's temperamental proprietor, had been remarkably put out about having to answer the door.

Isabelle located the key easily, and the door opened without so much as a sigh to notify Miss Standish that she'd returned. In the four days she'd been staying there, she'd learned it was best to avoid her.

Isabelle quietly closed the door behind her and returned the key to her pocket. But then…what was that? The key had clinked against another heavy, brass object. She removed it, frowning.

It wasn't brass, actually. It was William Stanton's gold watch.

Good God, she'd stolen it after all.

Chapter Three

It was a typical, damp English afternoon. Will was in his drawing room, weighing the effort of walking to his club against the gloomy pleasure of perusing his paper in search of bad news. He turned the page, allowing inertia to win. A portly tabby cat curled in the carved giltwood chair across from him, shooting aggrieved looks every time he rustled the paper. He appeared to be in as bad a temper as his owner.

Will's bad mood could be blamed entirely on the female sex. His mood had soured soon after he'd turned his back on Isabelle Thomas the previous afternoon. At first, he'd actually felt rather pleased with himself as he'd crossed the road, leaving her to wait. His mind had only been half on the argument between his driver and the greengrocer, so much so that he hadn't even balked when the man insisted he be compensated for his entire cart of vegetables when most still seemed perfectly saleable. Instead, he'd been thinking about the intelligent, beautiful, mysterious girl who would unexpectedly be visiting his house—a prospect that suggested many interesting possibilities.

He didn't mind buying her necklace, or even paying over the odds for it; it was a small price to pay to keep her off the street. And he'd hoped that once he'd taken care of that small matter, he might convince her to have supper with him, or perhaps go to the opera. He wondered how she'd react to that sort of invitation. Her blushes suggested she wasn't terribly experienced, but she appeared to be old enough and independent enough to make up her own mind. He'd felt inordinately satisfied when he'd finally succeeded in making her smile. He usually charmed women with ease, but her…well, it felt like a real achievement. Her adorable smile had more than made up for her prickliness.

Of course, he'd changed his mind once he realised that she was a thief, and a thief so skilled she hadn't even had to steal. She'd so beguiled him with her charms that he'd simply given her his watch—and sixpence, for good measure. The whole thing was gallingly ironic since he'd accused her of lacking common sense.

After he'd realised that she'd fled, he'd spent two angry hours searching the slums before finally giving up and returning home. He'd been damned fond of that watch; it had belonged to his grandfather.

Only once he'd reached his house, his mood got even worse. A letter awaited him there, from Miss Hume. She must have sent it within hours of his departure from her blasted school. It seemed that Mary was being sent home, and since he was her guardian, her home was now his. According to the letter, sometime during the evening after he'd left, Mary had snipped a large segment of hair from one Major Fitzgerald's daughter's head, using a sharp pair of scissors. Her possessions had been packed posthaste, and she would arrive, courtesy of Miss Hume, some time tomorrow morning. Miss Hume did not plan on inviting her back. She was Will's responsibility now, and he didn't have the faintest idea what to do with her. He knew nothing about children, girls in particular, and it might take months to find another school that would accept such a hoyden.

He lay down his paper and took the letter from his inside pocket, glancing yet again at the strident lines of text. Bloody unpredictable females, young and old…

A quiet knock on the drawing room door interrupted his ill-tempered thoughts.

'Yes?'

Bartholomew, his butler, entered cautiously.

'Good morning, my lord. It is your cousin.'

This wasn't welcome news. Will had several cousins, but all but two of them were considerate enough to leave him alone in the mornings. It was certain to be one of the demon twins, Henrietta or Venetia.

'What—here? Which cousin?'

'Which cousin indeed?' an arch voice called in from the hall. 'Surely you must know that Venny's at Waddlehurst with Philip and the children.'

Henrietta Sandon-Drabbe sailed into the drawing room, not waiting for permission to enter. She was a year younger than he, and the top of her head stopped just shy of his chin. She'd once been very pretty, and her pale blonde hair and blue eyes undoubtedly continued to appeal to most casual observers. Will, however, had a difficult time separating her personality from her appearance. She was intrusive, manipulative and bossy, as was her sister. Since they normally travelled as a pair, he considered himself lucky to have only one to deal with that morning.

Bartholomew wisely eased out of the room, closing the door behind him. Will folded the letter and laid it next to him on the sofa, forcing a smile as he rose. 'I hope she'll be away for a long time?'

'Until the end of the summer, sadly. But I know she would approve of my mission this morning.'

He groaned. 'Oh, Henny, don't say you're on a mission.'

'Well, I am,' she replied. Her gaze sharpened as it lit on the cat. 'And why is that foul creature not in the kitchen? Surely you have rats enough to keep it occupied. Shoo!' She waved her hand at it, and it insolently shifted its fat mass, but did not otherwise move. She glared at it before selecting another chair.

Once comfortably arranged, she said, 'I cannot imagine why you're being so disagreeable. You haven't even said good morning. I trust your mood will improve by tonight.'

Will resumed his seat. 'Good morning, Henny. What happens tonight?'

She gave him a patient, patronising look—the sort she reserved for dense, unobservant men and her husband, Edward. 'Constance

Reckitt's ball. You've known about it for weeks, and you promised you'd come.'

Will frowned. He'd forgotten that he'd agreed to attend the ball, and he'd only done so because Henrietta had nagged him about it almost incessantly.

'Edward going to be there?' he asked.

'No, he has developed a tickle in his throat.'

'How convenient for him.'

'Yes, suspiciously so. You, however, get no such reprieve. It is essential you make an appearance.'

'I'd hardly call it essential. I don't even know why you want me there, since all you'll do is scold me under your breath. You know I detest these things.'

For just an instant, her composure looked set to snap. In a tight, controlled voice, she said, 'I want you there because you are the Earl of Lennox. You are four and thirty. Have you no concern for your duty?'

He shouldn't have posed the question, since the answer was always the same. He didn't need his cousin to remind him of his duty. He was responsible for carrying on his family's name. If he didn't produce an heir, then eventually there'd be no more Stantons living at Wentwich Castle, his estate in Norfolk, and no more Earls of Lennox. Since he was the seventh Earl of Lennox, it was a tradition worth protecting.

'I've never said I won't marry. Just not right now.'

'When? What will happen if you don't produce an heir?'

'James is married now—'

'Yes, but your brother's wife has managed to produce just one, tiny girl in three years. Do you not think you should make some attempt at respectability? You need a wife yourself, William. Not some unending string of…of *women*.'

'You've been reading the scandal sheets again.'

'I'm not the only one. Your misdeeds have been widely reported for years, and you now have the most appalling reputation. I'm not even certain anyone *would* marry you.'

He closed his eyes momentarily, searching for patience, reminding himself that he didn't *really* dislike Henrietta. Bossy she might be, but she did mean well. 'Listen, Henny, I don't gamble and I haven't had a mistress in months, not that it's your business. So let's speak of something else.'

She backed off reluctantly. 'You *are* in a foul mood.'

'And you've done everything in your power to make it worse.'

She sighed, looking around the room in search of another topic of conversation. Her gaze settled on the letter next to him. 'But then why, I wonder, are you so put out this morning? Have you received bad news?'

He looked at the letter, too. The last thing he wanted was to give her another reason to interfere in his life, but then again, he wanted to change the subject. Besides, he hadn't the faintest idea what to do with the child when she arrived in less than a day. All three of Henrietta's brats were girls; she might be able to help him.

He rose to hand her the letter, sure that he'd eventually regret doing so. 'I suppose it is rather bad news.'

She started reading, but only got about halfway down the page before looking up with some alarm. 'I don't understand at all. Who's Mary Weston-Burke?'

'My goddaughter. Arthur Weston-Burke's only child.'

She laid the letter down, knitting her brow. 'Your school friend? He died a few months ago, did he not?'

'Yes, and she became my ward.'

Henrietta raised a sceptical eyebrow. 'You didn't tell me that.'

He was already beginning to wish he hadn't shown her the letter. He returned to the sofa, feeling defensive. 'No, well, I didn't think it would come to anything. She's been at school the whole time—'

'You didn't assume she'd be at school for ever, did you?'

He frowned. 'I thought I'd worry about what to do with her next when the need arose. Frankly, I assumed she'd be at school for a few more years at least. She's only twelve.'

She shook her head disapprovingly. 'Hasn't she any other family?

I cannot imagine why you've been selected for this task. I can't think of anyone more unsuited. You know nothing about children.'

'My nieces adore me.'

Henrietta snorted. 'That's because you spoil them. You're far too soft-hearted.'

'I'm not soft-hearted at all,' Will protested. He didn't think he was, either. He was a rake of the first order, at least by repute. But maybe she was right, and he was losing his touch. Maybe that's why he'd given his watch to a woebegone thief with big violet eyes.

'I don't think Arthur would have asked me to be her guardian,' he continued, 'except his entire immediate family lives in India. The only reason he ended up in England was because he was sent here for school. And, I suppose he knew I'd the funds to support her.'

Henrietta was looking increasingly concerned. 'What about the girl's mother's side of the family?'

'Her mother died about ten years ago, and she came from a rather unfortunate background. Father was some kind of a wastrel, and they haven't two farthings to rub together. It isn't an option.'

'But there must be someone! I can't believe she's no suitable relations. Surely there's a beneficent aunt lurking about *some*where.'

Will mulled over the possibility. 'Arthur had a sister, but she's in India with her own family, I think. Obviously she was too far away to attend the funeral, or I'd have enquired.'

That information brightened Henrietta slightly. 'Maybe she'll take the child. Write to her today. How long would it take a letter to reach India?'

Will thought of the scrawny, unloved girl. It didn't seem right to plan her departure before she'd even arrived. 'By the time word reached her, I'm sure another school will have agreed to take her.'

Henrietta brandished the letter. 'Really? I wish you luck convincing another school to take her. It says here that she cut off Amelia Fitzgerald's hair.'

He sighed. 'Apparently.'

'Your lack of concern is most alarming, William, considering you plan to allow this assassin into your home. I know the Fitzgeralds vaguely. They're a most respectable family, and Amelia has an angelic head of golden curls.'

Will thought of Mary, who he'd met just a few times. Tall, plain and quiet—not someone for whom the adjective *'angelic'* would ever be used. 'She had, you mean.'

'What are you talking about?'

'The curls. And I'm sure there's an explanation for this. Perhaps Amelia asked her to do it. Maybe short hair is becoming—'

'Becoming what, fashionable amongst twelve-year-old girls? I assure you, William, it is not. You'll have to take Miss Weston-Burke firmly in hand.'

He'd always bristled at authority, and he didn't like the domineering tone of her advice. 'Unlike you, Henny, I am not a natural despot. I met this Miss Hume a few days ago, and she's quite fierce, so you see a firm hand doesn't always work.'

'You don't know what you're talking about. It's supposed to be an excellent school.'

'Yes, well, apparently Mary didn't think so.'

Henrietta realised he wouldn't be persuaded. 'If the girl is this ill mannered now, I shudder to think how'll she'll behave after spending the summer with you. You'll have to hire a governess immediately. You'll have to change your entire way of life.'

'Have you finished?'

'Quite.'

'Then you'll help me, won't you?'

'Help?' She cocked her head slightly, ever sensitive to the rise and fall of the upper hand. 'How can *I* possibly help you?'

Will suppressed a sigh, knowing he was temporarily at her mercy. 'Well, as you pointed out, I don't know anything about children.'

'Yes, and if you promise to come tonight I'll consider advising you on occasion. I'll certainly place an advertisement for a governess for you—I know just the journal. And, if you dance with Vanessa Lytton, I might even offer to select your governess.'

'I'll have some say, Hen, as I'll be paying her salary.'

'You don't trust me?'

'Not in the least.'

'Very well—I will winnow the list down for you, and you can make the final decision. It will save you hours of tedium.'

Since Will had no desire to interview scores of potential governesses—and, for that matter, to spend another minute with his cousin—he agreed instantly. 'It's settled. You've won.' But then he thought it wise to ask, 'By the by, who's Vanessa Lytton?'

Henrietta smiled. 'She's a definite prospect, I should say. Well mannered and exceptionally pretty. Accomplished, too.'

'And no doubt well connected.'

'The granddaughter of a marquess. Or would you rather marry some farmer's daughter?'

He didn't want to marry anyone, but he knew she had a point. His own parents' marriage had been convenient and for mutual benefit, but not for love—although he'd never actually witnessed their relationship firsthand. His mother had died giving birth to him, and his father remarried a year later, this time to a woman he'd been in love with for many years. Will loved his stepmother, too; she was beautiful, intelligent and charming. But she'd also been an actress, and her background had caused a serious rupture in their family. The marriage had led, if he wanted to be brutally honest, to a great deal of unhappiness for many people.

So when it was his turn to marry, he would be more practical about things.

Luckily, he didn't have to admit to his cousin that she was right. She'd already risen and was arming herself with her parasol. He rose, too, out of courtesy.

'You're leaving?'

She nodded. 'I have to prepare for tonight. It takes me longer these days to look presentable. I'd avoid these dratted débutante balls all together if it weren't for you. They make me feel practically ancient.'

'And if it weren't for you, then I wouldn't go, either. It's most illogical of us. Perhaps we should reconsider?'

The look she gave him as she exited the room was answer enough. He would see her later that evening or pay the consequences.

Isabelle's tiny room was on the top floor of Hannah Standish's boarding house. It measured about seven feet by eight and the ceiling sloped sharply, making it suitable only for leprechauns and sundry members of the fairy world. The only personal items it contained were three sturdy, leather bags—stuffed full of clothes and books—and a plaster bust of Athena, given to her by her father. Other than that, it contained a bed, a dresser and a threadbare but clean carpet. A child's sampler, worked in violent red letters, hung above the small fireplace; FEAR HIM, it said, followed by the entire alphabet and all the numbers from one to ten.

That was the last advice she needed at the moment. She was terrified. What would—could—she do? She probably already faced debtors' prison, and now she was a thief, too, through no fault of her own.

From her tense position on the bed she could see William Stanton's watch, gleaming and golden on top of her dresser—proof that yesterday wasn't just a bad dream. She couldn't help wishing she'd begun her criminal career in less expensive style.

She *could* sell it, of course. She needed money, and it was probably worth more than she could earn in a decade as a governess. But selling it would only make things worse. Then she'd be an actual, rather than merely an accidental, thief. She shouldn't even entertain the thought. She'd think instead about what she could do to improve her situation.

Like finding employment, and since she had an interview later that afternoon, she felt justifiably sanguine. True, she'd no real skills, nor any history of employment. But at least she was well educated, thanks to her father's tutelage. A good education and a large debt were practically the only possessions she had left. Her father was responsible for both counts, in fact.

He'd raised her alone since she was six, when her mother died; he'd been, as far as she could surmise, unable to cope with the responsibilities of parenthood without a wife to guide him. He led a rarefied life as a dealer of ancient sculpture, and she…well, she was left feeling rather inconsequential most of the time, if not downright inconvenient. So, she'd learned to be interested in his interests. She could speak intelligently about Roman sculpture, Etruscan painting and Attic vases. She could read Greek and Latin, as well as French and German. In retrospect, it probably hadn't been much of a childhood. She certainly didn't love these topics in the same way he did, but she'd always hoped her aptitude might make him love her, as well. At least they'd have something to talk about together.

Her early memories of her father were few. Before the war made maritime travel impossible, he'd gone to the Continent for months on end, and it was only when he returned from a long voyage that she realised he did care about her, despite his awkward way of showing it. He always brought back the most exotic treasures: mysterious fragments of crumbling buildings, bits of sculpture, and, when she was seven, a beautiful, carved marble goddess taller than she. Even Napoleon hadn't impeded his purchases; when hostilities prevented him from travelling, he'd had large numbers of artefacts shipped to London, sight unseen. He'd be so pleased with himself when they arrived that he'd tell her stories about each object, stories that lasted well beyond her bedtime: about Daphne turning into a tree to escape Apollo's embrace, about Diana turning Actaeon into a stag. However, her father's finds had filled the corners of their large house only until they found a buyer, and everything inevitably did. His ledgers read like a guide to the great and good, and he became renowned in his own right. George III had even created him *Sir* Walter Thomas—an ultimately useless title that had died with him three years ago.

Unfortunately, it turned out that much of what he'd sold to those many fine gentlemen wasn't what he claimed it to be. She'd learned that soon after his death, when Sebastian Cowes first came to call.

He'd bought many objects from her father over the years, and when he looked at her his pale, liquid gaze had glided unpleasantly over her body, as if she, too, were for sale. She had disliked him immediately, but she'd still endeavoured to be polite…even when he had imparted terrible news.

He'd just returned from Rome, he told her, where he'd seen a marble bust in a shop window. On closer inspection he realised it matched one he'd bought from her father, down to every chip and crack. When he queried the shop owner, Signor Ricci, he learned that the bust wasn't old at all, but rather had been made by Signor Ricci himself in the antique style. Ricci claimed to know her father well, although apparently he'd visited the shop only once, and that many years ago, just as hostilities were breaking out in earnest with France. He'd arranged for Signor Ricci to send several large statues to England—a request he was to make repeatedly by correspondence throughout the course of the war. Only Ricci had not known that her father had sold his replications in England for many times his own asking price as genuine artefacts. Neither had Isabelle.

Sebastian Cowes wanted his money back, and she agreed that he should have it. The problem was, she didn't have much money to give him. She was shocked when he showed her the receipts for his purchases. Where had all her father's profits gone? She could only assume he'd used them to fund further travels and further purchases, since all he'd left her was a modest annual income and a good house with a leaky roof.

So she started to sell her possessions—china, dresses, silver, jewellery at first, and then finally her home. These monies, even combined with her inheritance, had covered only half the debt, and thus she'd ended up in London, looking for work. As if a governess's meagre salary would help.

She told herself she wasn't running away. She knew she had to face Mr Cowes sometime…she just wanted to postpone the inevitable. Before she'd left home he'd hinted that they might come to some other arrangement if she couldn't pay him. She wasn't certain what he meant by that, but she sensed she wouldn't like it.

She also had to accept that he wasn't the only man her father had swindled. She'd examined his books carefully. He'd meticulously recorded the sources from which he'd acquired every object, as well as each object's eventual buyer. Nearly everything he had sold during the last fifteen years of his working life had come from Signor Ricci. Luckily, those items had been dispersed to only eleven buyers, but each of them had spent a fortune. If anyone else discovered the secret, she'd be ruined. Out of malice, Mr Cowes might start contacting her father's other clients—and since the world of collectors wasn't very big, he could easily determine who they were. How could she be certain that he wouldn't tell them?

It would be a disaster, and now she'd nothing left to sell—nothing that anyone wanted, anyway. She needed her remaining clothes, and she refused to part with her necklace for less than it was really worth.

She glanced at the gold watch.

No, she couldn't.

A loud noise interrupted her thoughts. Isabelle rose from her bed to look out the window. Her room faced the narrow mews that ran behind the house, and a rickety cart had just halted by the back door. Samuel, the coal boy, leapt from his perch and began unloading a week's supply of fuel into the coal chute. He'd leave in a few minutes.

She gave William Stanton's watch one last, baleful look before sweeping up his sixpence from her dresser and racing down the stairs. Much as she'd like to sell it, she'd have to return it instead. There was a slim chance that Samuel could discover where he lived. He'd been useless when it came to pawnbrokers, but his job must take him all over London. He might be of some help yet.

She slowed when she reached the ground floor, and then tiptoed past the sitting room, not wanting to disturb the pair of spinster sisters who were her fellow lodgers. Miss Standish had introduced them as Respectable Women, and when she'd said this she'd looked suspiciously at Isabelle's red hair, as if it alone were indecent. They were always in the sitting room and always knitting, like two grey spiders. She couldn't wait to escape from the oppressive house. *Please, let her find a position soon...*

She walked faster as she neared the back door. When she stepped outside, Samuel had just finished his job. He was wiping his blackened hands on the front of his apron and preparing to leave.

'Good morning, Samuel.'

He blushed and mumbled something incomprehensible.

Isabelle fumbled around her pocket for the sixpence. 'I...I was wondering if you might help me. I, uh...you deliver coal all over town, do you not?'

'Yes, miss.'

'To lords and ladies, even? In Mayfair and Belgravia?'

He nodded.

'I'm trying to locate someone. The Earl of Lennox. Do you think you could find his residence?'

He didn't answer immediately, so she removed the sixpence. 'I'll double that if you're successful.' She descended the short flight of steps and gave it to him.

He stared at the coin for several seconds. 'Yes, miss. It won't take long.'

She wasn't so sure. He was perfectly respectful, but his mind wasn't as quick as one might wish. 'Shall I write down his name?'

'Can't read, miss. The Earl of...?'

'Lennox. William Stanton, Earl of Lennox. Please don't forget.'

He nodded again and climbed on to his cart. She watched as he jostled down the pitted road, feeling apprehensive. Sixpence meant a lot to her these days. She couldn't afford to be so generous.

Chapter Four

A fortnight later, Isabelle stood on William Stanton's doorstep, flanked by fluted, white columns and facing a glossy, black door. The house was so imposing she almost hoped she'd come to the wrong address. Which was silly, since she should be used to grand houses by now. During the two weeks that she'd waited for Samuel to return with his information, she had attended interviews for five governess positions at large houses in Mayfair—although none, perhaps, quite as large as this one.

Unfortunately, she hadn't been well received at any of those houses, which now only added to her discomfort. She'd actually felt quite optimistic at her first few interviews; she was polite and neat and well spoken, and even though she didn't know how to be a governess she hoped those qualities would count for something.

But the mothers of Mayfair didn't see it that way. On one occasion she'd even been turned away before setting foot inside the house, although not before the awful woman who lived there, Mrs Grubb— pronounced *groob* as Isabelle was mortified to learn—had looked her up and down disapprovingly and said she simply wouldn't do. Perhaps she appeared to be too young. Maybe it was her dratted red hair again.

At any rate, returning Lord Lennox's watch could hardly be much worse. She took a deep breath and knocked.

A footman answered promptly. He seemed surprised and confused to see her, as if she were the last person he expected.

'You're here to see his lordship?' he asked.

She nodded uncertainly. It was an oddly direct greeting.

'There were only six names on the list,' he said accusingly. 'I thought we'd finished for the morning. What is your name?'

Now it was her turn to feel confused. What list? 'Miss Isabelle Thomas. I...perhaps I should explain—'

He sniffed disapprovingly and ushered her inside. 'Quickly, quickly. There's little time for explaining. His lordship had hoped to complete these meetings half an hour ago and won't be too pleased to see you. You might as well sit, Miss Thomas.'

And then he briskly crossed the hall and disappeared behind a door before she had another chance to protest. She sat on a mahogany hall chair, nervously fingering the watch in her pocket. This wasn't going as planned. Perhaps she should just leave the watch on the table, cross her fingers and run.

She didn't have time. The footman reappeared. 'This way, Miss Thomas,' he said impatiently.

She rose, feeling unsteady. But she didn't need to feel scared. The theft had been an accident, and she was now returning the watch as was correct and honourable. Lord Lennox would surely understand. He'd been kind to her before.

The footman held the door open wider for her to enter and, somehow, she did so without fainting. She stood anxiously, keeping her gaze fixed on the grey marble chimneypiece that dominated the room. Only when the footman closed the door solidly behind her did she allow her eyes to focus on the tall, masculine form sitting behind the desk.

He was staring right back at her, and he didn't bother to rise out of respect. He was as handsome as the memory she'd carried around with her for the past fortnight, but now his green eyes were cold and assessing. She should say something...something...*anything*...

Instead she turned the colour of a radish.

He smiled at her embarrassment, but it didn't reach his eyes. 'I must admit, when Rogers told me that a Miss Isabelle Thomas was waiting I thought it must be a coincidence. But it *is* you, isn't it?'

'I…perhaps I should have written first?'

'Oh? Would you have warned me to hide my silver? I assume that's what you've come for.'

'I—' She frowned at his sarcasm. 'No, I have not.'

'You haven't seriously come about the position, have you?'

'I don't know what you're talking about.'

'You saw the advertisement. You must have.'

She shook her head. 'No—'

'Then why have you come?' He leaned back in his chair and crossed his arms.

With unsteady hands, she removed the watch from her pocket. She crossed the room and placed it on the desk in front of him. 'I've come to return it,' she explained, when all he did was stare at it. Then she took three steps backwards.

The room remained silent for several uncomfortable seconds. He picked up the watch and opened the case to examine it. His eyes showed no emotion when he returned his gaze to her face. 'You were just…borrowing it, I suppose?'

Oh, God, how could she explain? Her words spilled out in a jumble. 'No, I mean, I never intended to take it. I saw…' *Start at the beginning.* She took a calming breath. 'When you saved me from that pickpocket… I—I mean the reason I wasn't paying attention then is that I thought someone was following me, and I was trying to locate him in the crowd. I'd seen the same man several times that morning. And, well, my point is that I thought I was safe while you were accompanying me, but then when you left to converse with your driver I saw him again. I had little choice but to run. I didn't realise until too late that I'd taken your watch with me. I was too afraid to go back to see if you were still there.'

He was silent for several seconds. 'Who was he?'

Please let him believe her. 'I don't know, but I know it was the same man. I…I'm sorry it took me so long to find you, but all I had was your name, and I had to pay the boy who delivers coal to locate you. But I've finally found you. Please believe me.'

He deposited the watch on the desk in front of him. Any anger in his expression had been replaced by curiosity.

'Please sit, Miss Thomas.'

She did, flushing again as she realised that, as was habit, she'd said too much. 'I'm so sorry.'

'You can stop apologising. Have you seen this man since then?'

'No.'

'That area is teeming with criminals. He was probably another pickpocket.'

'I think so.' But she felt certain he wasn't. It was much more likely that he'd been sent by Sebastian Cowes to make sure she didn't flee. He could have discovered her London address easily from her house-keeper. Kindly Mrs Vincent would've worried terribly if she'd gone without telling her how she could be contacted, but Isabelle now wished she'd given false details.

He turned slightly in his chair and pulled the bell cord that hung down the wall.

She tensed and rose. Maybe he didn't believe her after all. Maybe he was going to send for the authorities. 'What are you doing?'

'Having a tray of…' He paused when the door opened. This time a butler entered. 'Oh, Bartholomew, please have a tray of tea brought.'

'Mrs Graham is just preparing one now, my lord. Shall I ask her to include an extra—?'

'Yes, yes, enough for two, obviously,' Will said with a touch of impatience.

The butler left silently.

He turned his attention back to her. 'You can sit again, Miss Thomas. You've nothing to be afraid of.'

'I must go. Really.'

'No, sit.'

It was an order, but she continued to stand. Because even if he didn't want to have her arrested for theft, he still did funny things to her insides. Funny things that made her blush and speak like an imbecile. 'No, no. I have to leave.'

'Why? Do you have plans for the afternoon?'

'Yes.' That wasn't true.

'I don't believe you.'

'I do. I'm having lunch. With…uh—'

'The king?'

Her gaze met his, and he challenged her to come up with another excuse. His eyes were so disconcerting that she couldn't think fast enough.

So she sat uneasily on the sofa. 'I can't stay for long.'

'You'll have a cup of tea. And thank you, by the way.'

'Why?'

'Because even if you didn't mean to take my watch, you still didn't have to return it. It belonged to my grandfather. I could not have replaced it. I must reward you.'

'I don't need a reward for returning something I took in the first place.'

Just then, a maid arrived with a finely chased silver teapot, a milk jug and a sugar bowl. Another maid followed, carrying cups and saucers. They quietly placed everything on a side table before leaving without saying a word or making eye contact.

Will rose when the door closed and crossed the room. He began pouring the tea.

'Milk?' he asked over his shoulder.

She'd have to stay. There was no polite way out of it, and for all her faults she did try to be polite. 'A little, please.'

He brought her a cup and saucer and then sat again, this time on a chair next to the sofa. He was coming closer, and she regarded him warily as one might an approaching shark. 'I'm still willing to buy your necklace.'

She shook her head firmly. 'No. No, I've changed my mind about selling it.'

And then he asked, completely unexpectedly, 'You said it was a gift—who gave it to you?'

She shrugged. She didn't want to talk about it. Doing so would only sadden her.

'Who?' he pressed her. 'A beau?'

Hardly that. 'My mother.'

He looked as if he wanted to ask another question, but he changed the subject at the last minute as if to spare her further discomfort.

'I assume you've found employment, then.'

Had she told him she was looking for work? Yes, of course; he'd said she was too pretty—and even though she didn't think he'd meant it, butterflies had started flapping their wings in her stomach. 'Why?'

'Because if you no longer want to sell your necklace, then that can only mean you're less in need of money.'

'Oh.' She didn't want to tell him about her many rejections. She sat forwards and placed her teacup on the table beside the sofa. 'Well, I've met several people—'

'And they've responded favourably? You've been offered a position?'

She shifted her weight, and the room descended into awkward silence. She looked at the wall. Why was he keeping her?

'Then…perhaps you might help me,' he said slowly.

She returned her gaze to him, warily this time. 'How do you mean?'

He rose and walked back to his desk. He shuffled through some documents until he found what he wanted. A newspaper, folded open to one of the back pages. He handed it to her as he resumed his seat. She stared at it, not knowing what to think. All she saw was line after line of advertisements—for tutors, governesses, lady's maids…

'I advertised for a governess last week,' he explained. 'One of those listings is mine…somewhere in the middle column, I think. I've been interviewing candidates all morning. My footman assumed you were another one, and he told me as much when he announced you.'

She was so bewildered that all the words started swimming together, and she couldn't tell which posting was his. She focused on his face instead. 'Oh. No, that's not why… You want a governess?'

'Yes. Rather urgently.'

'I see.' His words finally made sense. He wanted a governess, which meant he obviously had a child. Children, maybe, as well as a wife, since the two normally went together. The thought caused a sudden, dull pain in her chest. Just another reminder that she was well and truly on the shelf and that, in her current straits, she'd never get married and have a family of her own. It was foolish for her to feel any excitement when he looked at her with his green eyes. And why had he flirted with her if he was married? Perhaps it hadn't been flirting; it wasn't as if she was so accustomed to male attention that she'd necessarily know the difference.

'I hope you found someone appropriate?' she said neutrally.

'Well, my cousin did most of the interviewing—left just a few minutes before you arrived. I'm afraid we've different ideas about what makes a person suitable. She supplied me with six terribly proper women of mature years. They were nothing like you.'

She flushed with anger. 'I've been reminded of my shortcomings all week. You needn't remind me, as well.'

He frowned slightly. 'I didn't say you had any. The women were ghastly, and the post is still open. Just thought perhaps you might also want to apply for it, while you're here. It wouldn't be any trouble.'

Work for him? She couldn't think of anything worse. She could barely look at him without her knees turning to porridge. 'I'm not qualified.'

He sighed patiently. 'Right. Well, for the future that's probably not the best way to begin. Have you introduced yourself like that to everyone you've met?'

'No. I should have, though, for it would have saved a lot of time. Additionally, I've no references.'

He leaned back in his seat and crossed his legs. She suspected he was laughing at her silently. 'None? And you expected someone to hire you?'

She rose. 'I think our interview is over.'

'Sit down, Miss Thomas,' he ordered, rising himself. His voice was firm, and he looked prepared to pick her up and toss her back on to the sofa if she didn't obey him.

So she sat. He might be warm and kind most of the time, but she still didn't want to test the limits of his generosity.

He didn't return to his seat. He crossed the room again to deposit his teacup on the side table. 'What you ought to be doing is drawing attention to your strong suits. For example, you're honest.'

'You don't know that.'

'I know that you returned my watch. Still short sixpence—'

She reddened defensively. 'I forgot about the sixpence. *Do* add absentmindedness to the list.'

'—but you've a sense of humor. You're attractive, too—some might see that as a drawback in a governess, but I for one see it only as an advantage.' He turned around as he spoke, and she was reminded once more of how very attractive *he* was. But he must be teasing her. She didn't think she was very pretty—how could he?

She wouldn't let him fluster her. 'Surely my education is more important.'

He sat again, not looking terribly interested in her education. 'I was getting to that. What languages do you know?'

'French and Latin, a bit of Greek and German.'

'Far too many. How old are you?'

'What?'

'How old, Miss Thomas? I wouldn't normally ask such a personal question, but it is relevant.'

She was touchy about her age. 'I'm seven and twenty.'

He considered that for a moment. 'Well, that's a very sensible age. If you were a flighty nineteen-year-old I'd have to worry that you might elope with one of my footmen.' He paused. 'So why are you not married?'

Because she'd known very few men her age. Because she hadn't had a mother to introduce her to new people and take her to parties— just a rather cerebral father who didn't see the point of such trivial things. 'I've been holding out for a duke.'

He burst out laughing.

'Do I amuse you?'

He stopped, but he couldn't get his grin in order. 'Very much so, Miss Thomas.'

She rose and headed straight for the door. 'I will not waste your time, nor do I wish you to waste mine.'

Unfortunately, he beat her to it, literally standing in front of the door to prevent her from leaving. He looked as if he were losing patience with her. 'But I thought you wanted a job.'

She just raised her chin.

'I'm offering you one, you know. It wouldn't be too difficult. Mary's twelve, so she's fairly independent. You'd just have to spend a few hours doing lessons with her each day.'

Perfect, if only he wasn't be part of the deal. 'I imagine her mother would prefer to make these decisions.'

'Her mother is dead.'

Isabelle's irritation fizzled instantly, and she experienced a tinge of unwanted sympathy. He wasn't married after all. A widower. It was rather sad, and even rather romantic.

Stop it, you fool, she ordered herself. Be sensible, like your father taught you.

'I'm sorry for your loss, my lord. If you'll step aside, then I will bid you good morning.'

He looked momentarily confused, but then it dawned on him what she'd meant. 'It wasn't my loss, Miss Thomas. Mary is my ward. She was left in my care when her father died three months ago. Her mother's been dead for years.'

She took this in slowly. Not a widower. Not his child. She'd no reason to feel sorry for him. Instead, she felt suddenly defensive, as if he'd been misleading her. 'It was brave of her father to entrust her to you.'

'Then you agree I need your help?'

'Help, yes, but not mine. I've no experience, and you've seen half-a-dozen competent governesses this morning alone. I suggest you hire one of them.'

'But I prefer you.'

Strange sensations, making even her toes tingle. 'I've already told you how I feel about your charity.'

'I assure you, my motives are completely selfish. I did mention I was desperate? You wouldn't have to work here for very long. I'll soon start looking for a school to take her in the autumn, so I'd probably only require you for a matter of months.'

Ah—an escape route. 'Months? But I need a permanent position. It will be better if I just keep looking.' *And keep getting rejected...*

'You won't find one without experience.'

It was true, and she knew it. He'd persuade her if she didn't leave soon. 'I recognise that is a problem—'

'Do you think I would simply leave you to wander the streets with no money?' he asked, irritation entering his voice. 'Do you know what happens to penniless young women with nowhere to go?'

'I imagine many such women wander the streets without you noticing them.'

He couldn't argue with that. She'd managed to fluster him, but not for long.

'If you accept this position, Miss Thomas, I will give you a reference.'

'For a summer's work?'

'It would be better than nothing.'

It would be. She realised that he would continue to obstruct the door until she agreed, so she returned to the sofa, feeling deflated.

She closed her eyes briefly and saw an image of Sebastian Cowes, who most likely knew where she was staying and had sent a man to follow her. Who she suspected had the most ignominious designs on her person and who would no doubt have her charged with debt if she didn't give in. She didn't know if the charges would hold, considering she hadn't committed her father's crimes, but they might if it could be proved she'd known about and benefited from them. And if not…well, no matter how badly her father had behaved, she didn't want his reputation to suffer—as it surely would, if his secret was made public.

She thought also of her diminishing funds and of the long list of people who might one day realise what a fraud her father had been. Lord Lennox had returned to his desk, and she looked at him out of the corner of her eye. She felt, instinctively, that he wouldn't hurt her, and living in his house would at least offer her temporary protection. True, she half-suspected that he harboured dishonourable designs of his own, but she was fairly certain she was imagining most of it. He probably flirted with every woman he met.

As it turned out, when she reasoned his offer through, she had little choice but to accept. It was the best she could hope for. She couldn't pretend that she was a sheltered young lady any more.

'I will consider it.'

'There's nothing to consider,' he said without looking up from the documents he was perusing. 'I need an answer now. You can always leave if you find you don't like working for me.'

'I will…yes, I will do it.'

He met her gaze, and she found herself startled by the emerald intensity of his eyes. Greener than she'd seen them before, and mesmerising. It must be the light.

'Then you can start tomorrow. I'll expect you here at ten.'

And that was that. He rose to open the study door and she found herself floating into the hall, unmoored and uncertain.

He spoke to Rogers, the footman, who was waiting to open the front door. 'Miss Thomas will return tomorrow morning. She is to be Mary's governess.'

Rogers nodded impassively. She turned around, looking for Lord Lennox, but he'd already returned to the study.

So she faced instead the bright afternoon, thinking that only the devil could have eyes like that.

Chapter Five

All of Isabelle's possessions fit snugly into her three bags. Lord Lennox had made no provision to help her transport her things, probably overlooking the fact that unlike him she didn't have her own carriage. For the time being she carried only one bag, containing just enough clothes for the next few days. If she hadn't been sacked by the end of the week, she would come back to collect the rest.

She opened the front door, but hesitated before stepping outside. Portentous grey clouds filled the sky, and the smooth paving stones were already lightly specked with rain. She turned her head and glanced behind her. The other two bags were neatly stowed beneath Miss Standish's dust-free hall table; her umbrella was at the bottom of one. Which one, she'd no idea, and she'd no time to look.

She stepped out and debated not going at all as a raindrop gently hit her cheek. What would happen if she simply didn't show up? Will didn't know where she lived, and he'd have no way to find her. She'd been awake half the night wondering if she'd made the right decision. *Had* she made a decision? As was her lot these days, she'd never really had a choice to begin with, and she was starting to think that Will had behaved rather highhandedly.

These were just cavils, though. He'd offered to help her, and she'd never been more sorely in need. She descended the steps, telling herself that it wasn't raining very hard and that the light shower would soon pass. The bag tugged heavily on her arm as she walked down the street, but she tried not to think about it. If she didn't get lost, she would reach his house in less than half an hour.

'Miss Thomas.'

She started at the familiar voice, but she quickly regained her composure. What was he doing there?

'Mr Cowes. Good heavens, you frightened me.'

Sebastian Cowes smiled slightly. He was attractive enough, with light brown hair and eyes, but Isabelle thought there was something unpleasant about his appearance, something calculating and cold in his overly starched, elaborately arranged cravat. 'I apologise, Miss Thomas. I've been waiting for you.'

'You might have knocked on the door, then. It's more respectable than lurking in bushes.' She spoke sharply, but she immediately wished she could revoke her words. Obviously the reason he hadn't gone to the door was that he wanted to find her alone, with no one to protect her, and it wouldn't be wise to provoke him. Although he was just a fraction of an inch shorter that her, she wasn't going to fool herself—in any physical struggle he'd easily be the victor.

She started walking again. He fell in next to her. She glanced at him sideways, wondering if he planned to lead her down a deserted street and force her into a carriage.

'How did you find me?' she asked.

'Were you hiding?'

'No, of course not,' she said irritably. 'But I don't recall telling you where I was or inviting you to visit. Have you had me followed?'

'Your housekeeper told me where to find you. She must not have known it was a secret.'

'It isn't,' Isabelle said, wishing again she hadn't given Mrs Vincent the boarding house's address.

'Not any more, at least.'

She flushed with anger. She'd always been intimidated by him, by his wealth, and power and handsome face. But she felt less impressed now. Compared to Lord Lennox, Mr Cowes seemed completely second-rate.

'Why are you here?' she asked, gaining confidence.

He put his hands nonchalantly in his pockets. 'I was worried when you disappeared so suddenly—visited your house one day and found it occupied by perfect strangers.'

'Yes, I sold it to pay you. And I *did* pay you.'

'Not in full. You do realise that if you fail to uphold your side of our agreement, then I'll have to approach the authorities.'

'I'd hardly call blackmail an agreement.'

'You've paid me only half of what you owe me, and you seem dangerously close to breaking your word. Since you've nothing left to sell, I can't fathom how you'll acquire the other half.'

'I'll use my imagination,' she said sarcastically.

'Even your imagination can't be that good,' he said, pausing to look at her face. 'But then, perhaps you *do* have something to sell?'

She was going to ignore that insinuating remark. He was too insignificant to fluster her. She could handle him.

She could.

She just wished her audible voice sounded as robust as the one in her head. Instead it quivered slightly. 'I…I did not come to London to hide from you as you suggest, you know.'

He looked amused. 'Oh?'

'Yes. I knew I needed further funds, so I came to find employment.' Feeling surer, she added, 'And I have.' As she spoke, she was eternally grateful that she'd accepted Will's offer.

'You'll be that well paid, will you? And what is it you're doing?'

'It is none of your affair.'

'I can think of only one position in which a woman could earn enough. Shall I tell you what it is?' He leaned in closer as he spoke, grabbing her tightly by the arm. Her stomach listed dangerously, and she thought she might be sick. This was the bit where he pushed her in a waiting carriage. Why had she been so impertinent?

'Do you not want to know?' he asked.

She shook her head. Softly, she pleaded, 'Let me go. I will be late.'

He released her. She was so surprised that for two seconds she just stood there, waiting for him to grab her again. But he didn't.

She took two steps backwards without taking her eyes from his face before turning to run. She didn't care if she drew attention to herself, and she didn't stop until she reached the end of the road. At the corner she paused, to see if he had followed, but he still stood where she'd left him, watching her smugly. She kept running.

Even though Isabelle had been to Will's house once before, she still managed to lose her way. It didn't help that she'd gone down an unfamiliar road in order to distance herself from Sebastian Cowes. Only after winding down a series of unfamiliar streets had she regained her bearings.

Then it began to rain in earnest.

She was sponge-wet when she finally reached the house, her hair dripping at the ends and her shoes squelching with every step she took.

She was also almost an hour late.

She knocked, consoling herself with the fact that at least her day couldn't get much worse. Rogers, the footman, opened the door, looking annoyed with her yet again. 'We were expecting you at ten, Miss Thomas.'

Oh, what an awful way to begin. 'I'm sorry.'

'Haven't you an umbrella?'

It was a stupid question, with an answer so obvious she didn't bother to reply. She stepped inside, trailing water behind her. She dropped her bag on the polished marble floor. 'I accidentally went down the wrong road. I got lost.'

He harrumphed. 'His lordship wished to see you when you arrived.' He walked to the study door and knocked, looking over his shoulder at her as he did so. 'Do not move, Miss Thomas. You are dripping.'

A few seconds later, Will emerged from the study. If it were possible, he looked even more handsome today. His attire possessed none of the fussiness of Mr Cowes's ludicrous cravat—his own was simply tied, and his jacket and breeches were again a sober blue and buff. Normally, the austerity of his dress was tempered by the playful spark in his eyes, but today he seemed merely irritated.

That is, until he looked at her. Then he just seemed confused. 'Good God, did you swim here?'

She glared at him. She knew she was late and that she'd annoyed him, but she didn't want to be the butt of his sarcasm. 'You may have noticed the rain.'

'It didn't rain that hard here.' He turned to Rogers. 'Tell Mrs Wright to come.' And, to Isabelle as the footman walked off, 'I have rather a busy morning.'

He still sounded peeved, and an awful sense of dread settled around her shoulders. Would she ever learn to control her temper and hold her tongue? For all that she might have protested yesterday, she truly needed this position—particularly in light of what had just happened. At least she'd be safe in his house.

Some humility was in order. 'I am sorry. I hope I haven't inconvenienced you.'

He sighed and actually sounded a bit contrite. 'No, no, I'm sorry. It's obviously been something of an ordeal getting here this morning. Uh…perhaps you should…' He held out his handkerchief.

She took it gratefully. A mirror hung on the wall a few paces away and she walked towards it, dabbing her face. But the reflection she saw…heavens, for the first time she realised just how dishevelled she looked. Positively amphibious. Her cheeks were flushed and most of her hair had slipped from her chignon to hang wetly around her shoulders. She immediately began smoothing it back, but then she noticed her dress. Thick, chaste cotton most of the time, but right now it clung to her in a positively…

'Oh, dear.'

'What's wrong?' Even though he'd apologised for his abruptness, his voice sounded gruff and irritable.

She raised her gaze from her suddenly conspicuous breasts and realised that he was watching her in the mirror. She turned around immediately, slouching her shoulders forwards in an attempt at modesty. 'Nothing.'

His gaze lingered on her face for just a second longer than was proper, but before she had a chance to turn an even more intense red, a matronly, middle-aged woman walked purposefully into the hall.

He dragged his attention away from Isabelle and cleared his throat. 'Ah, Mrs Wright. This is Miss Thomas.'

The woman—obviously his housekeeper—smiled warmly, her manners too good to reveal any surprise at her appearance.

He turned to Isabelle, assiduously keeping his gaze above her neck. 'I thought Mrs Wright could show you around the house this morning. Perhaps you would prefer to…uh, go to your room directly to change?'

She nodded silently, and with a nod of his own, directed at both her and Mrs Wright, he returned to his study.

'Well, then,' the housekeeper said cheerily, clapping her hands together, 'shall we begin?'

Before setting off, Isabelle restored her modesty by fishing a shawl from her bag and wrapping it around her shoulders.

'You poor duck. I'll lead you straight to your room, although I think we can see most of the house on the way.'

Isabelle followed her up the staircase to the first floor, feeling rather awed by the woman's efficiency. She talked practically non-stop as they walked, and Isabelle hoped she might be an ally. She'd obviously already offended the footman.

'I'm afraid most of the rooms on this floor are formal and won't pertain to your duties,' Mrs Wright was saying. She opened one half of a pair of massive, mahogany doors. 'Here is the ballroom. Rather nice, don't you think?'

Nice? It was the largest room Isabelle had ever seen, not that she had much to compare it to. The parquet floors gleamed, uncluttered by furniture except for a long suite of damask-covered chairs that lined the walls and four carved mahogany side tables. Tall windows, framed by red velvet, tasselled curtains, filled the room with light, making it bright even on a cloudy day. And beyond the windows, gardens—gardens of a size she hadn't realised existed in London. It was like a palace.

She couldn't help smiling. 'Yes. Rather nice.'

Mrs Wright had apparently grown jaded by this level of opulence and didn't waste any time gawping. She walked briskly across the room, and Isabelle struggled to keep up. At the other side, she opened another door, leading them into a dim corridor.

'This is a servants' passage. It connects most of the principal rooms. This door here…' she paused to rap on it gently '…leads to steps that will take you all the way downstairs to the kitchen. Mrs Graham is the cook. She doesn't like anyone to take food from the kitchen between meals, and I'd advise you not to get in her way.' She laughed, but Isabelle didn't find the prospect of a truculent cook amusing. They kept walking.

Mrs Wright pointed out the door that led to the dining room as they passed, but she didn't bother opening it. At the end of the passage, they came to a set of stairs. Standing beneath the staircase, Isabelle looked up, feeling dizzy. They appeared to spiral up for another two storeys.

'These will take you to your bedroom. There's another set of servants' stairs on the north side of the house, and you should try to use them unless you're accompanying Miss Weston-Burke—you're not as low as a scullery maid, my dear, but still it's best to keep out of sight. And you should use the servants' entrance in the future, as well. I will give you a key.' Isabelle blushed—she'd already used the front door twice. Had that been wrong? She wasn't used to thinking like a servant.

Mrs Wright mounted the steps and Isabelle followed behind her, forcing herself not to look down or think too hard about how securely the stairs were attached to the wall. They stopped at the second floor, and Mrs Wright opened a door. It led into a small vestibule containing a walnut armchair and a tall, Chinese vase. A fat tabby cat slept peacefully on the chair. The tip of one of his ears appeared to have been torn, and his tail trailed down crookedly, as if it had been broken at some point.

'I won't bother showing you this floor since you'll never need anything on it. His lordship's rooms are at the far end, and all the other rooms are vacant bedrooms. And that fine creature,' she added, motioning towards the cat, 'is your other charge.'

The cat yawned and stretched.

Isabelle stared at it. 'My other charge?'

'Yes, and he's very demanding. He's called Tobias the Third, and you mustn't be too kind to the scoundrel. He followed his lordship home one afternoon about two years ago, and his lordship made the mistake of feeding him and letting him inside. We've been trying to evict him ever since…he's supposed to stay in the kitchen, but Mrs Graham's terrified of cats and keeps letting him out. Silly woman always pretends it's an accident.'

'Why is he the third?'

'Tobias the First died three years ago. The Second lives in his lordship's country house in Norfolk. He's a talent for taking in strays—an honourable quality, I suppose, but I told him I'd leave the minute Tobias the Fourth appeared nonetheless. Not one yet has been a good mouser, so they're no use to me. Come along.'

They returned to the dark staircase and walked up one more flight. Mrs Wright was short of breath when they reached the top.

'The rest of the servants reside in the north wing, but you'll sleep on this floor, amongst the children's bedrooms. Ceilings are still quite high.' Isabelle followed her down the corridor. 'The nursery is the fifth door on the right. This room is yours.'

Isabelle peeked inside. She was pleasantly surprised, as she had been by every aspect of the house. Being a governess, she could enjoy a position better than a servant's, but still a long way from being a guest or a family member. Yet even though her room was not on one of the principal floors, its ceiling was embellished with a simple cornice and a central rosette. The walls were painted a buttery yellow, making the room warm, bright and cheerful—not grand like the rooms she'd already seen, but by any other standard quite impressive.

She couldn't believe her luck. 'It's perfect. Thank you for showing me.'

Mrs Wright nodded. 'T'isn't any trouble. You may also use the small bedroom next door as a sitting room if you like, as no one else will if you don't. The house is one of the largest in London, and it was never intended to be so empty. These rooms should be full of children, but his lordship is in no hurry to marry.'

Don't look too interested. 'No?'

'No—women have thrown themselves at him since he was a lad, and I suppose he's never seen the sense in limiting himself to one woman for the rest of his life. But he will marry some day soon, I'm sure. He understands his duty.'

Isabelle frowned slightly, but she didn't know why exactly.

'You'll find Miss Weston-Burke in the nursery.'

'Can you tell me anything about her?' Isabelle asked as Mrs Wright turned to leave.

She paused in the doorway, frowning. 'She's been here for less than a fortnight, and she's kept mostly to herself.'

'What sort of things does she like to do?'

The housekeeper shrugged. 'I've no idea. Don't know if she likes to do anything at all.'

That was a queer thing to say. 'What do you mean?'

'From what I've gathered, mischief and mayhem are her only pursuits. According to her school report, which I took the liberty of reading as his lordship left it open on his desk, she's the most sullen and disobedient girl they'd known in a decade. They sent her away, you know. That's why he hired you.'

'Oh?' Lord Lennox had failed to mention that.

'Indeed,' Mrs Wright said with a smile. A rather knowing smile, Isabelle thought, as the older woman sailed away, humming.

Chapter Six

Isabelle allowed her hair to dry and changed into a fresh gown, unfortunately very wrinkled from travel. She'd hoped to hang it up overnight. Then she pottered about for another twenty minutes, opening every drawer in hopes of finding telling artefacts to illuminate the rakish Lord Lennox. Billets-doux from past mistresses, threatening letters from creditors…but she found nothing more than a broken fan and a ten-year-old receipt for roof repairs.

Finally, she knew she could put the meeting off no longer.

She left her room and walked down the corridor to the nursery. She knocked lightly, and when no one answered after several seconds she opened the door with trepidation. The walls inside were covered with rather tatty Chinese paper—birds and blossoming trees picked at by generations of young Stanton fingers. A dollhouse, made to resemble the grand house that contained it, stood on a stand to the side of the room. Its inhabitants made up a sorry skeleton crew: a wax-faced mother and her three children, each in a state of dishabille, a wild-haired maid and a decapitated butler. Other than that, the room showed little sign of recent occupation.

It was occupied, though. It took Isabelle a moment to locate her. Mary Weston-Burke sat cross-legged on a battered armchair, the arms so worn that the filling showed through the striped fabric. She'd been reading a book, but she lowered it when Isabelle entered. Her grey gaze was rather cool and assessing, Isabelle thought.

But still, she rose politely, her arms and legs unfolding like the ivory wool-winder the spinsters used, all straight lines and angles. She was tall for her age, too thin, and had hair as red as Isabelle's— a fact that made Isabelle's apprehensive heart warm slightly with camaraderie. The girl had not been blessed with beauty, Isabelle thought, but she had an open expression that probably brightened when she smiled.

If she ever smiled.

Isabelle had no idea where to begin. She'd even less experience with children than the average female, since she had no siblings. Her father had always talked to her as he would have to an adult. Isabelle had barely spoken to a child since she'd been one.

And this child was the most disobedient her school had seen in a decade.

She smiled unconvincingly. 'Good afternoon, Mary. I am Miss Thomas.'

The girl curtsied. 'How do you do.'

Isabelle looked around the room, hoping some object would provide her with something to say. It was a bright space with views looking down on to the square—rather forlorn, like the girl inside it, but not without scope for improvement.

'I'm told you left your school.'

Mary nodded.

'I take it you didn't like it.'

'No.'

This was going brilliantly well. Isabelle realised she'd never discussed her salary with Lord Lennox. It had better be generous. 'Then I hope you'll like me better.'

Mary looked away, unwilling to offer any reassurance, and Isabelle realised that she was failing already.

'Shall we get started, then?' she said matter of factly.

Will didn't seek Isabelle out until the next afternoon. It was a deliberate choice, since his plans had started to crumble the moment she arrived at his house, an hour late. He hadn't given a damn about her tardiness—the reason he'd been so annoyed was that he'd started to think she wouldn't come at all. That thought, and the fact that he'd have no way of finding her if she didn't appear, had caused an entirely unexpected feeling of disappointment. He shouldn't care; she was as replaceable as any pretty girl…although not so the novel master-servant relationship he'd been clever enough to devise. At the time, hiring her had seemed like a stroke of genius from which both parties would benefit. Now, however, he wondered if his spur-of-the-moment decision didn't signal the onset of madness—which did, after all, run rather strongly through the Stanton blood. He couldn't *actually* seduce Mary's governess. Not while she was still employed in that capacity, anyway. He'd merely set himself up for months of torture.

He entered the nursery after they'd finished their lunch. The door was ajar and made no noise as he pushed it open. He was surprised by the room, which looked barely changed from when he'd used it as a child. He'd been inside only a few times since.

They were both sitting on the floor. Scattered on the carpet around them was evidence of a busy morning—one bible, a novel, two books of French grammar and a workbasket overflowing with scraps of fabric and yarn. Mary noticed him immediately. Her cool grey gaze, remarkably like her father's, lifted from the white linen handkerchief she was pretending to embroider. She showed no emotion, but Will thought he saw—just maybe—a flicker of curiosity. He smiled, and she looked away diffidently.

Isabelle didn't register him, however; her attention, and a rather dark frown, was focused on pulling a stubborn stitch through a piece of silk. He watched her for a second, enjoying the way she pursed her lips in frustration. There was something delightfully imperfect about her face, something that made it more memorable and more pleasing than a face that conformed to every convention of beauty.

'Good afternoon.'

She looked up with a small start and immediately began to rise. 'Oh, good afternoon. I didn't see you come in.' She looked uncertainly at the mess that surrounded them. 'I, uh, we began the day at the desk, but found the floor more conducive to work. It is…sometimes one needs to spread out.'

He let his eyes savour the smattering of freckles on her nose. 'I don't care where you work. You can come downstairs, if you like. No need to stay in the nursery all day.'

'I wouldn't want to bother you.'

It undoubtedly would bother him, having her any closer at hand. It just wouldn't bother him in the way she imagined. 'I thought we'd have an outing.'

He could see her struggling with the pronoun, wondering who he meant by *'we'*. Mary and him? All three of them? 'Oh. Yes, of course.'

'Mary?'

The girl nodded after a moment's thought. Will felt a slight pang of guilt. She'd lived in his house for nearly two weeks, and he should have offered to take her out before now. But what did he have to say to a sulky child? All they had in common was a mutual acquaintance: his friend, her father. But such a topic of conversation was no doubt too painful for her so soon to his death.

'Tidy up, then, and we'll go.'

As Will waited downstairs, he debated the wisdom of his proposal. He didn't really know what the protocol was for taking outings with members of one's staff, nor, he imagined, did Isabelle. But since it was considered appropriate enough for her to live in his house, he didn't think there should be anything *so* odd about being seen out of doors with her—which was, after all, far less intimate. It was the only way he'd ever manage to have a conversation with her, at least one that wasn't strictly professional, since he couldn't start frequenting the nursery without causing his servants to gossip.

But when Isabelle and Mary descended the stairs a few minutes later, he was struck by the fact that the protocol for her would be different. If she were matronly and plain, he could take any number of outings with her without raising an eyebrow. But she was young and beautiful. She'd obviously spent a few minutes titivating her person, and her efforts had resulted in a slightly squashed hat and a chignon at her nape. Already, though, her hair was beginning to sneak free from its confines. There was something delightfully untidy about her appearance, necessary to soften the severity of her grey dress. But even dull grey couldn't conceal her perfect proportions and tiny waist. He admired her tailoring for a second, then realised he was actually just admiring her...

He cleared his throat and fixed his attention on Mary. 'Shall we?'

Chapter Seven

'Where are we going?' Isabelle enquired, her voice rather hesitant.

Will had been waiting for her to ask. They'd been in the carriage for twenty minutes and barely a word had been spoken. Mary sat quietly on the seat across from them. As usual, her opaque expression revealed nothing of her thoughts.

'The British Museum.' It wasn't a venue he'd have much desire to visit on his own, and he'd decided on it merely because it sounded suitably edifying—just the sort of place he might request Isabelle to take Mary anyway as part of her tutorial duties, ignoring the fact that he just wanted an excuse to sit next to her in his carriage.

In fact, he now rather wished he wasn't sitting next to her. She was too close—not from any effort on her part, since every time the carriage turned a corner she all but clung to the wall to avoid leaning in to him. But the fact was, at six foot three he simply took up quite a lot of space, and there was no preventing his leg occasionally touching hers. Like most ideas he'd had since meeting her, it had seemed a good one at first, but now her proximity was causing his body more inconvenience than pleasure.

'Have you been before?' he asked.

'Yes. A few times, but not for years.'

'Oh?' He waited for her to expand.

She looked at him only briefly before lowering her gaze. Reluctantly, she explained, 'My father was an antiquary, and he used to visit whenever he was in town. Sometimes he brought me along.'

'So that explains your rock collection.'

She wanted to glare at him—he could tell from the set of her profile—but she caught herself in time to change tack to a mild-mannered shrug. He smiled. Talking to her was never boring.

'What's an antiquary?' Mary asked. Will glanced at her, rather surprised. These were among the first voluntary words she'd uttered, and she had a lovely, clear voice, reminiscent of her father's in its timbre.

Isabelle didn't look as if she wanted to discuss the subject in depth. 'He was interested in ancient objects...uh, Greek vases and sculpture and that sort of thing.'

'Why?' Mary asked sensibly.

'Why? Um, that's a very good question. Well, he collected these things and then, uh, he sold them. It was his profession.'

'It's not anymore?'

She looked out the window. 'He died three years ago.'

Will wondered why she seemed so uncomfortable, although he supposed Mary's questions were rather blunt. She didn't have the polished manners of many girls her age, although he didn't think there was anything unfriendly about her. She was just a touch defensive, and rather plain and awkward to boot. He wondered if he should buy her a new wardrobe. He hadn't paid much heed until that moment, but the girl's clothes were hardly more fashionable than Isabelle's. It would be a small price to pay to cheer her up. Then again, perhaps she didn't care.

They rode the rest of the way without speaking. Will was relieved when the carriage finally stopped. He climbed out first, needing to put some distance between himself and Isabelle. The sun shone and a gentle breeze rustled the trees, bringing pedestrians out in droves: scholarly-looking gentlemen, couples out for a stroll and busy families all milling about on the street in front of the large, pediment-topped building.

They entered the cool, marble-clad hall silently, as if entering a church—although it was, Will noted, better attended than any ecclesiastical service he'd been to in years. In addition to its immense collection of antiquities, the museum was a repository for all sorts of strange and wondrous things: beetles from Africa, Antipodean seashells, a pair of stuffed giraffes. He hadn't been since he was a boy, but the beetles had impressed him most at the time.

Mary walked quickly ahead, probably hoping to get the visit over with as soon as possible. Isabelle walked slowly beside him, looking after the girl with concern.

'Are you all right?' he asked.

She glanced at him anxiously. 'Yes, of course. Why?'

'You seem rather distracted.'

'No. I'm sorry. Have you been here before?' It was a polite question, awkwardly asked and obviously only intended to direct his attention away from her.

'I came with my Uncle Henry many years ago, when I was about fourteen. He wanted me to see some collection of Greek vases and assured me the experience would be salutary. I'd just failed a Greek exam in spectacular fashion, and he thought I needed inspiration.'

'Did you improve?'

'I'm afraid that whenever anyone tells me something's good for me I take an instant dislike to it. And since there was nothing I disliked more than my Greek tutor, Mr Dunster, I was determined to pay no attention.'

'You were not a good student?' There was a welcome smile lurking behind her question. He could tell that she was beginning to relax.

'Terrible, but I never had a teacher as charming as you. How is your pupil?'

The smile faded, and her expression became worried again. 'Well…quiet. She seems determined not to like me. I might be her Mr Dunster.'

'You're no one's Mr Dunster, I assure you. I wouldn't take her aloofness personally. She doesn't seem to like me, either. Or anyone, for that matter.'

'Yes. You neglected to tell me she had something of a reputation.'

He liked the way she couldn't resist a gibe, even if it was at his expense. 'I'm not sure I believe it. She hasn't cut all your hair off yet, has she?'

She frowned at him. 'No, but she's barely spoken. I can't imagine her being wicked, although Mrs Wright assured me that was the case. I suppose sorrow can cause one to act…erratically.'

'According to Miss Hume, her misbehavior long predated her father's death.'

Isabelle thought that over. 'She's very clever, I should think.'

'Arthur was clever. The only reason I passed my exams was because I copied from his.'

She rolled her eyes. 'I don't believe you.'

'Oh? You think I might be a bit clever, too, do you?'

She blushed, but managed to retort, 'No, I don't think you passed your exams.'

He sighed. 'I shall have to work hard to impress you, Miss Thomas.'

She looked at him sideways, again with a smile tugging at her lips. 'If anything, I'd say she's a bit too clever. Perhaps boredom caused her to be mischievous.'

Will considered her suggestion. Arthur, too, had been in endless scrapes at school, always the result of an active imagination and too much time on his hands. 'I wouldn't worry much about it. You need only entertain her for a few months to keep her out of trouble. Hide the scissors.' He looked around the room to avoid the dark look that she now directed at him. 'Rather impressive, isn't it? I'm sure you know far more than my Uncle Henry. Did your father educate you?'

She nodded. 'Unfortunately.'

'Why is that?'

Her gaze followed his around the vast room. 'Girls don't need to know these things.'

'No?' he asked. 'But you do.'

She blushed. 'Only by osmosis, and I assure you, it hasn't done me a jot of good.'

'Maybe it has. Maybe that's why I hired you.'

'My knowledge of Greek sculpture?' She sounded highly dubious.

'Yes, of course. Why else?' He knew exactly why he'd hired her; he wondered what she thought.

'Charity, remember?'

No, not that. Not really. He *did* feel a powerful urge to protect her, but at the same time his motives could hardly be more ignoble. 'You're wrong again. I hired you because you were far prettier than the other candidates.'

'Be serious.'

Will liked the way her eyes started to flash in annoyance, the way she opened her mouth slightly as if preparing an insult, and then closed it quickly once she thought better of it. Her peppery remarks had been what attracted him to her in the first place. She was so different from the trained poodles Henrietta and Venetia insisted on introducing him to, young ladies who made only anodyne comments and would never dream of disagreeing with him.

'I apologise. I forgot, for a moment, that I was in the presence of a bluestocking. I shall be entirely serious from now on.'

She frowned sternly. 'I am not a bluestocking.'

That only made him start thinking about her stockings, which he'd caught a glimpse of when she'd climbed into the carriage. They weren't blue at all. They were white and sensible, but they covered a slim, promising ankle. He shouldn't be thinking about her ankles, either. Or her legs.

Before he embarrassed himself, he turned his attention instead to a giant, sandalled foot, three feet long and carved from marble. It sat on a plinth in the centre of the room. 'What is this?'

'I haven't the faintest idea,' she said rather grumpily.

'Liar. I'm sure you could tell me exactly.'

'No, I cannot.'

'You're not a bluestocking. I take it back. Now tell me.'

His cajoling tone worked. She smiled reluctantly. 'It's Roman, the foot of a god, I imagine, and I'm *not* a bluestocking. Not really. I'd have far preferred to spend my time doing the sorts of things other girls did. It's just that my father was in charge of my education and upbringing, so he saw that I learned the sorts of things he thought were important.'

'What about your mother?'

'She died when I was young. Her father was a professor of Latin at Oxford, and my father was his pupil. He was there as a scholar— poor as a church mouse, and he showed his gratitude by eloping with his tutor's daughter when she was seventeen.'

'How scandalous.'

'It was, I suppose.' Her smile grew, as if at some distant memory. It had an unaccountable effect on him. He caught her eye, and she looked away, blushing. He put his hands in his pockets, trying to control the urge to touch her, and they walked along quietly for several minutes.

He couldn't help glancing at her from time to time, though. He liked looking at her. There was something natural and unaffected about her that he found extremely appealing. He liked talking to her, too, especially during the rare moments when she let her guard down.

He realised he probably shouldn't be strolling around with her like this, as if they were alone, but Mary was a blessedly unconcerned chaperone. She'd walked ahead and was at the far end of the room, uninterestedly inspecting a large cabinet of terracotta vases. She looked bored, and Will experienced another twinge of conscience. She was so unhappy, and he hadn't done much to help beyond hiring a governess with his own entertainment in mind. He simply didn't know what to say to her, though. He knew nothing about children, and although he managed well enough with those he was related to, they were mostly quite young and all it took to please them was presents every time he visited. He'd assured Mary, when she'd first arrived, that he'd send her to another school soon, but if anything his words had made her more sullen. What could he do?

'Are you interested in this sort of thing?' Isabelle asked rather suddenly.

Will looked around the room, feeling no flicker of excitement at the endless rows of vases. 'Not particularly. They all look the same to me.'

'You've never bought any, then?'

'No. M'grandfather collected Chinese teapots.'

'But not ancient sculpture or anything of the sort?'

She seemed oddly interested in his answer, and peculiarly anxious. 'No. Sorry to disappoint you.'

Instead, she actually looked slightly relieved. 'Not at all. It's just that I've heard there are a lot of disreputable dealers out there, and I should hate for you to have fallen victim to one of them.'

It was an odd thing to say, but perhaps less so considering her father's profession. She *had* been in possession of several forgeries when he first met her, but to her credit she'd readily declared them as fakes. He didn't press her about it. 'Thank you for your advice, Miss Thomas. I shall be vigilant.'

She blushed again at his teasing tone. 'What are you interested in, then?'

'Interested?' Was she trying to change the subject?

'Yes. Everyone has an interest.'

Will had to think for a moment, not least because it was a more direct question than he was used to being asked by a woman. It also made him feel momentarily insufficient and rather purposeless for the first time in many years. But he wasn't, not really. He might have spent much of his life being thoroughly irresponsible, but when he had inherited his title four years ago that had changed. Suddenly he'd had two large houses to take care of and more tenants than he could count. He took everyone's happiness and health very seriously, perhaps more seriously than most would because he knew he had to make up for years of fallowness. He was still a long way from perfect, but when it came to protecting those in his charge, he thought he managed rather well.

She was looking at him, patiently waiting for his answer. Of course he wouldn't tell her all that, like some sort of maudlin fool.

'Horses,' he said. 'Do you ride?'

His remark just made her look uncomfortable again. 'Not well. I told you I wasn't very accomplished.'

He wondered if asking about riding had made her self-conscious. Everyone he knew rode well, but just about everyone he knew had grown up on large country estates with acres and acres of land. 'You could learn.'

'I know how,' she clarified. 'I…but I've never hunted, or anything like that…'

Her voice trailed off, and he noticed her staring into one of the crowded cases. A grey, stone woman stared back, her nose broken off and her head wound round with carved plaits.

'Miss Thomas?'

'What? Oh, sorry. Did you say something?'

He tried to alleviate her discomfort by asking a question he was sure she could answer. 'So…what's this statue you're looking at? Is she Greek? Roman?'

But instead of looking more confident, she blushed and looked away. 'I'm not certain.'

'Come now, don't pretend you don't know. I shan't accuse you of being a bluestocking again. What else would it be?'

She hesitated before answering. 'I'm sorry. It's Greek. I imagine it's a bit more than two thousand years old.'

She seemed bothered by saying that. 'Are you well?' he asked. She didn't look well. She looked pale and hot, and he felt suddenly worried.

'Yes,' she said. 'No. Perhaps I'm just tired?'

'There's a bench by the wall. Shall we—?'

He didn't get a chance to finish before a hearty greeting interrupted him, resonating from somewhere behind his left shoulder. 'Lennox? Is that you?'

Will turned around slowly, a feeling of dread brought on by the familiar voice. Two handsome gentlemen, one dark, one fair, were crossing the room, looking well dressed, well fed and well oiled from a self-indulgent lunch: his friends, John Dewhurst and Charles Prestwick. John had been the one to address him, but both gentlemen now regarded Isabelle with keen interest.

'We've just come from the club and are walking off the effects. What are you doing, old chap?' Prestwick asked, smiling at Isabelle as if she, too, might offer an answer. They were both obviously waiting for an introduction.

Bloody hell, he wasn't in the mood for this. She didn't look like she was, either. If possible, she'd grown even paler.

'I'm taking my ward around,' Will replied, quickly scanning the room for Mary. Was she even still there?

Dewhurst grinned engagingly at Isabelle. 'Are *you* his ward?'

'No, you…' Will managed to avoid an obscenity. He motioned towards Mary, whom he'd finally located. 'The girl over there. Tall thing with red hair. She's an old friend's daughter. Miss Thomas is her governess.'

'A governess. How interesting.' They both grinned broadly. Isabelle stared awkwardly at the floor. Will glared at them.

Prestwick caught on and grinned. 'Yes, well, we must be going.'

'Not so soon,' Dewhurst said. 'I wanted to ask Miss Thomas—'

'*Not* soon enough,' Will cut in. Isabelle was biting her lip, pretending not to be present.

The gentlemen made their excuses and wandered off. Will was sure they'd rib him about it when he saw them next. He really was a fool for taking her out in public.

'Sorry about that,' he said once they were out of hearing.

'You've nothing to apologise for.'

He felt he did, though. They'd ogled her as if she were his mistress. Fair enough for them to think that, but he hadn't liked it. It had made her uncomfortable.

'They're idiots,' he said.

'They're your friends?'

'Yes. And idiots. We might have tea somewhere. Or perhaps just sit.'

'Perhaps…I'm afraid I don't feel terribly well. I'm sorry.'

His gaze wandered over her face, trying to gauge what had bothered her. 'Home, then.'

She nodded after a moment's indecision, and then walked off to inform Mary.

What had caused the change? She'd seemed relaxed, and now she was practically wringing her hands. He doubted it was just his friends' asinine behavior—she'd seemed upset before they'd even arrived. He wondered if he'd ever get the chance to understand her better.

Chapter Eight

Isabelle spent the rest of the day feeling wretched, although not unwell as she'd told Will. She simply felt overwhelmed by her problems.

She hadn't expected to see one of her father's pieces at the museum. She was certain it had once been in his collection, even though she couldn't have been more than eight when she'd last seen it. She remembered the way the woman's plaits curled like snakes around her shoulders, and the flaking black paint around her eyes. He'd brought it back from one of his trips, and it was probably as old as it purported to be—if she remembered correctly, he'd bought it before his reliance on Signor Ricci began. But just seeing the statue had caused her to experience a sharp stab of insecurity. Who could tell what was true and what was false?

The experience had rendered her useless for the rest of the afternoon, barely able to concentrate long enough to give Mary her arithmetic lesson. She knew she couldn't afford to repeat this erratic behavior. Will had hired her to instruct the girl, not to behave like a ninny. And, oh, she'd made a hash of things even before she'd recognised the statue. She *must* be unfailingly polite to him. He was her employer, and her welfare was in his hands. But he kept provoking her, and she found herself responding as if they were equals. Worse, when she wasn't being downright impertinent, she was too bowled over by him to manage a sensible sentence. She shouldn't let his flirtation rattle her so. He certainly meant nothing by it.

But it did rattle her.

She looked out of her bedroom window. The pale moon had just appeared in the clear sky. Mary was in bed with a book, so Isabelle's duties, for now, were finished. She'd bid Mary goodnight, and although the girl's response hadn't been warm, it hadn't been unfriendly, either. She didn't know why Mary resisted every overture so stubbornly, but perhaps with patience she would understand more.

Her stomach grumbled, and she remembered her supper, which the cook, Mrs Graham, had promised to leave on a tray in the kitchen. Along with the officious Rogers, Mrs Graham promised to be stubbornly unpleasant. The risk of running into her made it almost worth forgoing supper. Hunger, however, won out in the end.

She rose from her seat, pulled a shawl around her shoulders and headed out the door. She guessed it to be about nine o'clock, and the house was quiet. What a relief. She walked briskly down the stairs, humming quietly as she went.

She didn't notice Will until she was six steps away from setting foot on the marble hall floor. He was standing by the front door, wearing severe black evening dress, impeccably cut clothes revealing broad shoulders that tapered to narrow hips and long, muscular legs. She stared, thinking there would be no way to improve him. He really was perfect.

He was staring at her.

And then she suddenly remembered that Mrs Wright had told her not to use the main staircase unless she was accompanying Mary. Another mistake to add to her long list.

He continued to stare, waiting for her to complete her descent. 'What's wrong?'

'I'm not supposed to walk down these stairs. I forgot.'

He seemed nonplussed by this answer. 'What's going to happen if you do?'

'Mrs Wright instructed me to use the servants' staircase. She said I must stay out of sight.'

He walked closer, to stand at the base of the staircase. 'That wouldn't be terribly sociable.'

It occurred to her that they were alone. Odd, since in her limited experience Rogers was never far from his post at the door. He must have noted her confusion, since he explained, 'I sent Rogers off to find my walking stick. Haven't the faintest idea where it…were you looking for him?'

Looking for…? 'For Rogers, you mean? No. I'm going to collect my supper.'

Slowly, she walked down the rest of the stairs, trying to ignore the fact that she'd have to pass right by him.

He spoke again just as she reached the hall floor.

'You're feeling better?'

He was just two feet away. She took a step to the side before answering him; she couldn't very well ignore a direct question. 'Yes, thank you.'

'And how is Mary?'

'She hasn't said.' She opened her mouth to say more, but then paused in thought. She knew she should bid him goodnight and carry on her way—that's what a servant would do. But she was curious about something, and her deferential role didn't yet quite fit. 'How…' she began slowly, 'if you don't mind my asking—'

'Not at all.'

'How exactly did she end up in your charge?'

He put his hands in his pockets. 'Mary's father was my best friend at school. He made me her godfather when she was born, and when he died I was the only person in a position to take her.'

'And you plan to keep her only until you find a school to take her.'

'That would be best for her.'

Isabelle wasn't so sure. It couldn't possibly be nice being shifted around. Little wonder the girl was permanently stand-offish. Obviously, though, she couldn't voice her concerns. 'Well, goodnight.'

He sighed. 'It won't be.'

She paused once more at his cryptic words. 'You're going somewhere?'

'Yes, a ball.'

She shouldn't say another word, but other than Will, she'd hardly spoken to anyone in weeks—a predicament, given her curious mind and voluble tongue. 'You don't sound as if you're pleased.'

'I find this sort of thing a tremendous bore.'

'Then why are you going?'

He leaned back against the banister. 'Afraid I've no choice. My cousin, Henrietta, has asked me to come, and I owe her a favour.'

'Oh.' She'd wondered about his life and his family, and here was a titbit to chew over. 'Have you many cousins?'

'Not compared to most people. I've got seven—all girls, and all younger than me. But I only see two of them often. Remember I told you about the uncle who forced me to go to the museum?'

'Uncle Henry?'

He smiled. 'That's the one. Extremely bossy. He had twin daughters, Henrietta and Venetia. I see far too much of them, in fact.'

'You don't like them?'

He frowned. 'They take after their father. They like to give orders. But…I'm fond of them. In as much as I'm fond of nearly everyone I'm related to. I'm quite loyal that way.'

She was trying to imagine him being ordered around by a woman, but couldn't. 'You're lucky. I was an only child, and I've just two cousins. I hardly know either of them.'

He tilted his head slightly, as if he were about ask her something. But then all he said was, 'Will you sit, Miss Thomas?'

He spoke casually enough, but his words set off a tremor of nerves in her stomach. She suddenly realised that she'd been far too free. 'Sit? Oh, no, I mustn't keep you.'

'You won't be, or I shouldn't have asked. I'm waiting for my carriage, you see, and I'd rather like to sit m'self, since I'll be standing for the rest of the night. But as long as you keep standing it would be terribly rude of me.'

A pair of hall chairs flanked the wide set of doors that opened into his study. She crossed the floor and picked one, nervously smoothing her skirts around her as she sat. 'I'm sorry. Did you wish to speak to me about anything?'

He took the other seat, only about six feet away. 'Not really...' He paused as if mulling something over. 'But perhaps, being female, you might offer me some advice, Miss Thomas. Concerning my cousins.'

She didn't want to give him advice. It seemed too intimate a proposition. Furthermore, Rogers would no doubt return any minute and she'd rather he didn't see her sitting there, so inappropriately alone with his master. Better make it quick. 'I doubt I'll be of any use. I don't know them, and I don't know you.'

'You know me a bit, and living in the same house as we do, I expect we'll know each other very well before too long.'

She hoped he couldn't see the spots of high colour staining her cheeks. 'What is the problem, my lord?'

'Their bossiness.'

'Surely you can simply ignore them?'

'I've been ignoring them for years, and it doesn't work. Only makes them more tenacious.'

'What...what is it they pester you about most?'

'They want me to get married.'

His words caused a small, illogical pain in her chest, perhaps since she knew she would never get married herself. He sounded so matter of fact about it, which she supposed was fair enough since marriage wouldn't be a difficult endeavour for someone like him. Finding a wife would be as easy as buying a new waistcoat. 'To anyone in particular?'

'No...well, that's not quite true. They have one or two young ladies in mind, but at this stage just about any sentient female of distinguished parentage would satisfy them.'

She tried not to frown at his blunt cynicism. 'Why should they care so much if you get married?'

He seemed surprised by that question. 'Because if I don't marry, then my title is likely to die out and I'll have failed in my duty. I've a younger brother, but he's had only one daughter himself. So…my cousins keep insisting on introducing me to suitable girls.'

'And what makes a girl suitable?'

'A host of things, I suppose. My cousins only care that she should be rich and well bred. Dullness, too, seems to rank quite high in importance to them.'

She shouldn't have asked. Obviously red hair and insolvency wouldn't feature prominently on the list. 'How…how very calculating.'

He raised an eyebrow at the current of anger in her tone. 'I assure you, I didn't invent the rules.'

She rose stiffly. 'I suggest you buy yourself another horse instead.'

He also rose, and he walked closer, not stopping until only a foot separated them. 'I'm afraid a horse wouldn't quite fit the bill.'

'No? I'd think you'd have a lot in common.'

He digested her insult slowly. 'Are you suggesting I'm…an ass, Miss Thomas?'

She was, in a roundabout way, and it was one of the stupidest things she'd ever said. He should dismiss her right there. But he didn't look angry. He looked as if he were trying not to laugh. Infuriating man.

But infuriating or not, humility was in order once more. She took a deep breath. 'I apologise if you interpreted my statement that way. I just meant that you were fond of horses. You told me so this afternoon. Buying a horse would be a more straightforward transaction.'

'I assure you, I'm much fonder of women.' He paused, allowing his gaze to linger on her lips. 'Can't kiss a horse, you know.'

He was too close, and he was talking about kissing. She was completely out of her element and, worse, she was red. Red hair, red face. 'I don't suppose you'd want to.'

He leaned in. 'I have to strain my neck with most girls, but you're rather a good height for kissing, Miss Thomas. Hypothetically speaking, of course.'

She needed distance. Ten strides to the servants' passage, and about fifty beats of her racing heart. She stepped to the side and started walking. 'Goodnight. I wish you luck with your brood mare.'

'Do you?'

She turned to give him one last look, wondering momentarily if he felt as affected as she did. There was something in his eyes…

'Yes, my lord, I do. I think you'll need it.' And with the turn of a knob she was out of the hall, away from his disturbing gaze. Into the dark corridor and passing right by Rogers, who gave her a most suspicious stare.

'William.'

Will turned around at the familiar but not entirely welcome voice. He'd been…not exactly hiding from his cousin, although he had been trying to make himself inconspicuous next to a small, potted tree. This was the third ball he'd been to since falling prey to her manipulation, and thankfully it would also be the last. He didn't need her help any more, since Isabelle had worked out so nicely.

Henrietta was waiting impatiently for his response.

'Henny. Aren't you pleased to see me here?'

'I'd be more pleased if you could manage to look like you wanted to be here.'

'You *did* insist. I recall telling you I didn't want to come.'

'Well, never mind. Here you are, so you might as well accept it. Look over there.'

He glanced in the direction she indicated. The Richardsons' ballroom was vast and contained a small army of débutantes. 'What am I supposed to be looking at?'

'Who, not what, and the answer is Vanessa Lytton. I introduced you to her two weeks ago at Constance Reckitt's ball. Do you not remember?'

He frowned as the memory came back. That ball marked the commencement of her blackmail. There, at Henrietta's heavy-handed insistence, he'd asked Vanessa to dance. She was, as had been promised, very pretty, but that was about the only compliment he could pay her. Of the string of young ladies Henrietta and Venetia had put forward over the last several years, she was the silliest, the vainest and the most vacuous.

He finally located her in the pastel-coloured throng. Her golden-blonde hair was pulled back neatly, except where it fell artfully around her temples. There was something very practised about her appearance, as well as about the way she demurely cast down her dewy gaze when she noticed he was looking at her.

'Yes. Yes, of course. Very memorable. She looks well.'

'Of course she does—never seen her have a bad day. Why don't you ask her to dance again?'

'Her dance card will be full, no doubt.'

'I suggested she keep several dances free for your arrival. You made quite an impression on her at your last meeting.'

He sighed. 'Henny, I have to warn you, it's a lost cause. I'd sooner marry a goat. Or a horse,' he added, thinking of his bizarre conversation of an hour ago. He still couldn't entirely believe Isabelle had been bold enough to insinuate he was an ass, but he rather wished more girls were like her.

'William—'

'You can't manufacture these things. You can't simply decide I should take an interest in a girl and expect it to happen. She's awfully dull.'

She crossed her arms. 'Very well. And I suggest you seek advice elsewhere when Miss Weston-Burke sets fire to your house. I offer you no help.'

He'd been waiting to launch his counter-attack. 'Ah, but I've already found a governess, thank you, without your help. I won't be needing your advice. So after tonight, you've nothing to hold over my head.'

She opened her mouth wide to retort, but apparently could think of nothing to trump him with just yet. 'All right. But I've already promised Miss Lytton that you'd be eager to dance with her. She's been waiting for you all night.' She turned and walked off in the Lyttons' direction, confident that he would follow.

He almost didn't, and in the end his decision to join the Lyttons had nothing to do with Henrietta. The fact was, although he didn't like Vanessa, he'd no desire to embarrass her publicly. Since his cousin had promised he would dance with her, any failure to do so would be interpreted as an insult. It would be best to get it over with quickly and then leave—Henrietta's machinations be damned. He had Isabelle now to help him. And what delightful help she was turning out to be.

'Mrs Lytton, Miss Lytton, what a pleasure to see you again,' he said as he approached them. He bowed and kissed Vanessa's gloved and scented hand. Henrietta watched him warily.

Vanessa was unaware of the tension. She giggled into a curtsy. 'Lord Lennox, I didn't know you were here!'

That was a lie. He knew she'd seen him, and he couldn't stand her coyness. He smiled tightly, noting that the musicians were conveniently just about to begin. 'But I could not have missed you. Shall we dance?'

'Oh, do, dear,' urged Mrs Lytton. 'I need a word with Mrs Sandon-Drabbe.'

Will gave Henrietta a dark look as he led Vanessa on to the dance floor, daring her to make any more promises on his behalf. He wouldn't be so polite next time.

Vanessa glided gracefully beside him, and when she turned around to take his hand he realised for the first time how small she was. At eighteen, she was hardly more than a child, and the top of her head didn't even reach his shoulders. Her high-waisted, pale pink silk gown fell to the floor in a gentle bell shape, making her look as delicate and empty as an inverted teacup.

And after spending the day with Isabelle, Vanessa seemed far less beautiful, even though he could admit she was more conventionally pretty. He'd meant what he told Isabelle—the fact that her lips were only a few inches lower than his made him want to kiss her all the more. Whenever he looked at her, as a matter of fact. When she'd so conveniently stumbled upon him in the hall, he'd been wondering if he could think up an excuse to seek her out again that night. And in that brief moment when he'd thought she'd come there seeking his footman—who might be considered, now that it occurred to him, a handsome enough chap from the feminine point of view—he'd felt…was it jealousy? He liked her very much, he realised; his feelings for her constituted more than simple lust.

· 'Are you enjoying yourself, Lord Lennox?' Vanessa asked.

Not at all. 'Yes, tremendously.'

The dance required that they separate for several seconds to dance with the person across from them, but all too soon Vanessa was in front of him once more, regarding him with her bovine gaze. Her small, pearl earrings dangled prettily as she cocked her head to the side in solicitous fashion.

'Your cousin tells us you've taken in an orphan.'

'Uh, yes. My goddaughter, Mary Weston-Burke.'

'How charitable you are.'

He didn't like that. Of course he would take in his own goddaughter. It wasn't charity, it was duty. 'I suppose.'

'You glow with happiness,' Vanessa said.

Will realised she was addressing him again. 'Glow? Do I?'

She smiled patronisingly. 'Yes. Having a child about must suit you.'

He thought about Mary. He didn't mind her much, but she'd yet to make him radiate with pleasure. She'd barely moved beyond monosyllables. She certainly didn't make him want to settle down, as Vanessa seemed to be implying. 'Well, I don't know…'

'You needn't disassemble, Lord Lennox,' she said, lowering her lashes coyly. 'I can tell. Ladies know these things.'

'Dissa…?' She was weaving some sort of spell of bafflement around him, and he'd no idea what she was talking about. 'You mean *dissemble*?'

She swatted his arm playfully with her ivory fan. 'Yes, that's what I said. You were not attending! Anyone watching would think I hadn't a single intelligent thing to say.'

'Not anyone who knew you, my dear Miss Lytton.'

'You're too kind, Lord Lennox.' She paused, and then leaned in conspiratorially. '*Every*one knows me, you know.'

He didn't know what to say to that, so he said nothing. The dance couldn't last much longer. He savoured fifteen seconds of silence.

'You are quiet.' She'd lowered her voice an octave, hinting at depths of kindness and generosity he doubted she possessed.

'My apologies, Miss Lytton.'

'What are you thinking about?'

'Greek sculpture.' That should shut her up. Her knowledge extended only as far as the final fashion plate in the latest Paris journal. 'Fascinating stuff, no?'

'Oh?' She looked worried.

'Yes. Uh, Actidias the Cretan. The great sculptor. You're aware of his importance, I trust.'

She bit her lip. 'Actidias. Yes, certainly.'

He doubted it, since he'd made the chap up on the spot. This was unfamiliar territory, but he nodded keenly. 'I've a particular interest in funerary sculpture. Sarcophagi and that sort of thing. Yes, yes, all very interesting. Ah—here's your mother.'

He released her and bowed, fervently hoping he'd convinced her that he was too mad for matrimony. 'Alas, I must be going, Miss Lytton.'

Vanessa, flushed from mental exertion, curtsied limply. 'Lord Lennox.'

But before he could make a clean escape, Henrietta laid a silken hand on his arm.

'I told Mrs Lytton that you'd suggested to me that you might take Miss Lytton and her for a drive on Friday, William. You didn't forget, did you?'

'No,' he said tightly. 'I did not.' He meant he'd suggested nothing of the sort; Mrs Lytton interpreted his words another way.

'Well, I'm so very pleased you haven't forgotten. We're delighted to come, of course.'

Henrietta's clear blue eyes sparkled victoriously. Vanessa looked more nervous than delighted, but she nodded weakly nonetheless.

Apparently a mad earl was better than no earl at all.

Chapter Nine

Isabelle gave the window a determined yank, but still it wouldn't open. The nursery baked with August heat, even though it was only June. Outside, a gentle breeze rustled the leaves of the elm trees that surrounded the square. Brooding grey clouds promised rain above the white-painted stucco houses, but for now it looked comparatively cool and inviting.

'Have you tried opening these before?' she asked Mary while giving a final, frustrated attempt. She'd have kicked something if she'd been alone.

The girl looked up from the leaf of paper on which, in her loose and careless way, she was prasticing her handwriting. 'Yes. I think they've been painted shut.'

'Are you not hot?' Isabelle turned around, wiping itchy strands of hair from her damp brow.

Mary shrugged and didn't look as if she would bother to reply. 'Why don't we go downstairs?' she finally offered lazily.

Isabelle frowned at the sensible suggestion. Obviously, the ground floor would be cooler, but she wanted to avoid Will at all costs. She hadn't seen him since last night, when she'd been so impertinent, and she thought that the longer she could put off facing him, the better. She couldn't believe some of the things she'd said to him—and nor, for that matter, could she believe what he'd said to her. A nice height for kissing? He couldn't have meant that. He was simply punishing her insolence with his outrageous words, and she considered herself thoroughly chastened since she'd nearly turned into vapour on the spot. It couldn't happen again. He was her employer, and she needed this position desperately.

The problem was, his words had upset her. They shouldn't have, since all he'd done was speak the truth, but they did. Naturally he'd want to marry someone suitable, and for him that of course meant someone pretty and aristocratic. By those stark terms, she wasn't remotely suitable. Not that she'd ever deluded herself into thinking that someone like him might be interested in someone like her, nor did she desire such a state of affairs. He was an arrogant cad, and sometimes she didn't even like him.

Oh, but most of the time she did; she really did. And it might be irrational, but hearing him say that she wasn't good enough—even implicitly—had hurt.

Her mood wasn't helped by the fact that she'd spent most of the night thinking about what he was doing at the ball. She could imagine him dancing with beautiful young ladies with small feet and hands and expensive gowns. Ladies who could sail over any obstacle on a horse with every hair in place. Who knew the right things to say and who didn't make strange, awkward comments. Who'd never dream of insulting him.

'If we go downstairs, we might bother Lord Lennox. Why don't we go to the park instead?' she suggested.

'It looks like it might rain.'

'You haven't even looked outside.'

Mary lifted her languid gaze. 'I have now. It looks like it will rain.'

'Not immediately. We should have at least an hour.'

Mary narrowed her eyes suspiciously. 'What about my lesson?'

Isabelle glanced at the line of desultory letters scrawled across her paper. She hadn't exactly been working hard. 'You need exercise more than another lesson. The fresh air will be good for you.'

'I'll be returning to school soon.'

'Possibly,' she answered, wondering what that had to do with going to the park. Had Will even begun to think about finding a school to take her? It would obviously be the easiest option, at least for him.

'So you needn't worry about what's good for me.'

Isabelle had reached breaking point. 'Who said I was worried? Personally, I enjoy the fresh air. I merely asked you to come along because I'm not supposed to leave you to your own devices.'

That seemed to satisfy Mary in a way. She didn't complain further as Isabelle collected their hats and opened the door. She rose quietly and followed her out of the room.

Although she'd lost her temper, Isabelle felt quite good about the exchange. At least they'd had something like a conversation. She decided that at this point she'd nothing left to lose, so she tried again.

'Despite your appalling handwriting, you're actually quite advanced in your studies. When did you start school?'

Mary didn't answer immediately, but then she decided, no doubt following Isabelle's logic, that if they had to spend every day together they might as well speak. 'When I was eight.'

'So…' Isabelle paused to glance at Mary sideways as they started down the wide staircase; she'd have to speak carefully. 'Then that would make four years at Miss Hume's. How awful.'

The slight against Miss Hume's revered institution went down well—well enough, at least, for Mary to nod her assent. Well enough for her to ask a tentative question.

'Were you sent to school, Miss Thomas?'

That was progress, Isabelle thought. Perhaps she might be good at this governess business after all. Maybe children weren't such a strange and distant species. 'No. My father taught me at home, when he could be bothered. I wish I'd been sent away, though. I would have met children my age.'

'I didn't want to go.' There was a hint of defiance to her voice.

'No?' Isabelle looked at her curiously.

'No. Except for me and a few others, all the girls' parents lived in the colonies. Their parents *had* to send them away if they were to have an English education.'

'Did you tell your father you preferred to stay at home?'

Mary didn't respond. Isabelle sensed she was trespassing into un-happy territory, but she couldn't help asking, 'When did you last see your father?'

She didn't know if she actually expected an answer, but after a few pregnant seconds Mary replied, 'I saw him three times after he sent me away. The last time was almost two years ago.'

'Two years?' At first she couldn't quite believe it. That meant she'd never had a chance to say goodbye to him. She probably hardly knew him. 'But did you not go home in the holidays?'

'No. Sometimes I went to a friend's house. Most of the time I stayed at school.'

'He wrote to you, surely?'

Mary didn't look as if she would answer, but eventually she nodded.

Isabelle opened her mouth to ask another question, but then held back. There was anger in the girl's expression, and sadness, too, as if pressed on the subject she might even cry. But why on earth *hadn't* she gone home? It occurred to her suddenly that per-haps Mary had misbehaved at school because she wanted to be sent away.

But obviously she couldn't ask her if that had been the reason. She'd never answer such a question, at least not yet. Isabelle just hoped that, in time, she would feel comfortable enough to open up.

They soon reached the hall, where Rogers wordlessly opened the door. As they walked down the street, she asked, 'Did you really cut off that girl's hair?'

Mary paused. 'Yes. I…'

It was still hard to imagine her doing something so wicked. 'But why?'

She looked away guiltily. 'I hadn't much choice.'

'What on earth do you mean?'

She took a deep breath before launching into her story. 'It was an accident. Amelia was trying to curl her hair, and all the papers and ribbons she was using got tangled up. Miss Hume would have written to her father if she'd known what she was doing. We weren't allowed to curl our hair.'

'Oh?'

'No, because she thought it was precocious, and Amelia had already been caught with face paint her cousin had sent from Paris.'

'So she asked you to cut her hair free?'

'Not just me. All the girls took a turn, but since I'd been in trouble so many times before, Miss Hume chose to blame me.'

The story seemed convoluted and sounded rehearsed. Isabelle didn't quite believe her. 'Were you trying to get sent away?' she enquired gently.

Mary didn't answer. She'd asked one question too many.

They walked the rest of the way in silence. The girl's long strides easily kept pace with Isabelle's, and they reached the park in a few minutes. By then the sky had darkened and a strong breeze had picked up, moody weather to suit their tempers. Dust swirled around the iron gates, causing minor tornados of detritus. Once inside, Mary walked off on her own, heading briskly towards an avenue of trees. Isabelle didn't try to stop her, just walked fast enough to keep up. The girl had said more that morning than she had all week and probably needed to recuperate from the experience in solitude.

Isabelle slowed her pace slightly, regarding the haphazard row of bluebells that lined the path and waved happily in the breeze. She sighed, missing her old life and her old home, even if Will's house was one hundred times more beautiful than the one she'd shared with her father. If only things hadn't changed.

She blamed Mr Cowes entirely for her misfortune, although deep down she knew her father was ultimately at fault. Could Mr Cowes know that she'd changed addresses? With a bit of determination, it wouldn't be so difficult to discover her whereabouts. She'd foolishly told her former landlady, the dreadful Miss Standish, where she was going. For all her apparent probity, Isabelle had little doubt the grasping woman would tell Mr Cowes whatever he wanted for a fee. She shuddered, remembering his hateful innuendos. She'd never been kissed before—not even chastely on the cheek—and she'd not so much as danced with anyone. But even without firsthand experience, she knew what happened between men and women.

She glanced over her shoulder, half expecting to see him or the dark-haired ruffian he'd paid to follow her, but the path was clear. Just because she hadn't thought of him in a few days didn't mean he'd given up. And what would she do once her position at Will's house ended? Mary *would* return to school, and then she'd be out on her own again.

She returned her attention to the path ahead. It was still fairly early, but already fashionable carriages were moving gracefully along the smooth lanes. A trio of elegant ladies trotted by, their high-stepping horses blowing hard through flared nostrils. One of them glanced at her as they passed, and Isabelle followed the line of her patrician gaze to her own drab dress. She'd liked it when she had bought it five years ago; it was sensible, the sort of garment a capable woman with informed opinions would wear. But now, confronted by the modish ladies of London's upper crust, she became painfully aware of her deficiencies.

Standing alone in the park, she couldn't remember feeling so dejected. How had her life come to this? And where, while she was asking herself searching questions, was Mary?

She turned around, scanning the area, trying to remember what the girl had been wearing. Green? Yes, bright green…but no green dresses in sight.

Thinking that perhaps Mary had wandered far down the path while she'd been staring at the clouds, she picked up her pace. But after thirty seconds of brisk walking she stopped suddenly. She couldn't have gone *that* far in such a short time. Was she hiding? Had she been lured away by some villain?

If she had been, it would be entirely Isabelle's fault.

'Mary!' she called, quietly at first, but then louder. She didn't care if she caused a spectacle in front of the well-dressed denizens of the park. She had to find her—and hadn't she *just* been waiting for the silly girl to do something like this, true to form. She'd probably run off simply to get Isabelle into trouble. Mischief for mischief's sake.

She stood in the middle of the road, not knowing what to do. Dratted girl. Ungratef—

And then she was sitting on the hard road, feeling as if her legs had been stolen right from underneath her. A sharp pain in her foot, and a riderless horse galloping past. Her chest ached dully from having all the air squeezed so suddenly from her lungs.

Most of all, she was embarrassed.

'Miss Thomas?'

That was Mary. Isabelle looked up. The girl was standing fifteen feet in front of her, and her expression indicated she didn't know whether to laugh or express concern.

'It *isn't* amusing,' Isabelle said, wanting to clear up any ambiguity.

Mary bit her lip, trying to control her smile. 'I'm sorry.'

'Where were you?' she demanded.

'Sitting by that tree—just over there.' Isabelle glanced in the direction she indicated. A book lay open on the ground; she hadn't run off or been hiding after all. The urge to scold her dissipated. It wasn't Mary's fault that she'd lost track of her.

'I should not have panicked.'

Mary shrugged and extended her gloved hand. 'I didn't hear you until the horse was nearly on top of you. Are you…injured?'

She took a deep breath and ascertained that all her ribs were intact and unbroken. 'Just my pride.' She accepted her hand and rose, wincing sharply as she put pressure on her left leg. 'And perhaps my foot. I think the horse might have stepped on it.'

'Can you walk?'

She tried. Although it hurt, she didn't think it was broken. 'Slowly. I think we should be able to walk home, but it will take a while. There's no choice, is there?'

Mary opened her mouth to answer, but was interrupted by a raindrop landing on her nose. She cast her sceptical gaze up at the sky instead.

Then another character entered the scene. 'Miss? Have you in-jured yourself?'

Isabelle closed her eyes, dreading the sound of the unfamiliar voice. She'd been hoping to pretend that no one else had witnessed her humiliation. But when she turned around, a handsome, concerned-looking gentleman greeted her. He held his smart black hat in one hand and the offending horse's reins in the other.

She felt perfectly in order rebuking him. 'Is that your horse?'

'No, I've just come from my carriage. I saw you fall and I—'

He broke off as he noticed a stout, breeches-clad boy waddling in their direction. He appeared no older than Mary and was as red-faced as Isabelle.

'Does this horse belong to you?' the man asked sternly.

'Yes, sir.'

He handed him the reins. 'You will be more careful.'

The boy nodded shame-facedly, giving Isabelle a pitiful look.

As he walked away, Isabelle realised she owed the man an apol-ogy. He'd been trying to help, and she'd scolded him like a fishwife. 'I'm sorry. I assumed—'

'No need to explain.'

'There is, though. I deserved to be run over, standing in the road like that.'

'You're limping.'

'He grazed my foot, I think.' She took a careful step. 'I think I can make it home well enough.'

'It's raining,' Mary pointed out prudently.

He frowned slightly. 'I am a doctor, Miss…?'

'Thomas.'

'Miss Thomas. Shall I have a look?'

She shook her head. 'Please, no. It is merely tender.'

'Probably just a mild sprain. Still, you shouldn't walk on it. Allow me to drive you home.'

'I can walk.' The rain came faster, now. Walking home at a snail's pace didn't seem an appealing prospect.

'It will be no inconvenience. Please.'

'Yes, but—' A fat drop splashed on her cheek.

Mary was looking at her as if she were out of her mind. 'It's raining,' she repeated under her breath.

Isabelle wiped the water away and continued. 'We would be grateful.'

Their handsome rescuer was Dr Collins. His manners were very correct, and he asked only polite, impersonal questions, unlike Will who asked whatever strange questions took his fancy. Isabelle found it a relief, and by the time they'd reached the house she rather wished she didn't have to get out of the carriage. Any chance she'd had of avoiding Will for the day had pretty much vanished, unless—please God—he'd gone out for the afternoon. She hadn't been that lucky in years.

Matters were made worse by the fact that they had returned in such an unseemly fashion—damp, accompanied by a total stranger and, at least on her part, dirty and injured, as well. She now realised that she should have told Will she was taking Mary out in the first place. She'd no right to make such decisions, since she'd only been working there a few days. She wouldn't be surprised if he dismissed her on the doorstep.

She allowed Dr Collins to help her from the carriage. 'I must thank you again. I fear we've spoiled your morning.'

'My morning has been improved immensely by this meeting. Hold my arm, and try not to put any pressure on your foot.'

She did as he asked, since he was a doctor.

Mary walked ahead and rang the bell. Isabelle crossed her fingers and hoped she wouldn't announce that the reason they'd arrived in this state was that Isabelle had nearly lost her.

A footman opened the door—not the supercilious Rogers this time, but Mayhew, his kinder counterpart. He looked at them bemusedly. His brow furrowed slightly when he noticed that Isabelle was holding on to Dr Collins's arm.

'Good afternoon, Mayhew. I can…'

But she didn't get the chance to explain, or even to enter the house. Will emerged behind the footman, obviously having been drawn away from his work in the study. He looked at Collins, then he looked at her. His gaze narrowed.

'Miss Thomas? What in the name of God is going on?'

'I'm so sorry—'

Mary stepped in—literally, to stand in front of her. 'Miss Thomas took me to the park and was nearly killed by a runaway horse. Dr Collins brought us home because she can't walk.'

'Mary, stop. I can walk perfectly well. My foot's just a bit swollen and Dr Collins is being cautious.'

Will had walked on to the portico now. He looked at Dr Collins again, but still didn't say anything. Isabelle was mortified. How must she look to him, returning like this?

Dr Collins tried to alleviate her discomfort. 'It was my fault entirely. I saw the horse, but did not intervene in time. I'm Collins, by the way.'

Will looked completely unimpressed by this explanation, as well as uninterested in Collins's identity. He was uninterested to the point of rudeness and didn't bother to introduce himself.

'No, no, it's not your fault. I…I wasn't paying attention,' Isabelle hastened to explain, hoping Collins wouldn't be offended by this treatment.

'How careless of you,' Will said, his gaze roaming over her. She couldn't read his expression. It held none of the warmth and teasing of last night.

'It wasn't carelessness.' That was Mary. Isabelle cringed slightly, worried about what would come next. *Don't tell him I was panicking because I'd no idea where you'd gone…* 'Miss Thomas was just watching me so vigilantly that she didn't notice the horse.'

At least her words drew Will's attention away from Isabelle. Instead he frowned at Mary, but the girl just shrugged and walked inside.

Dr Collins looked over his shoulder at his carriage, obviously eager to exit the uncomfortable scene. 'I must go, Miss Thomas. Might I call on you tomorrow to see how you fare?'

Will snorted. She couldn't imagine a more churlish response. 'I assure you I feel better already, Dr Collins. I thank you again for your trouble.' She hobbled inside unaided to prove her point, but as she was about to turn around to bid him goodbye, the door closed with a loud bang. Will had closed it.

She stared at the door for a second, unable to believe what he'd done. She opened her mouth to say something, but then shut it when she saw the hard glint in his eyes.

'You will tell me in future if you decide to go out,' he said coldly.

She would. She knew she should have today. But he'd been horrible to Dr Collins and she didn't like his tone. She crossed her arms and stared levelly back.

'That was very rude.'

'Of him, yes, to propose to court my employee.'

'Rude of *you*, sir! He only asked out of concern. He's a doctor.'

'Well, that's bloody convenient.'

'It was my idea, actually,' Mary said suddenly, her cheeks heightened by Will's inadvertent oath. They both turned to look at her, having all but forgotten her presence. 'I told Miss Thomas that I'd told you we were going to the park—I did it because I wanted to avoid my lesson. I'm sorry I lied.'

Isabelle continued to stare at her. Why was she trying to protect her?

He sighed. 'Mayhew, see to it that Mary has her lunch and returns to the nursery. I will have a word with you, Miss Thomas. In my study.'

Isabelle didn't miss the worried look Mayhew gave her as he ushered Mary off.

Her hopes plummeted to the floor. She was dreading the conversation. Will would ask her to leave. She knew it. Because she'd endangered his ward, because she'd made a spectacle of herself, and because she'd been rude to him—each reason alone was ample justification. She walked gingerly to his study.

Chapter Ten

Will closed the study door behind him. Isabelle was sitting in an armchair, looking nervous. He didn't know why he was so angry, since she hadn't done anything wrong. He didn't really care if she took the girl to the park. Yes, she'd spoken out of turn, but he'd thoroughly deserved it. What was wrong with him?

He knew the answer instantly. He hadn't liked seeing her, from his study window, climbing out of another man's carriage and resting her hand on his arm, particularly when he hadn't even known she'd left the house in the first place. Using his arm for support was understandable, in light of her injury, but he hadn't known it at the time. He'd responded in the most primitive way.

'What Mary said isn't true,' Isabelle said, finally breaking the silence. 'She's trying to protect me, although I can't imagine why. I know I should have told you we were going out. I will next time.'

'Why didn't you?'

'I didn't want to disturb you.'

He walked a few steps closer. 'You needn't worry. You don't disturb me.'

She took a deep breath. 'And I was afraid I'd been rather… impudent last night. I thought you might, um…'

'I've got very thick skin, Miss Thomas, and I think impudence is quite refreshing sometimes.' She blushed and looked away, and he felt a strong urge to kiss her pink cheeks.

He crossed the room to pour himself a glass of brandy, needing to turn his back to her more than he needed the spirits. 'And I should apologise. I suppose I, ah, might have overreacted. You can, of course, go to the park whenever you please.'

When he turned around, she was looking at him again, seemingly more collected. 'I will always tell you in the future.'

He wished he felt as composed as she looked, but 'future' sounded delightfully promising and reassuringly permanent. Bloody hell, he'd known enough women—why was this one having such an effect on him?

She tried to rise. 'I must let you continue doing, um, whatever it is you're doing.'

He walked closer. 'Sit down.'

'You're busy.'

He put a hand on her shoulder. 'And you're injured. Sit, Miss Thomas.'

She did, instantly, as if his touch had burned her. He pulled up a chair to face her and sat down as well. 'Give me your foot.'

She didn't. 'Why?'

He frowned at her. 'Just give me your foot and don't act like such a ninny.'

He knew he sounded autocratic, but since what he really wanted to do was drag her into his lap, for the moment a bit of gruffness was in order. She lifted her foot warily, and he took it in his hand. She flinched when he made contact. 'I'm going to remove your boot, Miss Thomas.'

She nodded, but she was staring fixedly out of the window, patently embarrassed.

An angry streak of dirt left by the horse's hoof marred her soft leather boot. He loosened it and carefully pulled it off. Her foot had swelled slightly, but would probably be better in a day or two. He could tell that the pressure of his hands hurt her, so he lay her foot down gently on his thigh. It was a lovely foot, even swollen and encased in pristine white stockings. He could judge its normal size

by the slim dimensions of her ankle and the few inches of calf that
were revealed. Again, he found himself responding in the most in-
explicable way.

'Did Dr Collins look at your foot?'

She was still too embarrassed to meet his gaze. 'No. He offered.'

Will snorted.

'I'm sorry?' she asked, finally turning her head.

'Nothing.' He carefully removed her leg and placed it on his chair
as he rose. 'Keep it elevated. And, uh, perhaps some cold water for
the swelling.'

Normally he'd ring for a servant to bring the water, but this time
he left the room himself. He needed the distance. Hell, he probably
even needed the cold water more than she. It was utterly ridiculous
that his body should be so undisciplined around her. *For God's sake,
it was only a foot.*

He returned a few minutes later, feeling only somewhat more
composed. She was still sitting on the chair with her leg propped up,
although her posture had relaxed considerably. Tobias, the cat, had
appeared from nowhere and was sitting on the floor by the chair, contemplating the potential comfort of her lap. She stiffened and
straightened when Will entered.

'A footman will bring some cold water soon.'

He returned to his desk, where he'd been steadily employed until
she'd arrived. He couldn't concentrate now, though. His attention
kept straying to her flushed, pretty face. The sun streamed in from
a large window, making her hair glow like copper. Tobias had finally
settled on her lap and was allowing her to stroke his head—
remarkable, really, considering the cat's contrary nature. Periodically
he kneaded her thigh with a lazy paw. Will cleared his throat and
shoved some papers around, trying to look busy.

'I'm sorry I made such a disaster of today,' she said quietly.

He felt sorry himself. She must think he was permanently ill
tempered, when actually quite the opposite had been true until she'd
appeared in his life. He'd been perfectly good humored that morning,

his mood only souring when he'd seen her with Collins. He didn't know what was happening to him. He wanted to make her smile again, but instead he'd never been less charming to a woman. He wanted to protect her, from the dangers of the street and from the lascivious thoughts of the Charles Prestwicks and John Dewhursts of the world. Never mind his own lascivious thoughts; never mind his questionable motives. The problem was, he didn't know what he wanted.

Or, more precisely, he knew exactly what he wanted and also knew he couldn't have it. It was driving him mad.

Still, he couldn't excuse his boorish manners. 'There's no need to apologise, Miss Thomas. I'm sorry myself. Just a bit distracted today. Rather a lot that I have to do.'

'Oh.' She paused. Then, 'What…what are you working on?'

She asked it hesitantly, as if she were aware that it wasn't the sort of question she should ask her employer. It certainly wasn't, but he didn't care. He didn't class her with the other servants. She looked, spoke and thought differently, and her family background, if she told the truth, had at least been educated, if not terribly affluent. Besides, it wasn't as if he were doing anything confidential. Mostly he was just signing his name, giving his consent for various building works and requests from tenants. His steward managed Wentwich Castle when he was in town, and every week he forwarded Will a large batch of letters, all awaiting his attention.

'I'm seeing to estate business. More specifically, I'm signing my name, over and over.'

'Is it dreadfully boring?'

It should have been, but he didn't mind it. 'No. I mean, writing my signature is no great pleasure, but I care about it.'

'Your house, you mean?'

He paused before answering. He loved his house, as anyone would if his family had lived on the same piece of land for centuries. 'Yes…not just that, though. I care about the people who live there. I've known many of our tenants my entire life. The oldest is nearly ninety. The youngest was born five weeks ago.'

Rogers arrived with a large bowl of water just then. He placed it by Isabelle's feet, but she just looked at it with bemusement.

'You're to put your foot in the water,' Will explained. 'It's cold. To reduce the swelling.'

'I understand the principle, but I should do this in my room.'

'You'd have Rogers carry it up two flights of stairs when you can put your foot in it perfectly well right here?'

The footman shot her a baleful look. Will fought the urge to re-primand him harshly for doing so, but at least Rogers's ire had the desired effect. Isabelle's face assumed an expression of guilt, and her next protest was weaker.

'But you're obviously busy.'

'I've told you already that you don't bother me. I can easily ig-nore you.'

She frowned at his words, but he went back to his work, pre-tending to pay no attention to her. Rogers left, and they were alone.

He watched her from the corner of his eye debating how best to submerge her foot without compromising her modesty. She was clearly resolved against revealing any naked flesh, so she eventu-ally put her stockinged foot in the deep bowl—very carefully, so that she didn't have to raise her skirts more than necessary.

The water must have been icy cold, because she immediately gasped and pulled her foot out. The cat lifted a cross eyelid and jumped from her lap.

'Put it back in, or I'll hold it there,' he warned, continuing to pre-tend interest in his work.

She didn't test him. She bit her lip and eased her foot into the water. Then she was silent for nearly two minutes—which, he was coming to realize, was a long time for her to remain quiet. He could see her getting restless. She looked around the room and began drumming her fingers on the arm of the chair.

'Miss Thomas?' he asked.

'Yes?'

He looked up at her. 'Are you finding it difficult not speaking?'

She blushed. 'I talk a lot, I suppose.'

'Yes. You're most impertinent.'

She looked at him for a second, trying to determine if that was criticism or simple teasing. When she realised it was the latter, she took it as permission to proceed.

'I don't mean to be. I suppose I'm rather under-talked during the day, considering Mary doesn't say much. Although truth be told, I suppose I've always been like that.' She paused. 'I'm doing it again, aren't I?'

He didn't mind. She had a lovely voice, and there was something both sweet and mesmerising about the way she moved her lips and used her hands when she spoke. 'You may talk all you like. And no doubt Mary will communicate more freely soon enough. Suppose she's just very shy.'

'A bit, maybe. She's obviously sad—angry, too, I think. And she does communicate, just not with me. Writes at least a letter a day to a friend from school. Heaven knows what she has to say about me.'

He lay down his papers. 'About us, for that matter, and I'm confident you fare better in her letters than I.'

'*Us*' felt strangely pleasing as he uttered it, but the word clearly made her uncomfortable. She changed the subject. 'Where is your house?'

'Wentwich Castle is in Norfolk. Not far from the sea.'

'What sort of house is it?'

He smiled. His father had described their house as notable for size but not its refinement. 'In the Gothic taste. Very big, but a little coarse. Rather like me when I was taking you to task this morning.'

'Oh, don't, it is of no matter…' She blushed again as her words trailed off.

He rose and crossed the room to remove a framed watercolour from the wall. He handed it to her as he returned to his seat.

'My mother painted that. It's dated at the bottom…there—1786. My grandfather had the tower and all those funny turrets added. He had a better imagination than sense of proportion. It took three architects to complete the house, since he kept falling out with each new one over his unorthodox ideas. The result is…well, a bit of a heap.'

He watched her eyes move over the picture, taking in every detail.

Finally, she looked up. 'It's lovely. Perhaps just a touch eccentric, but all the better for it.'

That made him rather proud, although he didn't know why he should care. 'It's far too big, really. Once one thing is repaired, something else goes wrong. I employ a man whose sole function is to walk round the roof, repairing leaks as he goes. By the time he gets back to where he started, it's leaking again.'

She smiled at the image. 'You exaggerate.'

'Just a little.'

'But you like it nonetheless.'

'I love it—I'm there most of the year. If I can't find a school to take Mary before the autumn, I'll have to take you both there with me.' He hadn't even considered the possibility until that moment and surprised himself by suggesting it. It would be interesting, having her there. He'd rather she come in a capacity other than that of a governess, though.

Her smile faltered at the thought. 'By then I…I might—'

'You'll have something better to do?'

She frowned. 'It is not inconceivable that some better opportunity might come along.'

'Of course,' he said indulgently.

She stared at the picture again, no doubt in order not to look at him. 'Did you grow up in Norfolk?'

'Until my parents died when I was eleven, we were almost always there.'

She looked up, sympathy in her eyes. 'I'm sorry to hear that. You had to grow up quickly then.'

Yes, he had. 'Well…sort of. I'm a second son, you see, so I wasn't immediately head of the family. I spent the first three decades of my life being thoroughly irresponsible. My older brother, Richard, died four years ago—he was seven years older than me. My younger brother, James, is alive and well.'

'How tragic to lose both parents at once. And a brother, too, at such a young age.'

Losing his parents had been devastating, but Will had felt little sorrow at Richard's passing. 'My real mother actually died when I was born. I was referring to my father and stepmother. He married her soon after my mother's death, and she's the only mother I knew. They were killed in a fire—it was tragic. At any rate, she hated London, so we stayed in the country most of the time.'

She placed the watercolour carefully on a parcel-gilt side table. 'Which mother painted the picture?'

'My real one.'

He could see her hesitating, obviously wondering how many questions she could ask before being accused of impertinence again. Cautiously, 'Why did your stepmother dislike London so much?'

He debated telling her she'd overstepped her bounds—which she had—but decided in the end that there was no harm in answering her question. It just wasn't the sort of thing he discussed with many people. 'I suppose she felt like a bit of an…interloper. I think that's how she was treated, although to be honest I was too young to be aware of much. She didn't come from a grand family.'

'How "not grand" is not grand?'

'A long way from grand, in her case. Her father was an actor, and she started out on stage herself. My father saw her playing Ophelia and fell instantly in love.'

'But that's rather romantic,' she said.

He smiled ruefully. 'Might have been, except he was already betrothed to my mother.'

She looked mildly outraged. 'Did he marry her anyway? Even though he'd fallen in love with someone else?'

'Yes, and when she died he married again, for love. Everyone thought he'd gone mad for marrying someone so far beneath him.'

'I suppose love is the best reason to marry.'

He raised an eyebrow. 'Love has little to do with it.'

'Not marry for love? You mean you'd marry someone you disliked?'

'No…what I mean is…' She looked so appalled by the idea, and he realised it didn't sound particularly laudable. He wouldn't expect her to understand, though—her parents had eloped and left her a pauper. Marriage was different for people who didn't have much to begin with. They could marry for love because they had so little to lose. 'All I meant was that marriage should be a based on reason and sound judgement rather than impulsive emotions. Of course I'd have to get on with the person. But sharing a common background is more important.'

'Love isn't enough, then.'

'It's not even necessary.'

She frowned. 'Your poor mother.'

'Yes, I suppose you're right. She was only about nineteen when they married, and I don't think she was expecting her husband to be smitten with another woman from the start—to be keeping her as his mistress, in fact. But she got something out of the marriage. They both did.'

'What did she get?'

'Money. A title. And my father had a pretty wife.'

'Whom he didn't love,' she said pointedly.

Will shrugged, realising he wouldn't convince her. He believed everything he was saying, but for some reason saying it to her made him feel like an ass. No doubt he sounded like one, but experience had taught him that this was one area where it paid to be cynical. His father's first marriage, unloving though it might have been, had been sound and trouble-free. His second marriage had produced James, who would always be Will's best friend. Other than that it had just led to tragedy.

Bloody Richard…

'May I ask some questions now?' he said, wanting to talk about something else.

'I've been asking far too many.'

'Where did you grow up?'

She removed her foot from the water and carefully dabbed it with the hem of her dress so she wouldn't cause a puddle on the floor. She didn't look at him as she began speaking. 'Not far away. In

Hampstead. We needed to be close to London since most of my father's clients had houses in town.'

'Was your father successful at what he did?'

She finally looked up. She spoke slowly, reluctantly. 'Yes. Very, I think. He was knighted, you know. For advising King George about some purchase.'

'Then…' He paused, trying to find a delicate way to pose his question. 'I've been wondering, Miss Thomas, why he seems to have left you in such straits.'

He sensed she didn't want to talk about it. She became very still, and her expressive face turned a telltale pink. 'He was rather unwise with money. He made some mistakes. He, uh…'

How interesting, Will thought. She seems to have a secret. 'Come, now, let's be fair. I've told you about my family.'

She shrugged. 'Well, there's not much to tell. We always lived comfortably. I didn't know anything was wrong until after he died.'

'Debts?'

She nodded. 'A few. I've come to think that because my mother came from a wealthier family, he felt pressure to give her things he couldn't actually afford. Her family thought she'd made a mistake when she married him, and I suppose we lived above our means to prove that he could provide for her.'

He suspected she was lying. 'If she died when you were six, he should have had ample time to recoup his funds.'

'Yes…I admit I don't entirely understand it. But he also had to spend a lot of money, you see, in order to buy new artefacts—he had to travel quite a bit just to find them, and that itself was an expensive business. And if he didn't find buyers for them in turn, well, it was really a risky…' She paused to frown. 'And then, of course, the war meant he couldn't travel, and his business suffered because of it.'

'So the short answer is he spent more than he earned.'

'I've already confessed to a fondness for saying a lot when a little would suffice. I should see how Mary is.'

'I'm sure she's well. She didn't get run over by a horse. Sit a bit longer.' He wanted her to stay and to learn more about her. He sensed he'd only been given a glimpse of her prior life. 'What was your house like?'

'About a hundred years old. Red brick. Surrounded by pretty herb gardens. I had to sell it.' She bent over to collect her boot and then rose. 'I must go now. I will leave you to your affairs.'

'Then let me help.' He crossed the room and held out his arm.

She just stared at it. 'I assure you, I can walk. The water helped immensely.'

'Don't be silly. You shouldn't put pressure on it. You're no use to me injured. Take my arm.'

Reluctantly, she did, leaning on him to take the weight off her foot. He opened the door and walked with her across the hall.

'I suggest you spend the rest of the day in bed,' he offered, but then wished he hadn't. It was the wrong thing to say. It just made him think about her dishevelled and drowsy.

'I should be better tomorrow,' she promised, oblivious to his sudden discomfort.

'I'm sure you'll be waltzing in no time.'

She looked away again. He seemed constantly to be blundering into uncomfortable subjects. Why should *that* comment bother her?

'Do you like dancing, Miss Thomas?' he asked.

'I've done very little,' she said quietly.

'That's a pity.'

She looked at him. 'But I thought you disliked dancing.'

'When did I say that?'

'Last night. You didn't want to go to that ball.'

'Ah, it wasn't the dancing I objected to, but my partner. I'm sure you'd have been an improvement. I'm actually quite good. Shall we have a go?'

'No,' she said, too quickly.

'You don't want to dance with me? I'm offended.'

'I, what I meant…' She paused to collect herself. 'I am injured, my lord. I did not mean to be impolite.'

'Another time, then.'

She neither confirmed nor denied that possibility. They'd reached the bottom of the stairs, and she'd become shy again. 'Well, thank you, then.'

'I'll help you upstairs.'

'I don't need help.'

'Must you always be this argumentative?' He put her arm around his waist. 'You didn't complain so much when your Dr Collins was helping you.'

She held on to his arm and took the first step with her good foot, dragging the sore one behind. It required effort and concentration. 'Dr Collins is a gentleman.'

'What am I?'

She looked up the staircase with dismay. There were probably at least sixty steps to climb before she reached her bedroom. The landing seemed impossibly far away. 'You, sir, are not.'

'Really?' And before she could protest he'd picked her up into his arms.

After two seconds of frozen shock, she immediately started to struggle. '*What* do you think you're doing?' she hissed.

He held her tightly cradled, making it difficult for her to move. 'I *thought* I was being terribly gallant…what do *you* think I'm doing?'

'*Put* me down.'

'You said I wasn't a gentleman. I'm just trying to prove you wrong.'

'I take it back. Now, put me down.'

'If you don't stop wriggling about I'll drop you.' His lips were close to her ear, too close. She turned her head, and they accidentally brushed against her cheek. She went still.

He nearly groaned. He didn't know what had possessed him to pick her up: the thought of her clinging to Dr Collins's blasted arm or the painfully slow progress they'd make if he let her walk. But he was too stubborn to lower her now. 'Put your arm around my neck.'

She did as he asked her, too disconcerted to argue, and he made short work of the stairs. He didn't immediately lower her when he reached the third floor, either, but carried her all the way down the hall to her bedroom door. There, he let her down gently.

She looked at the floor, but her quiet voice was very angry. 'I hope no one saw that.'

'Who's here to see anything? You don't mean servants, do you?'

She glared at him, her eyes flashing. 'As a matter of fact, I do. I have to work with them, you know. If anyone saw, they will think...they will think—'

'*What* will they think?' he asked the question softly, but he didn't expect an answer. They'd think he was bedding her, that's what they'd think, and there wasn't a chance she'd utter those words.

But she was thinking them. He could tell by the blush staining her cheeks.

'I suppose I've never been too worried about what my servants thought,' he said, leaning around her to find the doorknob, trapping her in his arms. Stubbornly, she refused to lower her gaze, and he found himself lost in her blue eyes, her lush, full lips. It would be so nice, so easy to lean in and kiss her. Even angry, she wasn't immune to him.

Not kissing her tested his will far beyond the point at which he usually gave in, but this time he didn't. He knew he couldn't—not unless he planned to forfeit the game for just a kiss. If he kissed her, only three days after she'd arrived, he knew she'd pack her things and leave. Since he wanted much more from her than a kiss, he'd have to move very slowly.

He opened the door. 'Good afternoon, Miss Thomas.'

She blushed and looked away. 'Good afternoon.'

She stepped into her room and closed the door behind her.

Chapter Eleven

Isabelle's foot felt much better in the morning, despite the violent bruise that had started to develop. It was still tender to the touch, but as long as she was careful she could put weight on it without causing herself too much pain. Contrary to Dr Collins's supposition, it appeared not even to be sprained.

Unseasonable weather had again turned the nursery into a furnace, and at eleven o'clock they moved outside to the garden. It had been Mary's suggestion, of course. There was no way Isabelle would voluntarily increase her chances of seeing Will any time soon, and setting foot downstairs was sure to do so. But she didn't have any real argument against Mary's reasonable suggestion—she couldn't exactly explain that she'd nearly kissed the girl's godfather the night before and therefore was trying to avoid him.

So there they were, sitting on the lawn with several books spread out around them. They'd worked for a while, but now, as the lunch hour approached, they'd given up in favour of quiet contemplation. Mary, cross-legged, was held rapt by the rather sensational-looking novel she'd brought with her. Isabelle, lying on her back, just watched the clouds above. To her pessimistic gaze they looked alarmingly like wolves.

After some minutes, she turned her head to the side and regarded Mary. There was something she'd been meaning to say. 'Thank you for telling Lord Lennox that it had been your idea to go to the park yesterday, Mary. You needn't have done that. You shouldn't have. But thank you anyway.'

Mary looked up reluctantly from her novel. It appeared, for a moment, that she might acknowledge this thanks. But perhaps doing so was too sentimental. She just shrugged instead.

Isabelle went on. 'And also for saying that I'd been paying attention, when clearly I'd practically lost you.'

Mary put her book down. 'You didn't lose me.'

'Well, misplaced, then. I was daydreaming, at any rate.'

'Miss Pringle, my geography teacher, struck me with her ruler when I daydreamed. Which I guess I did a lot.'

Isabelle sat up, frowning. 'She sounds appalling.' She paused. 'What did you daydream about?'

It was Mary's turn to lie back on the grass. 'Home. Wishing I looked like Celia Bligh. She was the prettiest girl in school, and my best friend.'

'Is she the one you correspond with?'

She turned her head to regard Isabelle thoughtfully, as if weighing the wisdom of answering any more personal questions. But after a moment she nodded.

'Then perhaps she could come for a visit. Shall I ask Lord Lennox if you'd be allowed to invite her?'

'Do you think he'd let me?'

Isabelle almost wished she hadn't offered, since she didn't want to initiate any more conversations with the man. But Mary had spoken eagerly, and that alone made it worthwhile.

'Well, I don't know…there's no harm in asking. But I cannot promise anything.'

After a minute of companionable silence, Mary asked, 'What were you daydreaming about yesterday?'

Things she certainly wouldn't divulge: about her debts, her father, and the many suitable young ladies who'd been dancing with Will the night before. 'I can't remember. It must not have been important.'

'No?'

'No.'

Mary picked a long blade of grass and twirled it in her fingers. 'Dr Collins was nice. Handsome, too.'

'He was.'

She turned her head to the side, her face screwed up with curiosity. 'Why didn't you get married?'

Isabelle frowned. The girl had gone from taciturn to brazenly inquisitive in just a day. 'That's a rather intimate question.'

She sighed. 'I know. But Miss Hume told us the sole purpose of the female education was to prepare us to be wives, and since you're educated and…*quite* pretty, even with red hair, then why aren't you married?'

'I suppose I never found anyone I wanted to marry.'

'Yes, but why?'

Isabelle knew she was blushing. She should tell Mary to stop asking questions, yet she didn't want to discourage her too much. Saying *any*thing was an improvement on sullen silence. 'Has it occurred to you that maybe no one wanted to marry me? I suppose I've never met anyone who I considered to be…' she paused, realising she was about to use Will's favorite word '…suitable.'

'No?'

'No. I…I told you that my mother died when I was young, and I imagine my father never quite realised that he ought to introduce me to society. I didn't even know many girls my age, for that matter.'

'Celia's sisters—she has three—are all married. Well, no, one's just engaged. But they all went to scores of balls.'

'Yes, well, I didn't.'

'Not at all? Never?'

'Never.'

'Have you even danced before?'

Since she'd been forced to cover this subject just last night, she answered with undue grumpiness. 'No. Not with a gentleman, anyway.'

That was completely the wrong thing to say. Mary was undeterred and highly intrigued. 'With someone who *wasn't* a gentleman?'

Isabelle sighed. 'With my housekeeper. I wish we'd never got on to this subject. You should be doing your work.'

Mary was giggling already. 'What sort of dance?'

Isabelle frowned at her. 'A waltz. Our cook hummed. It's very rude to laugh at others' misfortune, you know.'

'I had a dancing master at school.'

'Bully for you.'

'Good afternoon.'

They both turned their heads at Will's voice. They hadn't seen him approaching.

Will had first seen Isabelle from his bedroom window. She was lying on the grass, looking radiant and lovely in the sun. He'd slept uncharacteristically late, having gone to his club after hc'd parted from her yesterday afternoon. He'd stayed into the small hours of the morning, hoping to drown her from his mind with brandy and long-winded conversations with the dour old men who took refuge there from their wives. It hadn't worked, and that morning as he'd lain in bed his mind had wandered back to far too pleasurable thoughts about her. Damned inconvenient that she'd chosen to plant herself right beneath his bedroom window. The warm, pleasant sound of her voice carried up, too far away to be distinct, but distracting none the less.

So, since the lunch hour neared, he stopped pretending she wasn't there and headed outside. He paused by the garden door, however, when he heard them speaking; he knew he shouldn't eavesdrop, but their conversation was just too interesting to miss. He listened, unde-tected, for several minutes. What he learned was rather illuminating.

Isabelle had led a truly sheltered life. It sounded as if she'd had very few male acquaintances, and she'd never even had danced with anyone. That probably explained why she was so uncomfortable when he broached the topic last night. If she'd never danced, then she'd almost certainly never been kissed. Until that moment, he hadn't fully appreciated how inexperienced she was, and he wasn't quite sure how the discovery made him feel.

On the one hand, he liked the idea. Her lack of experience explained her lack of coyness, something he found so refreshing. But on the other hand, her innocence rather made him feel as if he were taking advantage of her in the most churlish way—or at least as if he were contemplating doing so. She was penniless, powerless and alone, and he didn't want to hurt her. She didn't deserve it. He liked her. Rather a lot, he realised.

He felt strangely content as he watched them. He'd never seen Mary smile before, and here she was, laughing merrily at something Isabelle had said. It had a transformative effect: the girl appeared prettier, healthier and livelier. Isabelle must have that effect on people, he thought. She tended to improve his mood, anyway—at least when she didn't turn him into an uncharacteristically possessive lout. He'd hired her for his own selfish ends, but perhaps she really *was* just the thing Mary needed. He realised, quite suddenly, that he made a pretty useless godfather. He was good at paying for things, and when the time came he'd readily volunteer whatever funds were necessary for her school and wardrobe, but he hadn't yet given more consideration to Mary than that.

Finally he stepped outside. 'Good afternoon.'

They stopped talking instantly, and Isabelle went very still, suggesting she feared he'd overheard something embarrassing.

He pretended he hadn't, though. He wanted her to relax again, as she had been before he'd made his presence known, and as she had been yesterday, before he'd stupidly carried her upstairs. He shouldn't have done that, although he'd certainly enjoyed it.

He put his hands in his pockets and tried to look nonchalant. 'You look industrious.'

She blushed guiltily. 'We've stopped working for the moment. We *were* very busy…'

'You needn't explain. I can't imagine working out here on an afternoon like this. Thought I'd come out and enjoy the sunshine m'self.'

Isabelle's expression grew suddenly worried, and she rose, self-consciously dusting imagined bits of grass from her dress. 'Oh, I…I should have asked before we came out here. Would you prefer us to be inside? Did you wish to use the garden?'

He thought she sounded eager to escape. 'Not at all, except to have lunch with you. Shall we have a picnic?' He directed the question at Mary, suspecting she'd be more amenable to the idea. Asking Isabelle to have lunch with him outright would have sent her into an even greater panic.

Mary sat up slowly, and if Will wasn't mistaken her gaze passed between Isabelle and him for just a moment, as if she'd noted the undercurrent of tension. There was a quiet deliberateness to her manner, a thoughtfulness and perceptiveness that reminded him of her father. 'I am hungry,' she said.

'But we should really be working,' Isabelle protested. 'Your French. And it's a bit early for lunch.'

'You weren't working when I came out here,' Will pointed out. 'Am I to understand you simply don't want to eat with me?'

The brightening spots of colour that burned her cheeks confirmed it. 'Of course not. My opinion doesn't matter.'

'Well, then it's decided. Mary won't do any more work—pretend or otherwise—for the rest of the afternoon. I'll have Mrs Graham prepare a tray.'

He turned to go, but Isabelle started walking after him. 'No, you mustn't. I'll go.'

He stopped and examined her face, wondering if she had some plan. It wasn't so odd that she would protest. She worked for him, after all, and she should really be the one to do these dull tasks. But he rather suspected that if she went inside, she'd devise some reason not to return. 'But your foot, Miss Thomas. You should rest it.'

She stuck out her foot and rotated it to prove its soundness. 'I've recovered fully. I insist.'

'Then I'll go with you.'

That obviously wasn't the response she wanted. She looked flustered and not a little bit annoyed. He didn't care. If underhanded-ness were the only way he could be alone with her, then he'd be underhanded. He opened the door and waited for her to enter.

Isabelle hesitated and he wondered what debates were running through her mind. However, after that flicker of indecision, she set her lips and walked determinedly ahead.

He allowed her to lead the way through the silent, dim corridor that led to the kitchen. His gaze roved over her slender neck, tickled by a few wisps of red hair that had come loose from her otherwise neat chignon. His gaze travelled lower, admiring her narrow back and the gentle sway of her hips. They descended the stairs to the kitchen without speaking, and she didn't pause even once to check that he followed behind.

But then, just before entering the kitchen at the base of the stairs, she did stop, holding on to the doorframe with one hand and leaning in slightly. She let her head rotate subtly left and then right.

'Does something appear to be the matter?'

She turned around quickly, but then took two nervous steps back when she realised only a few inches separated them. 'Nothing. The kitchen is empty.'

'No Mrs Graham?' He'd dealt with many problems of graver importance, but preparing a tray of food himself would be a novel and not unintimidating task. He hadn't planned on going all the way to the kitchen in the first place—he'd intended to ring the bell just inside the garden door and wait for Mrs Graham come to him. Only that apparently hadn't occurred to Isabelle and she'd been leading the way.

Unlike him, she actually looked relieved by the cook's absence. 'She'll be in the servants' dining room along with the rest of the kitchen staff. They like to eat before you've had your meal. I told you it was too early. *My lord.*'

He frowned at the way she uttered the title, tacked on to the end of her admonition like an impudent afterthought. 'Right, then. What shall we do?'

'We'll manage, I'm sure. I mean, not we—*me*. I don't need any help. I'll make tea.' She walked purposefully into the kitchen and appeared determined to get rid of him.

And he was determined not to leave, despite the fact that he didn't even know where to find a spoon or a plate, let alone anything to eat. He wandered in behind her, looking around the vast room rather as he had the great hall of the British Museum. Copper saucepans gleamed in the sunlight, and two brightly plumed pheasants awaited Mrs Graham's ministrations on the scrubbed pine table. Presumably they'd reach his dining table that night or the next. *When had he last been there?*

'No, no. I'd like to help. Just tell me what to do.'

She stared at him for two seconds, but wasn't forthcoming with orders. She'd already located a kettle and was filling it with water.

He watched her for a few seconds before it occurred to him that he shouldn't just stand there enjoying the way her dress tautened when she lifted the heavy kettle. 'Here, let me do that.' He grabbed it from her, but then realised he didn't know where to put it. 'What do I do with it now?'

With a patient smile, she reclaimed it and placed it on its stand. A few seconds later, she'd lit a small fire beneath it, and it was on its way to boiling.

He watched her, wondering if she were enjoying her moment of superiority over him. 'You seem quite competent in here,' he remarked.

'Oh? We had a cook growing up, and I couldn't tell you what to do with those birds, but I *can* boil water.'

'Do I detect sarcasm, Miss Thomas?'

'Of course not, my lord.'

The room grew quiet. Still smiling, she walked away from the kettle and opened a cupboard, removing the necessary number of plates, cups and saucers from a brightly enamelled tea service. She began arranging them, as well as a small arsenal of utensils, on a tray. The clatter of china and the clink of silver filled the silence.

Stubbornly he waited for the kettle to boil, but like any other watched pot, it wouldn't.

She removed linen napkins from a drawer and began folding them. The lack of conversation seemed to be making her nervous.

'Is something the matter, Miss Thomas?'

'Why do you ask?'

'You've folded that napkin three times.'

She let it rest on the tray and turned around. 'I'm sorry.'

'Don't apologise. I wanted to congratulate you, you know.'

'Why?'

'That was the first time I've seen Mary smile. Out there in the garden. I don't know how you managed it.'

She looked back at the tray and began shifting things around. Compliments seemed to make her uncomfortable. 'I'm afraid she's terribly unhappy.'

'That's childhood, I suppose,' he offered.

She frowned. 'I wouldn't have thought yours was unhappy.'

It had been, actually, at least after his parents' death had left eighteen-year-old Richard in charge. Luckily, Will was eleven and already boarding at school, but James, two years younger, was not. Will had sensed that things weren't right when he'd come home during his breaks. Richard, never pleasant, was usually drunk, and James had retreated into mysterious silence. He only understood the abuse his brother had suffered years later, when he'd accidentally seen the legion of scars crisscrossing James's back. Ever since, he couldn't forgive himself for not having prevented it, even though he'd been just a child himself.

'No, I don't suppose it was too bad.'

She frowned thoughtfully. 'Do you know she rarely saw her father?'

'Rarely saw him?'

She nodded. 'Yes, only three times during the past four years. He apparently wrote to her, but he didn't visit or send for her over the holidays.'

Will didn't say anything right away. He knew why Arthur hadn't sent for the girl, although he supposed Mary might not. Arthur's death hadn't been sudden and unexpected; he'd been wasting away for years, weakening until he could no longer sit up. Will hadn't been aware of the seriousness of his illness until Arthur had invited him to stay just a few months before he died. They hadn't seen each other in years, since Arthur had grown reclusive after his wife's death. After such a long absence, Will had been shocked by the hollow face and sunken shoulders that had greeted him. He could only imagine what a child would have felt. 'I didn't know it had been that long. I suppose I'm not surprised.'

'Not surprised? Did he not care for her at all?'

He could see she was outraged by his apparent lack of concern, and he was impressed again by how unafraid she was of taking him to task when she thought he was in the wrong. He explained, 'He cared a great deal. He'd been ill for a long time, and I imagine he didn't want to frighten her. I didn't even know how ill he was until he contacted me, with only a few months left to live. I was…horrified by his appearance. That's when he asked me to look after her. Perhaps he should have let her see him like that. Probably. But I imagine he wanted her to have happy memories of her time with him.'

She was quiet for several long seconds. 'I'm sorry. I didn't mean to imply that he was unkind.'

Will shrugged. 'You needn't apologise. The kettle's boiled.'

She grabbed it quickly and set it on the pine table before he could offer to help again. She turned around more slowly, her brow furrowed thoughtfully. 'I don't think she knows how ill he was, either. She thinks he didn't want her—I mean, she didn't say so explicitly, but I'm sure that's how she feels. I rather suspect that's why she was always trying to get sent home from school. She simply wanted to be with him.'

'Perhaps.' He paused. 'Except she continued to misbehave even after he'd died. That's how she ended up here, remember?'

'Maybe she wanted to be with you, then. I imagine she just wants a family.'

'I'd never have pegged you for such a sentimentalist, Miss Thomas. If she wanted a family, then she'd hardly have chosen me.'

Isabelle blushed with a mixture of anger and embarrassment at his mild mockery. 'It seems odd to me, too, but I suppose she had no other options…'

'Ah, I'm the last resort of the desperate.'

'That's not what I meant,' she said defensively, rummaging through the cupboard doors in search of nothing to avoid his curious gaze. He wondered if she really did regard him as a last resort.

He also realised he'd hurt her. 'I'm being difficult. It's a bad habit. I don't think you're sentimental.'

After a moment, her posture relaxed slightly; apology grudgingly accepted.

He continued. 'Her father was one of my best friends, as I've told you. He was a bit unruly himself, so perhaps she just takes after him.'

She looked at him again. 'What do you mean?'

'I was at school with him, and he was constantly trying to get sent down. Only difference is, he never actually succeeded. So perhaps young Mary's merely surpassed him.'

She considered this information. 'You should tell her.'

'What, that her father nearly got expelled from Eton half a dozen times? Is that the good example she's been waiting for?'

Her eyes flashed with a hint of impatience. 'Obviously not, but if I didn't know my parents very well I think I'd like to know if I shared something in particular with one of them.'

He considered her words. They made sense. Will often wondered what his real mother had been like. He'd seen her portrait; he looked like her. And although he remembered his father, it was a child's memory—a big, handsome man who seemed brave and wise and capable of anything. He wished he could remember him as more than a father, though. As a man who made mistakes from time to time.

He didn't actually have too many happy memories, come to think of it. And neither would Mary.

'We'll need more than tea,' he said, changing the subject. 'Where will I find comestibles?'

'Mrs Graham keeps most of the food in the larder.'

He looked around the room. Three doors opened into God only knew where. 'The larder?'

She sighed. 'And to think you came along to help me. Have you even been in the kitchen before?'

'Are you teasing me, Miss Thomas?'

She suppressed her smile, but the slight tug at her lips made him rejoice quietly. 'Through that door and down the corridor,' she said, pointing. 'It's the first right.'

Chapter Twelve

Isabelle watched him until he vanished down the corridor. She could hear him moving things around and wondered what he'd eventually find and whether it would be edible.

She smiled to herself, but when she realised what she was doing, she stopped. Or tried to, anyway, for a few seconds later her smile broke through again. She'd never known anyone like him before. Most of the men she'd previously spoken to had been her father's friends—grey men with stooped shoulders and bad eyesight. She'd certainly never spent so much time with someone so charming and handsome, so completely winning that just being around him tended to make her lightheaded and buoyant. She hadn't had a friend since her father died.

That thought caused her smile to vanish. William Stanton wasn't her friend, and she mustn't forget it.

She needed to occupy her hands to make her mind stop wandering. She located a porcelain teapot that matched the tea service, and then the brass-inlaid rosewood tea caddy, perched high on a shelf. It was locked, but Mrs Wright had told her where to find the key, hanging on a nail behind the largest earthenware bowl.

Key in hand, she opened the caddy and inhaled deeply, enjoying the aroma before adding a heaped spoonful of tea leaves to the pot.

'What are you doing?'

Isabelle spun around at the sharp voice, sprinkling tea on to the table as she did so. Mrs Graham, the cook, stood in the doorway, glaring at her, her face red and her ample bosom heaving with anger. 'There you go, spilling it. You have to ask to use the tea, you know. You have to ask me or Mrs Wright. You've no business helping yourself like you own the place.'

'I'm sorry,' Isabelle said, sweeping the leaves into her hand.

'Just because his lordship's taken a liking—'

She stopped abruptly, blanching like an onion. Isabelle spun around to see what had ended her tirade. Will stood in the doorway behind her, a loaf of bread in one hand. He placed it on the counter. 'What did you say, Mrs Graham?' His expression said he knew exactly what she'd said and what she'd been about to say.

The cook began wringing her hands. 'I didn't know you were here, my lord. Is something the matter?'

'Miss Weston-Burke, Miss Thomas and I will be having lunch in the garden. You weren't here to prepare it, so Miss Thomas and I have been making do. I told her to make tea. Last I heard, I don't ask for permission in my own house.'

'No, my lord.'

Isabelle couldn't take her gaze off his face. He wasn't looking at her, but was looking unblinkingly at Mrs Graham. No anger showed in his expression, but he was definitely angry. The cook looked ready to cry.

It was very bad. She appreciated him defending her, but Mrs Graham would only seek revenge when he wasn't there to protect her. She took a deep breath. 'I'll carry the cups and saucers. If you could perhaps help with the food, Mrs Graham?'

'Yes, Miss Thomas, I'll prepare something.' The words were polite enough, but there was a hint of mockery in her tone. Not enough to be easily detectable, but Isabelle heard it.

She reached for the tray, but Will picked it up first. His eyes challenged her to argue. She didn't. She walked up the narrow stairs, with him following behind.

Mary had moved to the shade of a tree, her nose once more deep in her book. She glanced up as they approached.

Will deposited the tray on a wrought iron table and sat on the grass next to her. Isabelle stood awkwardly for a second, then she sat, too, although several feet away.

He leaned back, supporting his weight with his hands. 'What are you reading?' he asked Mary.

She regarded him suspiciously, considered not answering, and then replied, 'It's called *Orlando's Reprisal.*'

He snorted. 'What tosh. Little wonder you can't put it down. Shall we have a game of bowls?'

Mary put the book facedown on the grass. She said nothing, but a competitive sparkle appeared in her eyes.

'There should be everything we need in the summerhouse,' he continued. 'I think, anyway. Haven't been in there for years. Come along?'

He rose, and after a second's indecision, Mary rose, too. Isabelle just watched, feeling too dazed to follow them as they headed towards the back of the garden. The peaked roof of the summerhouse was just visible through a leafy rhododendron. They disappeared.

She leaned back against the tree, feeling shaken. Some of the servants disapproved of her, that much was apparent. Mrs Graham and Rogers the footman, anyway, and presumably a few others. *Just because his lordship's taken a liking...* What had she intended to say? That Will had taken a liking to her? He certainly hadn't. He probably thought her an eccentric oddity, amusing to tease and unpredictable enough to offer some entertainment. But that was surely the only reason he bothered speaking to her at all.

Will and Mary reappeared a few minutes later. He carried a battered wicker basket full of colourful balls; a wreath of cobwebs attested to the fact that these items had hibernated for years. He placed the basket at her feet, and she noticed dust marring his blue woollen jacket.

She rose nervously. Sport of any description made her uneasy. 'Perhaps we'll be a team?' she asked, not having the faintest idea how to play the game.

'It's not played like that,' Will protested.

'Yes—I've played with teams before,' Mary argued.

'You can't have teams with just three players. It'd have to be two against one.'

'You could play with Miss Thomas,' Mary suggested. 'I'm quite good, actually.'

Before Isabelle had a chance to protest, he snorted. 'Are you suggesting I'm not? I may not be good at much, but I can definitely beat a pair of girls at bowls.'

Mary shrugged, unconvinced.

'How…how is it played?' Isabelle asked hesitantly, following after them quickly. She was starting to feel inadequate again. She found walking in a straight line to be difficult enough, never mind doing anything with a ball.

'You take the little ball,' Will explained, rummaging through the basket. 'And you bowl it.' He demonstrated, leaning forward to send the ball in a smooth arc across the lawn. It stopped squarely in the middle. 'It's called the jack, and the goal is to get these bigger coloured balls as close to it as possible. That's the essence of it, anyway. Pick a colour.'

She peered into the basket and retrieved a yellow ball.

'You have four, actually.' He removed three more and put them on the ground in front of her.

She held her breath, concentrated, and rolled her ball straight at a rosebush.

Mary grinned. Will frowned at Isabelle.

'I don't think you're trying, Miss Thomas. Here, watch me.' He bowled. His ball stopped about a foot from the jack before rolling back another three inches.

'It's the slope,' he explained to his female audience. 'Ideally the lawn should be completely flat.'

'I don't see any slope,' Mary said, removing three balls from the basket. She frowned, looking for the fourth. 'I'm missing one.'

'Which colour?' Will asked.

'Green.' She took a step, bowled her first ball carefully, and knocked his out of the way. Her ball halted about five inches from the jack.

She smiled cheekily. 'Have you seen another green ball?'

'I saw some blue ones in the summerhouse,' Will offered. 'You could pretend one of them is green.'

She ran towards the back of the garden.

'I'm letting her win, you know,' he said.

'You are, are you?'

'Of course.'

Isabelle prepared herself to bowl again, but she was distracted. She glanced at Will, wishing she didn't find him so appealing.

He was watching her. 'Miss Thomas?'

'Yes?'

'I can see you're concentrating very hard, but perhaps a hint?'

She straightened warily. 'What am I doing wrong?'

'If you...' he stood beside her and took her hand in his '...try straightening your wrist.'

Straighten her wrist? When every bone in her body had gone limp? All she could do was stare at his hand holding hers, noting every tendon. She was so mesmerised that she didn't hear the door open until it was too late.

Mrs Graham again, along with one of the downstairs maids, each carrying a tray. Wide-open, scandalised mouths that they closed immediately when Will looked in their direction. With eyes averted, they put the trays on the table.

Isabelle jerked her hand away. She became aware that her hair had come loose; she could feel wispy strands tickling her face. She knew she looked suspiciously dishevelled.

He behaved as if nothing were amiss. 'Thank you, Mrs Graham. That will be all.'

The cook nodded without looking up. The maid, a girl of about seventeen, was blushing profusely. They walked quickly back to the house, but before they'd even reached the door their heads were bent in gossip.

'Are you not hungry?' Will called over his shoulder. He'd already walked over to the table and was inspecting the trays.

She didn't answer him. Her heart had sunk to her ankles. Simple gossip was the best she could hope for. At worst, the other servants might become truly spiteful. Why did he not understand how difficult he'd just made her life?

She answered her question easily enough. Because he had no interest in her. Because as far as he was concerned, he was merely helping her learn to play the game—any other interpretation was simply wishful thinking on her part. Nothing compromising had occurred, even if appearances suggested otherwise.

She stared at the jack, bit her lip and bowled. Her yellow ball halted about two feet from its goal this time. Mary, walking briskly back from the summerhouse with a ball in her hand, smiled shyly at the improvement.

'Well, at least it went straight that time,' Will said. Isabelle glared at him, in no mood for his sarcasm.

He took his turn, knocking her ball well into the sidelines. Mary tried to come to her rescue by knocking his ball out of the way, but her ball lost momentum one inch too soon.

'Drat.'

He just smiled with male satisfaction.

In the end, he won, but only narrowly. Mary came a close second and Isabelle trailed embarrassingly, her stroke of good luck utterly undone by her nerves.

'I think you cheated,' she heard Mary tell Will over a bite of cake.

'I did not,' he replied.

Isabelle said very little as she finished her own lunch. The scene made her heart ache and speech rather difficult. She wished she hadn't seen this side of Will's character—the side that was perfectly content playing silly lawn games with a scrawny girl and teasing her out of her sulk.

So what if he was wicked? He was also…good. Good enough to fall in love with if she weren't very careful.

Just not good enough to love her back.

Chapter Thirteen

Isabelle heard raised voices as she descended the stairs the next morning.

'Do be quiet.' It was Will, shouting irritably down at someone in the hall below.

She stopped mid-step, catching herself just in time to avoid the creaky eighth stair. Carefully, she retracted her foot. She didn't want to see him. In the first place, she was walking down the wrong stair-case again, and although he didn't seem to care, he could choose to care if he wanted. In the second place…well, avoiding him whenever possible was simply a good policy to follow. As quietly as she could, she turned around and started to shrink back upstairs.

'Miss Thomas?'

Drat. Not quiet enough. She turned around slowly. He was looking at her, waiting for some response. To make matters worse, he wasn't yet dressed. Not completely, anyway. He'd put on trousers and a white linen shirt, but his shirt was open at the neck and his hair was tousled. He wasn't wearing shoes. Why couldn't she remember to use the servants' stairs? Then this sort of thing would never happen.

'Yes?' Her voice was small.

'Where are you going?' he asked, leaning back against the wall. He didn't look pleased to see her.

'To locate a book,' she managed. 'That is, unless you—'

'Then why are you going back upstairs?'

She quickly invented a feeble excuse. 'I didn't want to bother you.'

'Must I keep reminding you that you don't?'

She frowned at his lordly tone. 'I might be convinced if you didn't seem so annoyed.'

He still looked annoyed, but he denied it. 'Well, I'm not. Did you sleep well?'

She would have said no, but a deep, impatient male voice called up from downstairs at just that moment.

'Would you *please* hurry?'

'My brother,' Will explained. 'He doesn't like mornings.'

Interesting. He'd mentioned his brother before. But it wasn't a time to ask personal questions, not when he wasn't wearing a jacket. 'I mustn't keep you.' She started down the stairs again, hoping to dart past him. But he stepped to the side, effectively blocking her path.

'How's your foot?'

'Entirely better, I think.' He continued to stand in her way, and she felt forced to respond to his solicitous question with one of her own. 'You are going somewhere?'

He nodded. 'For a ride in the park, followed by a visit to my brother's house. I shan't be back until late.' He fell quiet, and she had the impression that he was trying to think of something to say in order to prolong their conversation. His expression, at first so intimidating, softened slightly. 'I was wondering if you needed anything.'

She cocked her head. 'What do you mean?'

Explaining seemed to make him impatient again. 'I mean, do you have everything you need here? If not, inform Mrs Wright or go shopping yourself. She can tell you where we have household accounts, so you can put whatever you like on credit. Is your room lacking?'

She shook her head, bemused. She needed so much, but she certainly wasn't going to ask for anything. Although he was offering to help her, he seemed so grumpy about it. 'My room is perfect. Thank you.' She paused, however, thinking about Mary.

Her clothes were nearly as outdated as Isabelle's, and even though she didn't seem to care Isabelle wondered if new clothes might improve her confidence. And then there was that matter of her friend, Celia…

'Is there something else?'

'Well…'

'Yes?'

'Mary would like to invite a friend from school for a visit.'

He seemed surprised by the request. 'Yes, yes, of course. Can't imagine any responsible parent entrusting their child to my care for even a short period of time, but—'

'She would presumably bring a chaperon.'

'Really? How awful. But, no, it's all right. The girl needs friends.'

'She'll also need a new wardrobe. Most of her dresses are nearly an inch too short and not terribly fashionable, either. She also needs gloves and hats and…uh, other small, personal items. If you don't mind, I could take her shopping today.'

'By all means. I'd noticed she was looking a bit outmoded, but I suppose I forgot to do anything about it.' His gaze drifted over her body as he spoke, and she wanted to cringe. He was obviously taking in the dowdiness of her own gown and wondering, no doubt, if she could be trusted on such an errand.

'I'm afraid my own clothes aren't very stylish. One would assume I didn't pay much attention to such things.'

He shook his head slightly. His voice was thick. 'That's not what I was thinking. Would you…would you like more clothes? It never occurred to me to ask.'

She blushed. 'It should not have. I have enough. I…I have more at the boarding house where I was. I should really collect them soon—'

'Get them while you're out today. Take the carriage.'

'William!'

His brother again, this time sounding completely exasperated. His obvious disgruntlement saved her, at any rate. Will walked forwards to glare over the banister, and in that moment she walked quickly past him and carried on down the rest of the stairs with little more than a 'goodbye'.

Only once she'd reached sight of the hall, she wished she'd made a different decision. Will's brother was, indeed, waiting there. And, to make matters worse, he was staring at her. For just a few seconds, she stared back; it was hard not to. He was nearly as tall as Will and every bit as handsome, although in a different way. Darker. Scarier.

She lowered her gaze and finished walking down the stairs. Servants did not gawp, she reminded herself. Nor did they speak to their superiors, so she would just pretend to be invisible. She headed towards the servants' passage, thinking how difficult it was pretending she was invisible when he was still staring at her; she could sense it, even though she didn't remove her gaze from the oak floor. He must have been thinking some very amusing thoughts, because she also sensed he was trying hard not to laugh.

They slowed their horses from a canter to a trot and then eased into a walk. The horses puffed with the exertion and, although the day was early and still cool, a light lather appeared on their necks where the reins had rubbed.

Will loosened his horse's reins, and he gratefully stretched his neck almost to the ground.

'Shall we have lunch?' James asked.

Will glanced at his brother. James was his half-brother, actually, and the person who understood him best. Apart from sharing great height and green eyes, they appeared almost unrelated. James wasn't perhaps quite as broad as Will, and his hair was so dark it was almost black.

At the moment, Will's expression was also fairly dark. He rode in the park with James at least once a week, but he wasn't enjoying it much today. Damn Isabelle for taking him by surprise that morning. He'd responded gruffly, but who could blame him when she'd appeared so unexpectedly and his bedroom door was close enough for him to see it beckoning from the end of the corridor, pleading with him to carry her inside and toss her on the bed? It was either be gruff and unpleasant or give in to the lecherous voices that increasingly instructed his behaviour where she was concerned. He chose the former option.

'Very well.'

And damn her again for driving him from his own home. It was as if she were in charge, not him. That morning, he'd felt almost…nervous speaking to her, like some green schoolboy. His plan—if he could even call it that—had collapsed. It had seemed so simple when he'd devised it, but he'd quickly comprehended that he hadn't thought beyond getting her inside his house. And now that she was there, he couldn't seduce her. For one, she was, in effect, under his protection. For another, he'd always favoured brief affairs, but if he started one with her, what would happen when it ultimately came to an end? She'd still be Mary's governess. She'd still be in his house.

And he was just a little worried that he wouldn't want to end things. What was happening to him? Maybe Vanessa Lytton had been right, and having Mary about was having a softening effect on him.

On his mind, anyway. But definitely not his heart.

'You were late this morning,' James remarked. Will detected a smirk in his voice.

'Yes.'

'You're not usually late.'

'Today I was.'

Silence, while James prepared a new plan of attack. Finally he couldn't contain himself. 'So, Will…I'm curious about your improved domestic situation.'

Will glanced at him. 'I don't know what you mean.'

'Henrietta was by earlier in the week,' James carried on. 'She mentioned you'd asked her to help you select a governess for Mary.'

'I did.'

'And am I to assume that the red-headed beauty is your new governess?'

'Yes,' he answered tightly. 'What else would she be?'

'She doesn't look like the governess Eleanor just hired for Diana.'

'It's not my fault your governess is homely,' Will retorted. He didn't want to talk about Isabelle.

'I can't imagine Henrietta would pick a governess who looked like that.'

No, and he knew she'd have something to say about his choice if she ever saw Isabelle. He'd bar her from his house if need be. 'I managed without her help. Miss Thomas came along and I thought she was too good to dither about.'

'Came along? *Where* exactly did she come from?'

Unwise to admit outright that he'd met her in the slums. 'Well, sort of nowhere. I found her in a difficult situation—no family, no funds, no home.'

'Always a sound basis for inviting someone into your house.'

'You must admit she's pretty.'

James just shook his head. 'I don't believe you've hired your mistress.'

Will frowned. 'She's not, you ass.'

Pause. 'Then why isn't she? I presume that's why you took her on.'

Why indeed. That had been the plan, hadn't it? 'Shut up, James. I don't want to talk about it.'

James was chuckling to himself. 'Is she not co-operating with you?'

'No, I just don't want you bandying about the reputation of m'ward's governess.'

James snorted. 'Her reputation? Since when do you care?'

He didn't care about her reputation; she was a no one without a reputation worth speaking of. But no one or not, he did think he cared about her. Just a bit. As one did of helpless girls who were under one's protection. As he did of the tenants on his estate, and anyone else he was responsible for. Even the bloody cats who turned up. She was just another stray, as was Mary. Nothing more than that.

And yet hearing James speak so slightingly of her infuriated him. 'Well, I've never been in this situation before, have I?'

'I'd have thought you'd been in this situation *many* times.'

'Bloody hell, I told you I don't have designs on her. I wouldn't want any member of my household being spoken of like that.'

'Of course.'

The patronising ass. 'Very well. Maybe her more than the others, because she's in charge of m'ward. I wouldn't know what to do without her. Highly dependable.'

They rode on a bit without speaking. Will enjoyed the silence, knowing it wouldn't last.

'But she won't be in charge of your ward much longer,' James pointed out after another minute.

'Why not?'

'Because you're sending the girl back to school. You told me so before she even turned up. What will you do with Miss Thomas then?'

He'd barely thought about sending Mary away since Isabelle had arrived. The disruption to his household that he'd anticipated had never happened. Mary was quite amiable, really, once you got to know her. He'd thoroughly enjoyed their afternoon yesterday. Furthermore, sending her away would mean sending Isabelle away, too, and he wasn't ready to entertain those thoughts.

'Mary might not be returning to school.'

'No?'

'No. It's working out quite well.'

'I'm certain it is.'

'Don't be so damned cynical,' Will said irritably.

'Since when are you *not* cynical?'

Will didn't answer. 'It must be lunchtime.'

James was looking at him strangely, but he suppressed whatever question it was he wanted to ask. 'Very well.'

Will returned home at eleven that night. After lunch and a few too many drinks with his brother, they'd gone on to James's house. Will hadn't minded. He liked his sister-in-law, Eleanor, very much, and he adored his niece, Diana. They'd just one child, a two-year-old girl so small it seemed impossible that she should be related to his oafish brother. In a strange sort of way, Will actually liked visiting James more now that he'd married; marriage had lightened the dark moods he was prone to and had healed old wounds that Will once thought he'd never recover from.

To see him happy made Will happy, or at least it normally did. His brother's house, noisy and somewhat disorganised, offered a pleasing contrast to his own solitary existence. But today, seeing James and Eleanor together had made him feel an unusual emptiness. It hadn't helped that his old friend, Harry, and his new wife had joined them. They'd all traded anecdotes about married life and children, except for Will, of course, who'd just listened absentmindedly. As he pushed his food around his plate, he realised that he'd finally reached that unenviable stage where all his friends had wives and children, and he did not. He used to feel rather lucky to have escaped such commitments, but he wasn't so sure anymore.

James dropped the subject of Isabelle until the ladies had withdrawn after supper and Harry had stepped outside to promise his cantankerous driver that they'd leave in twenty minutes. James had accused him, like Henrietta had a few weeks ago, of softheartedness. Rubbish, Will thought, not even worth defending against—although a niggling doubt had entered his mind. When Harry returned, he had invited Will to visit him in the country that weekend, and he accepted immediately. Perhaps some time away from Isabelle was in order.

He slipped his key into the front door and opened it quietly. He generally didn't request any servants to stay up if he knew he'd return home late, and as was habit Bartholomew had left just a small lamp burning on the hall table. Will retrieved it carefully, so as not to extinguish the flame. He crossed the hall and began climbing the stairs.

At the top of the stairs, though, he noticed that the library door—just past the drawing room—was slightly ajar. That was odd. The doors were usually kept closed, even during the day, and at night Bartholomew locked them, too, as an insurance against theft. Perhaps it was an oversight.

He walked to the door and pushed it open further, although just enough for his body to fit through. The well-oiled hinges didn't creak, and the carpet absorbed any sound his footsteps might have made. At first, he saw no one; the library was the third-largest room in the house, after the ballroom and the drawing room, and any intruder could easily have hidden in the shadows. But then he noticed the dim light of a candle at the back of the room, and a slim female form silhouetted by the moonlight that shone through a window. She was standing rather precariously on top of the library steps and appeared to be balancing a candlestick in one hand and several books in the other.

'Isabelle?'

She turned suddenly at the sound of his voice, losing her balance slightly—just enough for the books to wobble and fall. She tried to catch them, but just lost her candlestick in the process. The candle extinguished before it hit the floor. He thought he heard her curse.

'Are you all right?' He entered the room more fully and started moving towards her.

'Yes,' she answered quickly. Without her light, he could see her less clearly, but he suspected she was frozen in place like a scared mouse.

'You couldn't sleep?'

'No, I...' He could hear the library steps creak as she began her descent, feeling her way clumsily in the dark. 'I thought you might have some books I could use with Mary. Bartholomew very kindly left the door open for me, but I should have locked it hours ago.'

'Wait till I reach you.' The darkness forced him to walk slowly.

'What? Oh, I'm down already. I shouldn't...oh...'

'What's wrong?' He was at her side now, and she was straightening, indicating that she'd been bent over.

'I've spilled wax on your carpet.'

He didn't care. In the warm glow of his lamp she looked...amazing. So sweet and pure that he held his breath, so tempting that it hurt. She wore the same simple dress she'd been wearing earlier, but she'd loosened her hair. Soft, wispy tendrils framed her face, tumbled to her shoulders. Everything about her was so pretty and fresh, more beautiful every time he saw her.

'It doesn't matter.'

She shook her head guiltily. Her voice was small, uncertain. 'I'm so sorry. I shouldn't be in here. Please don't blame Bartholomew.'

He swallowed hard. 'I don't mind that you're in here.'

'No? But I should have asked your permission.'

'Sweetheart, you can do just about anything you please and you won't bother me.'

'What?'

She blinked, as if she didn't quite understand what he'd said. He was baffled by his stupidity himself. Sweetheart? He hadn't meant to say that, even though he'd meant it. He shouldn't even call her Isabelle.

There was nothing to do but pretend it hadn't happened. 'Here, take my hand.'

The term of endearment had put her on guard. She didn't accept his offer. 'I can see well enough. If I just find my candle, you can relight it with yours.'

'Don't be ridiculous. A maid will retrieve your candle in the morning.' He took her reluctant hand in his and led her slowly through the dark library, around shadowy masses that he knew to be tables and chairs, and then out of the door.

The landing's white painted walls made it slightly brighter than the library. Bright enough to see clearly if one's eyes had adjusted. He discarded his lamp on a marble-topped table. She could have navigated her way back to her bedroom from there without any help from him, but Will didn't let go. She might have run off if he'd released her, but mostly he just didn't want to.

He reached around her to pull the library door shut, and her proximity struck him like a wave. How easy it would be to keep his arm around her and pull her even closer, to lean in, to tilt her head back and taste her velvety lips. And she was looking up at him like she was waiting for something to happen. Her blue eyes—bottomless, nervous—were curious, too.

He couldn't have avoided it if he'd wanted to, and since he'd been thinking about kissing her for weeks he was utterly defenceless. His hand moved up her arm, tracing a gentle line across her shoulder, her neck. He cupped the back of her head, drawing her lips to his. And then he was kissing her—not casually, but as if his life depended on it.

Too intense, too fast, he realised. He forced himself to slow down, to nibble gently on her closed, inexperienced lips. Then tentatively, perhaps even against her will, she parted them, allowing him inside.

It felt wonderful. Warm and soft, like a sigh of relief. Only he didn't sigh, he groaned. Weeks of tightly controlled anticipation suddenly released like floodgates. He found her tongue and teased gently until she was kissing him back. Touching his tongue with hers, duelling curiously.

Her hands had somehow come to rest on his shoulders, and she gripped him tightly. He took a step forwards, pressing her against the wall. Her tall, lithe body fit his snugly. Right and perfect like a missing piece found.

Eyes closed, she tilted her head back, and he allowed his lips to leave hers to trail down the column of her throat: smooth soft skin, light pulse beating quickly, and the welcome vibration of a soft, satisfied moan. Moving slowly had never been more difficult. He felt, again, like an untried schoolboy, wanting to tear her clothes off and make love to her right there, never mind a bed.

No, no, a bed would be nice. Necessary, too, since he wasn't sixteen and he'd bloody well remember it or he'd embarrass both himself and her. He began guiding her towards the stairs. She didn't protest, but she was probably only half-aware of what he was doing. He hardly knew himself. He'd told himself she was off limits; it was too soon, and she wasn't ready. But even though he knew he *should* stop, he didn't want to. He wanted to carry her to his bedroom without taking his lips from hers. He wanted to make love to her, in his bed as was proper, for the rest of tonight and tomorrow, too.

Oh, God, tomorrow. What would happen tomorrow?

He didn't want to think about it. Only that moment mattered. But then, that moment, suddenly—

Heavy, sensible footsteps walking down the oak floorboards. Footsteps he knew very well, forcing him to stop. He pulled away, cursing his butler quietly. He was the last person he'd want to see at a time like this.

Isabelle obviously also recognised the footsteps. Her eyes focused, and her dilated pupils narrowed sharply. She pushed against his chest and he released her slowly, his responses still dulled by passion. She darted up the stairs, heading to her bedroom, and he just watched her go. He leaned against the wall, letting his head fall back to rest on it; he hoped some of its coolness would permeate his brain.

Damn.

Bartholomew appeared with a lamp about five seconds later. He'd obviously heard something because, very discreetly, he glanced at the staircase. Will straightened, knowing his hair would be dishevelled, his colour heightened. His butler would draw conclusions.

'Bartholomew,' he said.

The man obviously already wished he hadn't come. 'Good evening, my lord. I am sorry—I heard you enter the house, but then I heard noises in the library…I assumed there might be some problem, or you might…need something. I didn't mean to—'

'Didn't mean to what?' Will asked. *Intrude? Interrupt? Ruin my night?*

He blushed. 'Nothing, my lord. Will that be all?'

'That is all, Bartholomew. Thank you.'

Relieved, the butler headed back to his quarters. Will continued to lean against the wall for several minutes. He wouldn't have spoken to his butler so sharply if he hadn't felt so keenly frustrated, if the blood hadn't still been coursing through his body. Bartholomew hadn't ruined his night at all. He'd prevented Will from making an already colossal mistake even bigger.

But he'd still made a big mistake.

Chapter Fourteen

Isabelle closed the nursery door with a click, leaving Mary to eat her lunch alone. She'd put on a good face that morning and hoped the girl had detected no change in her behaviour. She doubted she'd convinced her, not when she'd been so patently distracted. All she wanted to do was hide in her bedroom, but that wasn't an option. She needed to find Will. Needed to tell him she planned to leave.

She began walking down the corridor, dreading the task. Yesterday's events had disturbed her from start to finish, even during the many hours between his departure with his brother and his late-night return. Eager to get out of the house after two days' confinement, she'd promptly instructed Mary to prepare for their shopping expedition. But while she was waiting for her in the hall, Rogers had shown in someone unexpected and not entirely welcome.

'Dr Collins. I— Good afternoon.'

He hadn't looked very comfortable, had even allowed his gaze to search the hall, no doubt looking for Will or any other ogres that might be lurking. 'Miss Thomas—I do apologise for the imposition, but as I was nearby I thought I'd enquire about your foot. I hope your employer won't mind?'

Rogers had raised a dubious eyebrow, but thankfully said nothing.

As usual, the blood rushed to Isabelle's face. 'No. I mean, Lord Lennox has gone out for the day. I, uh, thank you for your concern. My foot seems to be fully recovered.' She felt at a loss. She couldn't exactly invite him in, but how rude to make him stand in the hall when he'd been so kind. 'I've just a few minutes, but—shall we take a walk around the square?'

He'd followed her outside. 'I should have come sooner, but I feared it might make your situation worse.'

'Worse?' She stared at the smooth paving stones, not comprehending.

He didn't answer immediately. Just walked beside her quietly as if ordering his thoughts. 'I must confess that your foot isn't the only reason I've come,' he said finally.

She glanced at him sideways. Oh, not him, too. Must all men have ulterior motives? 'I'm relieved to hear it as my foot has fared well enough without your attention. Is it my elbow that interests you?'

Will would have grinned at her and said something outrageous to make her regret her cheek. Dr Collins was too earnest. 'I've been worried about you.'

'Worried?'

'Yes. That you might be unhappy in your position. What I witnessed the other day… He has a temper, obviously. And a reputation.'

'Dr Collins—'

'Please, Miss Thomas, don't protest, and don't misinterpret my words. I'm an honourable man and offer my help without expectation of reward. If you *are* unhappy, if you should need anything at all…'

She stopped walking. She didn't doubt his honour, and, yes, Will had a temper. So had she. And if she knew anything at all, she knew Will wouldn't hurt her. She looked back at the house. They'd only gone down one side of the square, but Mary was already standing on the steps, scanning the street. 'I must go. She's waiting for me.'

Dr Collins had walked her back. He'd given her his card, too, although at the time she'd assumed she wouldn't need it.

One day later she wasn't so sure.

She definitely couldn't stay at Will's house, not when he'd nearly been her undoing just last night. The problem was, she didn't want to go anywhere else. She liked Mary and she liked him—liked him too much, apparently. She'd allowed him to kiss her and had kissed him back with unseemly enthusiasm. She'd never before received even a chaste peck, and his kiss… Well, perhaps she hadn't behaved in a ladylike fashion, but she didn't think a gentleman would kiss like that, either. If Bartholomew hadn't come along, she didn't know what would have happened.

She finally found him in the hall, shrugging into his jacket. Bartholomew stood by the door, holding his hat. Will was obviously on his way out. Isabelle nervously wondered if the butler had seen her as she'd escaped upstairs last night.

'Miss Thomas.'

She forgot what she'd planned to say. Her face filled with hot colour as he said her name.

'Did you need something?' he prompted.

'Uh, yes. I wanted a word with you, my lord. But it can wait.'

His gaze roamed slowly over her face, and she wished she knew what he was thinking. 'Or we can speak now.'

She nodded and followed him to his study. After closing the door, he immediately crossed the room to pour himself a drink. 'Please sit, Miss Thomas.'

She chose one of the large armchairs. He opted for the sofa that flanked it. He swirled his drink and waited.

'What did you wish to say?' he asked after several silent seconds.

How to begin? She folded her hands in her lap, then unfolded them.

'I… What I wanted to say…'

He interrupted her rather impatiently. '*Must* we have a word?'

She looked up at him warily. 'My lord?'

'I said must we? I think I know what you're going to say, and I should say first that I'm sorry.'

'Sorry?'

He leaned forward. 'Yes, Miss Thomas. Abjectly so, even though I can hardly recall what happened. I'd spent the day with my brother and, I'm ashamed to admit, I was completely foxed when I arrived home. But I've some memory of… Did I kiss you?'

Hearing him say it was more humiliation than she could with-stand. She rose stiffly from her chair, her cheeks burning. 'I must find a new position.'

He didn't seem to be anticipating that. His face remained expressionless, but she suspected she'd annoyed him. He leaned back into the sofa and crossed one leg over his knee. 'May I ask why?'

Because she was already thinking about kissing him again and finding it hard not to stare at his lips. Because she didn't think she'd ever be able to look at him the same way again. 'Well, I…I should do so anyway, since you'll return Mary to school soon.'

'I've made no plans to do so yet.'

'But you will. And I…well…'

He rose from his seat and crossed the room to look out the window. He turned around. 'I've apologised already, Miss Thomas. If you leave this house, I shall feel terribly guilty. Is that what you want? Is my apology not enough?'

He was trying to cajole her. 'No. I mean, that's not what I want.'

'Then don't leave. We'll just forget it ever happened.'

She wouldn't be forgetting it any time soon. 'I should still leave.'

He left his glass on a side table and walked closer. He stopped when he was just a few feet from her, his gaze wandering across her face. 'I've no intention of kissing you again, if that's what you're worried about. I don't know how it happened in the first place. Could I have thought you were someone else?'

But he'd called her Isabelle; he'd called her sweetheart. He'd tasted of brandy, but he hadn't been that foxed. 'I… Yes, you must have.'

'Well, then, I suppose we've finished our talk.'

No, they'd arrived at no conclusion. Nothing was settled, and he was standing so close, close enough to cause funny tremors inside her stomach. How could she continue to work here when she couldn't even stand beside him without turning to a jelly?

She took a rallying breath. 'I still think I should find another position.'

'But I quite like you here.'

His voice was soft, seductive, and she finally met his gaze, a mistake because she became trapped by his hypnotic eyes. Eyes that had gone dark, that travelled down her freckled nose to settle on her lips. He was leaning in—or was she imagining it? He'd just said he wouldn't kiss her again, and he certainly wasn't foxed now. He hadn't even sipped his drink.

She felt her eyelids begin to droop. There'd be little harm in one more kiss if she planned to leave anyway. Just one, and then she'd pack her belongings.

But there was no kiss. Just a firm rap on the door. Will stepped away.

'My lord?'

It was Bartholomew, on the other side of the mahogany panels. Her saviour for the second time in less than a day. He obviously wore angel's wings beneath his butler's jacket.

'Sit, Isabelle,' Will commanded.

She sat, not even pausing to object to his order. She folded her hands on her lap and tried to look blameless. Nothing had happened, after all. He hadn't kissed her, nor had she him. Thinking vivid thoughts about doing so didn't count.

Bartholomew entered, but he was too well trained to indicate if he detected the heavy tension in the room.

'Mrs Lytton and Miss Lytton,' he announced. 'They were expecting you to take them for a drive, my lord. It seems you should have collected them half an hour ago. They have, uh, taken it upon themselves to pay a visit to ensure everything is all right.'

Isabelle glanced out of the study door to see two attractive ladies, apparently mother and daughter, huddled in close conversation. Will saw them, too, and muttered something indistinct but impolite.

'Shall I show them in, my lord?' The butler's eyes betrayed him, and he glanced at Isabelle as he spoke.

Will looked at her, too. 'Yes, of course.'

'I'll leave,' she said awkwardly, but it was already too late. She'd have to walk right past them.

'Just sit,' Will said threateningly under his breath. 'If you leave, it'll look like…'

He didn't finish, but she knew what he was going to say. If she left, it would look like they'd something to conceal. She sank back into her seat as the two elegant ladies were shown in. One appeared to be about forty, and the other eighteen, but age seemed to be the only difference between them. They shared perfect, patrician features, pale blonde hair and complexions like fresh cream. Not a freckle in sight.

The older one paused as she passed through the door, her assessing gaze taking in Isabelle's flushed cheeks and Will's abandoned glass of spirits. She frowned.

Miss Lytton at first noticed nothing amiss. 'Lord Lennox, you didn't forget our engagement, did you?' she chided.

He choked slightly over the word. 'Engagement?'

'Yes—that drive you promised. We've been so looking forward to it. We shouldn't have come, I know, except we worried something might be wrong.' Here she paused to lower her lashes demurely. 'You do not think it too bold, I hope?'

Isabelle, for one, could hardly believe their audacity, coming to his house like this. But then catching a husband was a cutthroat sport, and anyone would bend the rules if the husband to be caught were Will.

He'd clearly forgotten his promise, but he responded to the contrary. 'Of course I didn't forget…just running slightly late. I hope you're well?'

Vanessa nodded and opened her mouth to speak, but then finally noticed Isabelle, who was trying assiduously—but without visible effect—to evaporate. 'We are well, Lord Lennox. I hope we've not come at a bad time.'

Isabelle had never seen Will truly flustered before—she could not, until that moment, even have imagined it. But now, trying to explain her presence on his sofa, he began to stammer. 'Uh…no, of course not. I was just…uh, having a word with Miss Thomas. She is Mary's governess. Mary's my ward.'

Mrs Lytton's eyes narrowed suspiciously. Vanessa's widened with practised excitement.

'Yes, of course! The orphan. I should be delighted to meet her. How old is she?'

'Uh…eleven.'

'Twelve,' Isabelle interjected.

Will gave her a frosty look. 'Yes, that's right. Twelve.'

'How charming. She must come with us.'

'Oh. Well…'

'Do go collect her, Miss Thomas,' Vanessa said. She didn't even bother to look at Isabelle as she made this instruction.

And Isabelle didn't bother to rise. She didn't like taking orders from just anyone. Especially not spoiled girls nearly ten years her junior.

'Are you waiting for something, Miss Thomas?' But that was Will this time. He was looking at her with impatience.

'What?'

He frowned. 'Please collect Mary.'

She rose unsteadily. Although Will had lost his temper with her more times than she could count, he'd never spoken to her so coldly before. He'd never treated her like a servant. She walked from the room, trying not to cry, all too aware that the women were watching her leave. She closed the door behind her and, for just a few seconds, leaned against it, praying she'd be able to collect herself before anyone saw her.

Will would have preferred dismemberment by rusty knife to spending an afternoon like this, trapped in his carriage with the ladies Lytton. He suspected Mary, looking sullen and uncomfortable in the seat across from him, felt much the same way.

He'd completely forgotten that he'd promised to take them to the park—understandable, since he hadn't been the one to make that promise in the first place. It was one of the last things he'd want to do any time, and particularly when he was a hairsbreadth from kissing Isabelle again.

He supposed it was Providence that had prevented his kiss, although he'd never have expected divine intervention to come in the form of Vanessa and her mother. There was nothing to cool his ardour like the pair of them, and he shouldn't have even been contemplating kissing Isabelle—not now, not when doing so last night had nearly driven her away. When she'd told him she planned to leave he'd felt…he wasn't sure what, but he hadn't liked it at all. Irritated, and scared and a bit ill. He didn't know if he'd convinced her to stay, but he'd try again when he got home. He wouldn't let her leave.

For now, he'd just have to get through the Lytton ordeal. He looked at Vanessa, who was chattering inanely to no one in particular and casting furtive, amused glances at Mary. It made him angry, her sense of superiority. She'd sized the girl up smugly when she'd come downstairs to join them, taking in her provincial dress and carrot-coloured hair. He'd given little thought to her clothes until Isabelle brought the subject up yesterday, and he wondered if she'd taken her shopping. She'd mentioned gloves and hats, but it would be worth having a modiste sent round to create a whole new wardrobe for the girl. He should have insisted weeks ago. Fashionable clothes would be necessary armour against someone like Vanessa—someone whose only strength lay in the way she looked.

Vanessa noticed that he was looking at her and smiled with calculated shyness, an expression she'd no doubt practised many times in front of a mirror. He tried to smile in return, as was merely polite, but he couldn't quite manage. He really disliked her. Not only had she belittled Mary, but she'd been rude to Isabelle as well. And as for the proprietary way she'd ordered her around—she was in for an unpleasant surprise if she seriously thought she'd one day be mistress of his damned house.

Of course, he'd also been rude to Isabelle, and he didn't expect her to forgive him easily. He hadn't wanted to speak so brusquely to her, but he'd been desperate to regain control. Nor did he want the Lyttons to read anything into the compromising situation, so he felt it was necessary to treat her like a servant. They'd obviously drawn their own conclusions anyway, or at least Mrs Lytton had. Even now she was looking at him with a coolness he hadn't seen before. Vanessa, however, was probably too vain to feel threatened by another woman.

'Mrs Sandon-Drabbe informed me you'd been at Miss Hume's school,' Vanessa said, still regarding Mary as if she were something unpleasant to be squashed.

Mary turned her attention away from the passing scenery, where her gaze had been fixed for a quarter of an hour.

'That's my cousin, Henrietta,' Will clarified. 'You haven't met her yet.'

'Oh.' She seemed diffident and unhappy again—quite unlike the smiling girl she'd been two days ago in the garden. All due, no doubt, to Vanessa's insensitivity. 'Yes, I was,' she said finally. 'For four years.'

'I was educated at home,' Vanessa went on rather pompously. 'I've never known a girl who was sent to school. Why did you not have a governess before now?'

Mary shrugged, and Will wondered again if she understood why her father had sent her away. She was only twelve and very well might not.

'Mary's mother died when she was young,' he explained so she wouldn't have to. 'Her father thought she'd be better looked after at Miss Hume's.'

Vanessa smiled patronisingly. Her mother chimed in. 'My daughter was lucky to have such a fine education. I wouldn't trust anyone to look after her away from home. She's been very sheltered. I believe that's how a young lady should be raised. Do you not agree, Lord Lennox?'

Will had serious doubts about Vanessa's education, and if a sheltered upbringing was what it took to produce a nightmare like her, then he was definitely opposed to the idea. 'I can't say I have much opinion on the subject.'

'Have you seen her watercolours?' Mrs Lytton asked. 'She's very talented.'

Before he had a chance to answer, Vanessa volunteered, 'I can show them to you next week if you would like. Would you?'

'Would I what?'

'Would you like me to show you my watercolours next week?'

'I…uh, well, I'm going away for the weekend and may not have returned by then.'

That was true. He'd agreed to visit Harry in the country. Mary didn't know that, however, and her dangerously twitching lips suggested she thought he'd made up the lame excuse on the spot. He frowned at her, but her grin broke through anyway. Vanessa noticed, and her expression turned downright hateful. She sensed she was being laughed at, but she didn't know why.

'Has your upbringing trained you to be amused by others?' she demanded.

Mary bit her lip and looked at the scenery again. The breeze tugged at her hair, creating a wispy halo around her head; her hair appeared more orange than ever in the bright sun.

Vanessa's haughty gaze travelled over her, and he found himself feeling unexpectedly but powerfully protective. 'She's merely daydreaming, Miss Lytton. She wasn't listening to you.'

Vanessa wasn't satisfied. 'What a pretty dress,' she said, sounding completely insincere. It was an awful dress; Mary was skinny and ginger-haired and awkward. And, damn it, he liked her for it. Vanessa had probably never had an inelegant day in her life, and he couldn't stand her.

Before Vanessa could give free rein to her vitriol, her mother grabbed her hand and applied subtle pressure. 'Perhaps, my lord,' she said, looking at him meaningfully, 'a more fashionable governess might do the girl some good. I'm not sure your Miss Thomas has the first idea how a girl of Mary's gentle background should behave. I'd recommend finding a replacement immediately.'

He'd no doubt she would. 'Miss Thomas is very clever.'

Mrs Lytton smiled patiently. 'Cleverness is all very well, but there's so much more a young lady needs to learn. About clothing and manners. We could help you replace her—'

'I like Miss Thomas, and I don't care about clothing,' Mary interjected.

'Or manners,' Vanessa said under her breath.

Will stared at her. He wasn't surprised by her petty viciousness, but he hadn't expected her to display it in front of him, in his own carriage. 'What did you say, Miss Lytton?'

She was wise enough not to repeat her words. Her mother attempted to smooth the situation over. 'It is a pretty dress, dear. We are merely tired.'

'Then I will take you home.'

Mary returned her attention to the scenery. The only sound, for several uncomfortable seconds, was that of the birds and the rustling trees outside.

'Pleasant weather, isn't it?' Mrs Lytton said finally, relying on the one dependable subject when all else failed. 'Hope it doesn't rain tomorrow…'

Georgina Lytton shooed her daughter upstairs and closed herself inside her private sitting room. She crossed the floor to her orderly satinwood desk, pulling the bell on the way.

What an unspeakable disaster. Her head throbbed, and as she sat down she covered her forehead with a cool, smooth hand. She closed her eyes briefly, willing the pain to ebb.

She'd been depending on an alliance between her daughter and Lord Lennox, and she'd told everyone she knew that it was a certainty. Now the only thing that was certain was that Lord Lennox would *not* marry Vanessa. When he hadn't seemed bored by her, he'd been downright irritated. Georgina was a realistic woman: she knew her third daughter wasn't a skilled conversationalist and that her views were narrow and provincial, despite her sophisticated upbringing. But none of that should matter when her face was taken into account.

The audacity of Lord Lennox—it wasn't as if he'd make much of a husband. She'd certainly never deluded herself into thinking he'd be faithful to her daughter, but he was so rich any number of infidelities wouldn't matter. With three daughters, no sons and their house entailed to a second cousin, they needed the money.

She located a clean sheet of paper and wrote three neat lines of text. Her footman arrived as she finished. She kept two footmen, actually, which strained Mr Lytton's finances but was completely necessary for appearance's sake. She'd never marry off Vanessa if the true state of their finances got round. This particular footman was George, the more handsome of the two. He was the one she'd been hoping for.

'Ah. I have an extra task for you, George.'

'Yes, madam?' he said without alacrity.

'Tomorrow I would like you to go to this address.' She handed him the paper and waited while his eyes slowly scanned the text. 'That is the residence of the Earl of Lennox. My daughter holds some tender feelings for the man, but I fear he might be a scoundrel.'

'Yes?'

'Yes. He has a ward, a girl of about twelve, staying with him, along with her governess. A very pretty governess—too pretty for me to believe that's her sole function in his household. Do you understand me?'

He nodded miserably.

She continued. 'You will speak to his servants and find out anything you can about this arrangement. Flirt with his chambermaids. I don't care *how* you go about it. I must know all I can about his character before I further encourage an alliance with my daughter.'

She opened her desk drawer and began rummaging through old letters by way of dismissal, but he continued to stand there. She realised he was waiting to discuss compensation. She glanced at him coolly. 'I *will* pay you, George. Not this very minute, of course. I'll add it to your salary. You *do* trust me, I hope.'

His uncertain expression indicated he did not, but her cold, challenging gaze kept him from voicing his objections.

She watched him leave. The gall. She'd pay him—perhaps—if he discovered anything useful. What was coming to the world? The man worked for her, and he'd do what she told him, no matter how distasteful. Servants were a grasping lot and one couldn't be too generous.

Chapter Fifteen

Will had deposited Vanessa and her mother at their house with relief, and he hoped never to see either of them again. He knew he was unlikely to be that lucky.

Mary had been silent for the rest of the journey. He looked at her now, as the carriage pulled away from the pavement and began heading down the street.

'Are you all right?' he asked.

She glanced at him slowly. He noticed, for the first time, that her big grey eyes were actually rather beautiful. She simply nodded before returning her attention to the street outside.

They rode in silence for several minutes until Mary asked suddenly, 'Are you going to marry Miss Lytton?'

He was surprised by the question, but answered it easily. 'No.' There wasn't a chance in hell he'd marry her, and there never had been.

'I could have been nicer to her. I shouldn't have laughed at her.'

'Perhaps. She didn't make it easy.' He didn't feel a speck of anger. He hated when the strong picked on the weak. As Richard had James, when James had been too young to defend himself. He didn't know if that experience had conditioned him to feel the way he did, but he supposed it must have. 'I thought you handled yourself quite well.'

The compliment seemed to please her. Warm colour filled her cheeks, and Will felt rather good himself.

He remembered what Isabelle had told him.

'You take after your father in that way, you know. He was very good at recognising a fool.'

That certainly captured her attention. 'What do you mean?'

'I mean he'd have had little time for Vanessa Lytton.'

'Even though she's pretty?'

'Pretty's not so important.'

'How long did you know Papa?'

'More than half my life. We met at school, when we were fourteen. We'd already been at school together for a few years before then, but our paths had never really crossed. We were very different, but he was still my best friend there.'

'How were you different?'

'Well…we didn't tend to move in the same circles at first. Your father was much more bookish. I suppose I spent most of my time at sport. We might not have met except we both got into a scrape with the headmaster on the same day—'

'Why?'

'I'd been caught sneaking out the night before…' He trailed off as the memory came back, and he couldn't help smiling. The geometry master's daughter had promised to leave her bedroom window ajar, but he'd been nabbed halfway out of his own bedroom window…

'And?'

No need to go into prurient details. 'And your father had written an essay that was deemed too…uh, strongly egalitarian in its sentiments. We had to sit in the headmaster's office for most of the day, waiting for him to return to give us our caning. That should have been that, except when he finally arrived late that afternoon he realised that we'd been making free with his brandy for hours— which, I should mention, was your father's idea, not mine.' And a ruddy good idea it had been, he added silently. Lessened the pain of the inevitable blows.

Her eyes were wide. 'You mean you were…'

Isabelle had been completely wrong. He shouldn't be telling her this. 'Pickled. And we were great friends from then on—best friend

I've ever had, excluding my brother. That wasn't the last time we had to face Bittlesham's wrath, either. We were both terrible students, just in different ways. I miss him.'

Mary was silent, thinking it over. Then, 'I'm not such a bad student.'

'Isabelle says you're very clever.' Damn. Isabelle again. He mustn't call her that.

Luckily, Mary didn't seem to notice anything improper. She was watching the scenery go by once more.

'She also thinks you were trying to be sent home.'

She shrugged.

'I'm sure Arthur didn't want to send you away. He was very ill, you know.'

'I know,' she said softly.

'And without your mother—'

'I know.' Said this time with less patience.

'I didn't see your father much after we left Oxford. He fell madly in love with your mother and became completely countrified, tutoring local brats and growing turnips. I stayed in London, and I couldn't quite understand how one of my friends could settle down so soon, when I definitely wasn't ready. But he was happy, even though your mother's death was a terrible blow. I saw him about once a year at first, and then less and less. Miss Thomas tells me you corresponded with him.'

'No.'

He frowned. 'No? I'm sure she mentioned it.'

'It's not correspondence if only one person writes.'

'You mean he didn't write back?'

'No, I didn't. He wrote often. I hated him for not sending for me, and I wanted to punish him.'

'Don't say that,' Will said. He tried to sound stern.

'I'm sorry. I don't mean it. I don't feel like that any more. Wish I could change it now.'

She needn't have apologised. It wasn't difficult to imagine how she'd felt. 'Miss Thomas tells me you'd like to have a friend to visit. Why don't you invite her for your birthday? It's coming up, isn't it?'

He saw a glimmer of hope in her eyes. 'You know when my birthday is?'

'Of course—I came for your first three birthdays, you know. Took four long hours to reach your house. Suppose you wouldn't remember.'

She smiled, the slight, half-smile that reminded him so much of his friend. 'I remember meeting you once—I mean, once before that time when you had words with Miss Hume.'

'When?' His memory was failing now.

'In London. Papa took me for a visit. It was after Mama died, and I was about six. And I remember you sent me a doll one Christmas.'

He had done that—it'd been the least he could do as her godfather. He should have done much more, but what did he know about children? He didn't know what to say to them most of the time. But he was doing all right now. He thought he was, anyway. It wasn't so different from speaking to an adult.

'I didn't know how ill he was,' he said. 'Not until last summer, when he invited me for a visit. He'd lost a lot of weight…I think that's part of the reason he'd become reclusive. I don't think he wanted anyone to see him. He certainly wouldn't have wanted you to remember him like that, but he did think about you. That's when he asked me to look after you.'

'You regret it.'

'No. No, I don't.'

She looked out at the street again. He didn't think she believed him. It hadn't even occurred to him until that minute that he didn't regret it, but he didn't.

'You look like your father,' he said, trying to draw her back. 'You've your mother's colouring, but Arthur's expression. You're certainly more athletic. He was about as co-ordinated as Miss Thomas.'

Mary smiled again, but said nothing. He thought she looked happy.

The carriage halted to let a stream of opposing traffic rumble past, and they waited in companionable silence. Will looked out on the beautiful afternoon, on the rare, clear sky, and he felt a surge of goodwill. Regent Street was crowded with pedestrians, gazing into tempting shop windows. Hats and shoes, gleaming silver, tea from China, shawls from India and more, all on display. Everything anyone could possibly want, or at least a twelve-year-old girl.

'Would you like something?' he asked. He'd always been able to make women happy by buying them gifts, and Mary couldn't be too different.

'You don't need to buy me anything. I'll be leaving soon.'

'Not necessarily,' he protested.

'What do you mean?'

He didn't know what he meant. He shouldn't be making false promises, but it didn't have to be untrue. He'd assumed all along that she'd want to return to school, but perhaps not. It wouldn't be the end of the world if she stayed.

He needed advice. He'd ask Isabelle what she thought.

'Well, there's the rest of the summer. That's three more months. And then…honestly, there must be something you'd like. Never known a girl to turn down a present.'

She gazed out the window, examining the shops. 'A book?'

Three minutes later, Will's footman opened the door for them to alight. Will steered Mary across the road towards a busy bookseller's. Satirical prints hung in the large bow window, and he paused to admire a particularly rude one about the Duke of Clarence until Mary crossed her arms and frowned impatiently.

Once inside, they perused the shelves silently for several minutes. She moved about methodically, but he was more haphazard. He picked books up, skimmed them and left them on random tables. Now that Mary was happy, he started to dwell once more on that other troublesome female: Isabelle, furious. He needed to make peace with her.

'Maybe Miss Thomas would like a book, too?' he suggested.

Mary glanced up from the book she was reading. After a second, she nodded slowly. He hoped she didn't see through his question.

A book was the perfect gift. He didn't imagine she'd had many gifts, not in a very long time, at least, and he wanted to please her.

On grounds of propriety, she'd object to any present from him, but what could be more innocuous? A book wasn't a silk négligé. It wasn't intimate. But still…

'She won't accept it if it's from me,' he pointed out.

Mary didn't look up this time. 'Then tell her it's from me.'

'Very well. That I shall do.' He took her book from her hands and stared at the title. 'Appalling taste you have in literature.'

'Oh?' She didn't say anything else, just frowned at his waistcoat by way of retort. He frowned at it, too, wondering what the problem was.

'Does my waistcoat offend?'

'You're aware it's green.'

'No, blue. Matches the jacket. Did Miss Thomas take you shopping yesterday?'

'Green. We didn't buy anything. I don't much enjoy shopping.'

'All girls like shopping.' He knew that to be almost a fact.

'Well…the truth is we didn't have much time to look. Just as we were leaving the house Dr Collins came for a visit.'

'Dr Collins?'

She'd picked up another book and began skimming through the pages with irritating thoroughness.

'Mary?'

'What? Oh, yes. Dr Collins. He rescued us when Miss Thomas hurt her foot. You must remember him.'

Vividly. He realised he was gripping the book rather tightly. 'A bit. Don't remember inviting him back.'

'Miss Thomas was definitely surprised to see him. Flattered, too, I should think. What book shall we get her?'

'Flattered?'

She shrugged. 'He *is* handsome.'

'Is he?'

'Yes. I suppose you wouldn't notice. I think Miss Thomas noticed, though. He'll probably visit her again.'

'Why probably?' Something disturbingly like panic was forming a tight ball in his stomach.

'Well, wouldn't you?' she asked, her uninterested tone suggesting that the answer was as obvious as her red hair. Then—calculated, no doubt, to annoy him—she stifled a yawn. 'I think she'd like something on natural history.'

Isabelle had spent the day feeling…angry. It had taken her a while to put a finger on the emotion, but anger was it—and since Will hadn't been there for her to vent her rage at, by the end of the day she felt ten times angrier. Livid, because in the presence of those grand, ghastly ladies he'd treated her like a servant. Worse, actually, than he treated his servants.

He'd told her that he was contemplating marriage, and that loving his hypothetical wife wasn't a priority. The awful Miss Lytton could only be a candidate for the position. She appeared to possess every quality he valued: beauty, wealth and a good pedigree. Isabelle would add bad manners and stupidity to the list—traits that in her current mood only made the pair of them more compatible.

And how *very* like him to ask to speak to her and then make her wait. Bartholomew had informed her of his request a quarter of an hour earlier, and she'd been biding her time in the draughty hall ever since. She rose nervously from her seat to examine her face in the gilt-wood pier glass. Her freckles had begun to colonise her cheeks as well as her nose, something that happened every summer. She started to smooth back her hair, but caught herself just in time. She frowned at her reflection before returning to the unyielding hall chair. She shouldn't care that she looked pale and drawn; she despised him, and his opinion of her no longer mattered.

She leaned back in the chair, trying to find a more comfortable position. Undoubtedly anger was a healthy emotion. Until today, every time he'd so much as looked at her, her heart rate had quickened alarmingly. But now things would be different. His coldness had given her a new perspective, and she saw him for who he really was: a shallow, self-centred snob who didn't care about her. There was absolutely no point in wasting any more time over romantic daydreams about him.

She took a deep breath and exhaled slowly. *Good luck following your own good advice.* No matter what she told herself, she couldn't actually believe that he'd marry a toad like Vanessa Lytton, even if she was a beautiful toad. Nor could she accept that his apparent fondness for her was insincere—he'd always treated her, with the exception of that afternoon, as an equal. He'd provided her with a home, an income and a sense of safety, and although she had at times questioned his motives, she did believe that his kindness came with no ulterior motive.

Bartholomew reappeared to usher her into the small drawing room. She followed behind unenthusiastically.

He opened the door wide for her to enter and closed it promptly behind her. Will was standing, looking out the window, framed by the late afternoon sunlight that spilled in. He turned around when she entered, and she thought, for just a second, that she detected a note of apprehension in his face. But then, if it had been there at all, it vanished, and his expression became inscrutable. She found herself blushing, but refused to look down at the carpet. She would meet his gaze if it killed her.

'You wanted something, my lord?' She tried to sound indifferent.

'Will you sit?' He indicated an elegant armchair covered in red velvet. She shrugged and sat.

He crossed the room to stand in front of her, retrieving a small parcel from a side table on his way. He held it out. 'Mary bought you this while we were out this afternoon.'

She stared at it for three awkward seconds. It was disguised by brown wrapping paper, but had the dimensions of a book. Gingerly, so as not to brush her fingers against his, she took it from him. 'I will open it with her in the nursery.'

'She's not there. I've left her with my sister-in-law and niece for the rest of the day. She asked me to have you open it without her.'

He held her gaze slightly longer than was comfortable, and she found herself looking down at her lap despite her best intentions. Hoping to hide her embarrassment, she fixed her attention on the parcel and carefully untied the ribbon. Her eyes widened at the gift inside.

An atlas, bound in supple chestnut-coloured leather. She opened it and flipped through the pages. Lavish hand-coloured prints were interspersed throughout the text: detailed maps of places she'd never see, pictures of mountains, flora and fauna and exotic people in strange costumes. She closed the book slowly. Something didn't seem right. It would have been so expensive…

'It… This is from her?'

He nodded. 'Yes. She picked it. I think she inscribed it.'

Isabelle's heart was beating quickly, her palms sweating. She'd imagined for a moment that it was from him. But on the title page, in the girl's hasty and careless hand, it said, 'To Miss Thomas, from Mary'.

She closed the book again. 'That was very kind of her. I don't know how she paid for it.'

'Her father left her a robust allowance,' Will replied, smiling a smile designed to weaken any female resolve. 'And I helped a little.'

She wasn't ready to succumb. 'You should not have allowed her to pick something so costly.'

'Not that costly—not if you like it.' He looked slightly worried. '*Do* you like it?'

His question forced her to look at him. He seemed interested in her answer, and she couldn't fathom why. So she answered honestly, 'Yes, very much. It's beautiful. I will thank her in the morning.'

A moment of uncomfortable silence followed. Isabelle could tell that he didn't want her to leave, but didn't quite know what to say. Finally, he said, 'She, uh, tells me you didn't purchase anything during your shopping expedition.'

'No, my lord.' There was great power in answering with monosyllables.

'Were you able, at least, to collect your belongings from your boarding house?'

'Yes, my lord.' She gathered the brown paper in her hands, but before she had the chance to rise he spoke again.

'I also wanted to let you know that I'll be leaving tomorrow.'

Leaving? That made her pause. 'Oh?'

'Yes. Just for a week or so, to a friend's house in Surrey. I meant to tell you this morning, but...'

'But you were interrupted,' she finished for him as the memory of his curtness returned.

He detected her anger and frowned slightly. 'Yes, I was interrupted.'

'Well, consider me informed.' She rose and started walking to the door. She didn't turn to look at him. She could feel her lip threatening to tremble, but she would not cry.

Unfortunately, he followed her, and his longer strides allowed him to reach the door first. 'I didn't dismiss you.'

'I didn't know you had anything else to impart.'

He ran his hand through his hair in frustration. In a carefully controlled voice, he said, 'I thought perhaps you'd been upset by Miss Lytton.'

Yes. 'Why would she upset me?'

'I thought she treated you rather imperiously. I wanted to apologise.'

She turned around, no longer caring if he saw her tears. 'I thought *you* treated me rather imperiously.'

He shook his head slowly, his gaze wandering over her eyes, her lips. 'No. No, I just...I didn't want them to mistake the situation.'

'There was nothing to mistake, my lord.'

She tried to step past him, but he put his hand on her arm, preventing her from leaving. 'No, but I've realised that I'm perhaps...more familiar with you than one would normally be with one's employees. I enjoy your company, Miss Thomas. I like you very much—you must know that. But my familiarity with you could be misinterpreted. I wanted to correct any false impressions, and if I hurt you, then I'm sorry.'

'I see,' she said uncertainly. *Why* was he telling her this? She wished that he hadn't explained himself, that he hadn't apologised—her relationship with him would be easier that way, if she mildly despised him. There would be no more eccentric late-night conversations to make her laugh and lose her temper, no more insights into his character to make her think she might even love him. No more weak knees.

But she couldn't love him, and she needed her traitorous knees to stay strong. She carefully extracted her arm from his hand. She couldn't pretend that he was her friend; she'd already told herself as much. 'Is Miss Lytton the young lady you danced with the other night? The one you told me about?'

'She is,' he answered warily.

'Do you intend to marry her?'

His expression hardened. 'Did you intend to tell me about Dr Collins?'

'What are you talking about?'

'I will not have him in my house attempting to purloin my staff. I made that clear.'

She flushed furiously. 'He cannot steal from you that which you do not own, sir, and you do not own me!'

'Did you intend to tell me?' he repeated coldly.

'It is not your concern.'

'And so Miss Lytton is not your concern.'

She knew she should desist. She'd annoyed him, but she'd been angry to begin with and it only seemed just that he should be, too. 'Perhaps you ought to marry her. She seems to have so much in common with you, and you *did* say that was important.'

He didn't like that suggestion. He narrowed his eyes and took a step closer. '*What* exactly do you think she's got in common with me?'

It was stupid, but she said it anyway. 'She seems rather shallow.'

'You think I'm shallow?' He didn't raise his voice, but she could tell she'd offended him.

She wished she could take it back, because she didn't think it. What he'd said about marrying without love *was* shallow, but he wasn't the only person who thought that way. And why should she even care?

The answer came too readily. She cared because she knew she wasn't remotely suitable by his gauge, and it made her feel inadequate. Because if she'd come from an aristocratic or rich family, then he might even want to marry her. Because he liked her, but she wasn't good enough. But that wasn't his fault. That was just life.

'I don't think that,' she said softly. 'I'm sorry.'

He was so close, just a few steps away. Her whispered apology had diffused his anger, and his gaze warmed, drawn to her lips. Isabelle found herself looking at his mouth, too, wondering if he would taste as good today as he had last night. His anger didn't frighten her, but this…

'Miss Lytton isn't clever, or amusing, or kind.'

'She's pretty.'

'And you're much prettier.'

Her body swayed with the pleasure of his compliment, almost dizzy, and he cupped the back of her head to steady her. He tipped her head up, forcing her to look at him. 'I'm not interested in her, Isabelle.'

'Why?'

'Because I'm interested in someone else.'

He meant her. Maybe he didn't *really* mean it, but at that moment he seemed to believe it. Just by looking at him, she could imagine his lips on her neck, his rough, warm fingers tracing a path up her arms. She knew what it felt like. The memory of last night was so potent she could close her eyes and pretend it was happening all over again.

So she took a deep breath and she closed her eyes briefly, savouring the moment. Then she turned and walked away, taking the memory with her.

Chapter Sixteen

He left just after dawn the next morning. She watched from her bedroom window as his trunks were loaded into his carriage, enough possessions to last well over the week he said he'd be gone. Maybe good fortune had finally smiled on her and he'd stay away for a fortnight. She needed at least that much time; she had a lot to accomplish that would benefit from the absence of his curious eyes.

It would also be strange, though, not having him in the house. She was always so aware of his presence, even when she didn't know where exactly he was. The anxiety caused by the possibility of running into him had dictated her movements since she'd been living here. The house would seem empty and big.

She stayed at the window for many minutes after the carriage left, absentmindedly watching the street below as it began to rouse itself for the day to come. A delivery cart moved slowly along, the sway-backed grey that pulled it lifting its heavy feet with weary resolution. Soberly dressed maids appeared in window after window across the square, parting curtains to brighten drawing rooms and breakfast rooms, ballrooms and bedrooms. A slim boy with holes at his knees and bare, dirty feet limped along the pavement, no doubt looking for a handout from a kindly butler or cook. He wouldn't find such benevolence from Will's servants, Isabelle was dismayed to observe. Mrs Graham, stepping on to the street for an early trip to market, shouted at the boy to move on, swinging her shopping basket in his direction. Rogers, still lingering on the pavement after having loaded the carriage, laughed coarsely. Isabelle watched the cook and the footman banter; how confidently lazy they were now that Will had gone. Soon they were joined by a man Isabelle had never seen before, but who wore the livery of a footman—not Will's green livery, but that, perhaps, of a neighbouring house. They spoke closely for several minutes, and she wondered what they talked about.

Their conversation ended when Bartholomew came out to scold them for their indolence. Chastened, the cook hurried on her way and Rogers returned inside, nodding goodbye to his companion as he went.

Isabelle realised that she, too, had business to attend to. A lot of it, and she shouldn't be wasting time, either. She rose, crossed the room to her writing table, and read the advertisement she'd drafted during the night:

A young Lady experienced in tuition is desirous of a situation in a private home or school. She is qualified to instruct in French, Latin, Greek and German, together with History, Mathematics and all branches of the Natural Sciences. Music, Drawing and Dancing, etc. References upon request.

It had taken a long time to write, largely because she'd stretched the truth to filament thinness in parts. Experienced? Well, she doubted the experiences she'd gleaned in Will's employ would appeal to most potential employers. Mathematics was not her strong suit by any means, and although she could sing, she couldn't play a single instrument. She had debated whether she should profess any proficiency in dancing, and in the end had tacked it on to the end without making any claims at all. Let the reader interpret it as she saw fit.

She dressed quickly and folded the advertisement into her pocket, to be given to Bartholomew to be posted. It should arrive at the offices of *Belle Anglaise* by tomorrow and would appear in next week's issue. *Belle Anglaise* had the greatest circulation of all the ladies' journals; hundreds would read her plea. And for now…

She opened up last week's issue. She'd circled three advertisements already, posted by ladies seeking governesses. She'd spend the morning writing replies, and would hopefully be able to post them that afternoon. She could start Mary's lesson late. Her own well-being, for the moment, took precedence.

Four mornings later, she stood on the pavement in front of a large stucco house, only about a quarter of a mile away. Her first interview, and she'd be having another one tomorrow. It had been easy to get away from her duties at Will's house; Mary was never averse to starting her lessons after lunch rather than immediately after breakfast, and she'd asked no questions.

Nevertheless, Isabelle felt ambivalent rather than relieved by the swift progress she'd made. It appeared to be a nice house, almost as handsome as Will's. But would she be treated as well there? Would—she paused to glance at the name she'd written down— would Lady Grayson be as kind? She knew she couldn't work for Will any more, but she didn't want to say goodbye to him, either. She certainly didn't want to work for anyone else.

She straightened her back and approached the door. A bald-headed butler opened it, with a rail-thin, middle-aged Lady Grayson right behind him. Isabelle managed a perfunctory smile and after introductions followed the woman into her sitting room. The meeting seemed to be going reasonably well so far.

Then something odd happened. The woman, scanning her introductory letter, frowned. Isabelle watched her, feeling increasingly uncomfortable. Finally, she had to ask, 'Is something amiss?'

She looked up. 'You work for the Earl of Lennox?'

Isabelle had been worried she'd question her about her dancing and had dreaded being asked to demonstrate a *pas de deux* on the rose-coloured Aubusson. With relief, she replied, 'Yes. I've only been with him for a short while, though.'

'You've fallen out of favour already, have you?'

Was her question laced with innuendo? 'No, no. I think he's been pleased with me—' The woman raised an eyebrow, which put

Isabelle off her stride. 'He—it's just that he hired me to look after his ward, and she will be returning to school soon.'

Lady Grayson folded the letter and rose to hand it back to Isabelle. 'I don't think you'll be suitable for this house. I will show you out.'

Isabelle recognised the flimsiness of her résumé, but she couldn't believe the woman had rejected her so bluntly. 'I…well, you haven't asked about my other skills.'

'My husband might be interested in your other skills, but not I. Goodbye.'

Too rattled to understand what the woman implied, Isabelle followed her to the front door and left. She began to walk home, but decided on a detour through the park. It was still early and Mary wouldn't expect her to return for an hour.

She found an unoccupied bench and stared at the flat grey sky.

My husband might be interested…? Was she suggesting what Isabelle's naïve ears thought she was suggesting? She'd been treated badly at interviews before, but never as badly as that. Maybe she'd offended her somehow. It didn't seem possible anyone could be that rude without provocation.

She hoped her interview the following morning would be better, and from the start it seemed to satisfy her wishes. The lady of the house was polite, warm and generous, and unlike the hatchet-faced Lady Grayson, she was only a year or two older than Isabelle. She showed her around the house to make her comfortable, and as they settled into the woman's personal sitting room she introduced Isabelle, by way of gilt-framed portraits, to her three children and her portly, older husband. Much older, Isabelle thought, but she wasn't going to judge. She'd nothing but kind thoughts for this lady, and she felt, for the first time, that she had a good chance of walking out of the door having secured a place.

Then, during tea and cakes, Isabelle handed over her letter of introduction.

The lady read it carefully, a frown slowly marring her smooth forehead. 'Oh.'

Not again. 'Is there a problem?'

She glanced up. There was a look of pity, not disdain, on her face. 'You work for the Earl of Lennox. I did not know that.'

Why did this fact seem to matter? She'd taken the job with him so she could have experience and a reference, but his name acted like poison. 'I don't understand. I know I haven't been there long, but that is easy enough to explain. I'm not being asked to leave—it's just that he's sending his ward back to school and will no longer need me.'

'I am sorry, Miss Thomas. Despite your lack of experience, I really would be willing to give you a chance. In every other way you seem perfect. I would like to help you, but I cannot.'

Isabelle rose, furious. 'Why?'

The lady's kindness disappeared behind a cool mask. 'Now, now, Miss Thomas, I see no need to create a nasty scene.'

'Then tell me.'

'I would have thought you'd know. Lord Lennox is a prominent member of society. Did you think no one would notice?'

'Notice what?' she demanded.

The woman blushed. 'I'd really rather not say. Let it suffice that I do not wish to bring infamy upon my house. But that is your fault, not mine. Good day, Miss Thomas.' She rose, too, in order to show Isabelle to the door.

Isabelle just stared at her, still not understanding and not ready to leave until she did. 'Infamy? I have no idea what you're talking about.'

The woman sighed, glanced at the door as if wondering whether her servants were listening in, and then whispered, 'Your affair, Miss Thomas.'

It took several seconds for her meaning to sink in. 'You are accusing me of...of having...improper—'

'I am merely repeating what I've heard. Lord Lennox has been much talked about in the past few days, and your coming here only supports the accusations lodged against him. I can only imagine he asked you to leave his employ as a result of the scandal.'

'There is no truth to what you say!'

'None the less, I will not have someone such as you in my house. Should I invite you here to…to make love to my husband, Miss Thomas?'

'Your husband?' Isabelle said, staring at the round-faced man in the portrait. She couldn't believe what she was being accused of. With the exception of one stolen kiss, she was completely innocent. She no longer cared about being polite, and she nodded in the direction of the painting. '*That* man?'

The woman, apparently, no longer cared about being polite, either. 'How dare you?' She walked briskly the rest of the way to the sitting-room door, flung it open and called for the butler. Before Isabelle had the chance to be forcefully ejected, she pushed past the woman and marched across the hall to the front door. It didn't open easily. She yanked, yanked again, and then the butler was there, stepping in front of her to turn the doorknob in the opposite direction. With a withering look, he opened the door effortlessly. And she felt like a fool.

Dragging her dignity behind her, she left the house.

Isabelle wandered home slowly, weighted down by the knowledge that she'd very little chance of finding other employment—unless, that is, she chose not to use Will as a reference. But then she'd be back where she'd started, with apparently no experience and no one to recommend her. She'd have to stay in his employ—*if* he would keep her. He might not. He was already known as a rake and didn't seem to care, but even he couldn't be impregnable to such a damaging scandal. Carrying on an affair with the governess of one's ward went well beyond the pale.

But if she stayed…how long would it be until the rumour came true?

She turned down his street, wondering who could have started it. Was it simple, mischievous gossip, or was something more malicious afoot? Did Will have any enemies who'd want to blacken his character?

She stopped in front of his house, staring up at the imposing façade. Did any of the servants know? She'd detected no change in their behavior towards her; all were perfectly polite, except for Mrs Graham and Rogers who never bothered to speak to her unless necessary anyway. But eventually the rumour *would* trickle down below stairs. Servants liked to talk as much as anyone.

How could she go inside and give Mary a geography lesson now? How could she pretend nothing had happened? Maybe Dr Collins could help her. He'd offered, although he hadn't specified what form his help might take. She thought he could be trusted…

'Miss Thomas.' A man addressed her.

She turned around, his voice—familiar, but not immediately recognisable—slowly registering in her brain. It seemed like such a long time since she'd heard it, although in fact less than two weeks had passed. So much had changed.

'Mr Cowes. I—' She broke off, her gaze drawn to the stocky, dark-haired man who stood behind him, looking bored. She immediately remembered him as the man who'd followed her that day in the slums, although now he was dressed in a watchman's uniform. So he'd managed to find her after all. She'd been foolish to think Mr Cowes would give up easily. To forget that he remained a threat just because her life had grown so comfortable.

'What are you doing here?' she asked, taking a step backwards, bringing herself marginally closer to the house.

'For a moment I thought you might not recognise me,' he said, taking a step forwards to match hers. 'I should hope not. I was beginning to worry…you do remember what we discussed?'

'We've discussed nothing, sir.' She glanced at the house, wondering if anyone would notice her distress. Rogers tended to hover by the door, but she put little faith in him dashing out to rescue her.

She'd have to rely on herself. 'Have you been following me?'

'Afraid I've more important things to do. Robert, on the other hand…' he paused to nod towards his companion '…has been following you for weeks. Easily corruptible, London's watchmen—

he'd sell his grandmother for a pint of gin. But it *is* good to have the law on my side. He informed me immediately when he saw you leave the house alone this morning.'

'Well, consider me suitably reminded. I don't think there's anything further we have to discuss.'

'No? Well, there is that small matter of the money you owe me.' He, too, looked at the house, taking in its obvious grandeur. 'I imagine you're rather flush these days.'

Will paid her well. Governesses were normally paid in arrears every six months, but he knew her situation and had advanced her a liberal sum accordingly. But it wouldn't go very far. Not where Cowes was concerned. 'I can give you some. Not all, but a—'

'How, Miss Thomas? His lordship must be very generous.'

'I am merely paid for my services.'

'I've heard about your services and I must say I'm disappointed in you. Did I drive you to it?'

He was alluding to the spiteful gossip, and it suddenly occurred to her that he might be behind it. She flushed angrily. 'How dare you?'

He took a small step forwards. 'I'm sorry, Miss Thomas, but I've been extremely patient.'

Robert followed his lead and began moving closer, menacingly, as if to grab her.

She took another step back, but Cowes held up his hand to halt him. 'Unless—perhaps we could discuss new terms, Miss Thomas? Something suitable to your newly…elevated station in life.'

She couldn't bring herself to say anything at first, or even to nod or shake her head. She knew what he meant. He'd stated his terms implicitly before, and now he was forgoing subtlety altogether. He thought she was Will's mistress, and he was asking her to become his instead. She could capitulate or he'd punish her, by destroying her father's good name or worse. Fleet Prison itself wasn't an improbability, and although she'd prefer it to giving in to his evil demands, frankly she would rather forgo both options.

But perhaps she could play for time…

'This could all have been avoided,' he said, filling the silence, 'if you'd been willing to listen to me earlier. But I still might be persuaded to forgive you for putting me to this trouble.'

She nodded slowly, weighing her options. He was close, but not so close that she hadn't a slim chance of running away. But run where? She couldn't go to the house—that would solve nothing. It would only alert the servants, and she'd then be forced to tell Will everything when he returned. And she didn't want him to know—not about her debts, her father's crimes, about how low she really was…

And running off blindly into the streets wouldn't solve anything, either. She hadn't a chance of surviving on her own with no money and no place to stay, and she might not even get the chance to try. How much hope had she of outrunning two grown men?

So she stood her ground.

Cowes reached out for her face. She closed her eyes at the sight of his blunt fingers, but when they touched her cheek she jerked her head from his grasp in revulsion. 'Don't touch me.'

'So you're not ready to be reasonable.' He grabbed her hair this time, pulling painfully so she couldn't move.

Chapter Seventeen

Will had meant to stay at Harry's for at least a week, but after a few days he found himself longing for home. He felt relieved as his carriage began to rattle down familiar streets—unusual, since he much preferred the countryside to the cold, treeless elegance of Mayfair. He was afraid it had nothing to do with a newfound love for London, however, but rather with the freckled girl who inhabited his small upstairs bedroom and who was gradually inhabiting his heart and mind as well.

He'd missed Isabelle. Missed her a lot. It had been…odd not seeing her every day, she'd become such a habit. Odd and rather lonely not having her to tease or talk to, even though he'd been in a busy house with good friends. Harry had remarked that he seemed distracted, and he knew he had been. It didn't help that Isabelle and he hadn't parted on the best of terms, and he half-feared that she'd have disappeared during his absence. She'd seemed so unhappy the last time he saw her, and she'd already told him she planned to leave. He'd all but dismissed her words, safe in the knowledge that she didn't have anywhere to go. But what if she left anyway?

He now wished he hadn't gone away in the first place. The only reason he'd done so was… Well, blast it all, at the time he'd thought distance would give him some perspective. He hadn't anticipated that he'd only think about her even more.

What should he do when he arrived? Find her? Tell her how much he'd missed her?

No, he should not. Not immediately, anyway.

He stretched out on his seat and sighed. She had some strange effect on him. He should have enjoyed his short time away, but the happy family scene created by Harry, his wife and their child had made him feel Isabelle's absence even more acutely. For the first time in his life, he'd felt like he wanted a family himself. Like he wanted to come home to the same woman night after night, and to wake up each morning with a familiar warm body. The problem was, the only woman who figured into these novel fantasies was Isabelle. Isabelle, who he couldn't marry—and he wasn't yet so far gone that he proposed starting a family without the sanctity of marriage.

Then again, could he marry her? Although she worked as a governess, she was by no means base-born. She was merely…reduced in circumstances. After all, at one time she *had* been quite well off, and her father had even been knighted—not a hereditary title, not enough to make her his social equal, but worth something none the less. She was intelligent, beautiful—what would the response be if he were to marry someone like her? A great deal of amusement at first, mostly directed at him. But any man would just have to look at her to understand why he'd done it.

Will frowned. What was he thinking? Marriage did not apply to this situation. He didn't want to marry anyone. He wanted Isabelle as his mistress, nothing more, and there was nothing to stop that from happening—except, of course, for the fact that she'd certainly refuse him at first. Eventually, though, she'd come around. He knew she liked him and that she responded to his touch. It would be the best possible arrangement. He could give her everything she wanted, and as for himself…he'd be able to make love to her, to touch her whenever he felt like it and to spend every day with her if he bloody well pleased.

And it pleased him, at that moment, to see her, even if his impatience was unseemly. The carriage turned into Grosvenor Square, and he closed his eyes, imagining what she would look like. She'd be in the garden on a day like this, with the sun filtering through the trees to touch on her face and hair. He'd have to invent some excuse to take her away from Mary's lessons.

He opened his eyes as the carriage took a turn and eased to a stop. As he sat up, he realised that he would see her sooner than expected. She was standing in front of his house with a man. A man whose arm rested on her shoulders, whose hand appeared to be cupping the back of her neck.

A jolt of possessiveness coursed through his body, so strong and so primitive that his vision clouded. But then his vision cleared. Her pretty face showed terror. Her head tilted back slightly, forced into that position by the man's tight grip. Any attempt to pull away would cause her pain.

The welcome rumble of wheels. A carriage stopping—Will's carriage, and Will climbing out. He was supposed to be in the country, but he was here, instead. He'd come to save her. Isabelle's heart surged with relief and gratitude, eclipsing the enmity that had soured her week. Mr Cowes was no match for him.

He let go of her hair as Will approached, but he let his hand grip her shoulder instead, the pressure so strong it would leave bruises. He was not yet ready to give up.

'I think, sir, you should remove your hand,' Will said. He didn't raise his voice; he sounded calm, arrogant and firm. Cowes retained his hold, but she knew he was scared. She could sense the tension coursing into her shoulder.

'Remove your hand,' Will repeated, taking another step forwards.

Cowes eased his grip indecisively, but he still held on to her. Robert looked to him for instruction, but saw only fear on his face. No fool, he stuffed his hands in his pockets, turned and walked quickly off, abandoning his employer to fend for himself.

Will didn't bother to watch him go. His attention was focused solely on Cowes. 'Did you not understand?' Underneath his calm condescension there was fury, too. Barely concealed, but audible. He was walking closer.

Cowes coloured in anger. 'This is not your affair,' he sputtered.

'Let go of her.'

Then it was over. Cowes knew he'd been defeated. He released Isabelle and pushed her away. Will grabbed her and pulled her close to his side. He led her a few paces back, never taking his gaze from Cowes.

'What's happening?' he whispered into her ear.

With his arm around her, she felt safe and protected; she realised she was shaking. For a few seconds, she didn't even try to answer, just relished his warmth and his strength. If she said nothing, then maybe it would all go away.

'Isabelle? Who is that man?'

But reality wouldn't just disappear. She'd have to tell him. She looked up at his face. He glanced at her briefly, but then returned his gaze to Mr Cowes. That made it easier. 'He's called Sebastian Cowes. I owe him a great deal of money.'

He looked at her again, longer this time. 'I don't understand.'

'I…my father, as I told you, was an antiquarian—'

'Quickly, Isabelle.'

She took a deep breath and let the truth come out. 'He sold Mr Cowes several forgeries. And he—'

'Forgeries?'

'Yes, um, dishonest copies. Only he…he—'

Will understood the rest without her saying more. 'Only he claimed they were real. And Mr Cowes has learned the truth.'

She nodded unhappily. She'd admitted the worst—well, she'd not mentioned the scale of her father's transgressions, but at least she'd told him the nature of the sin. How would he react? She looked at his eyes, wishing she could read his mind. Did he hate her?

But there was no antipathy in his expression. Not directed at her, anyway. Cowes was another matter. 'Has he been blackmailing you?'

She nodded again.

'How long?'

Mr Cowes broke in, holding his frame as tall as possible, which still left him considerably shorter than Will. 'Sir, I am not leaving.'

Will released her and pulled her behind his back. He walked forwards, closing the gap between himself and Cowes. 'Then shall we have words inside? I don't think my neighbours need to witness this scene.'

Cowes now had a look of desperation about him, as if he realised his plan had crumbled. 'I don't care about your bloody neighbours,' he hissed. 'And if you're bedding her—'

Will pulled back his arm and punched him in the mouth. It was hard and unexpected, causing his head to jolt back and blood to trickle from his split lip.

Isabelle just stared, unable to believe the force of the blow. Will wiped his knuckles on his jacket.

'Go inside,' he instructed her quietly without turning to look at her.

She didn't obey. She didn't want to leave. Now that the immediate threat to her safety had passed she feared what Mr Cowes might say. She didn't want Will to learn any more about her, at least if it didn't come from her own mouth. 'Please, let me explain.'

'Go inside, Isabelle. I'll be in soon.'

She bit her lip and ran. Up the steps and through the front door. Bartholomew stared at her as she raced through the hall, but he didn't try to stop her as she dashed for the staircase. She passed Mary on the landing, but didn't pause, only mumbled a vague excuse for her haste. She didn't stop running until she'd reached her bedroom and closed the door behind her.

She crossed the floor and stood by the window. She could see the street below from that position, and what she saw…

Actually, very little detail from that distance, but it was enough to convince her she'd every reason to be worried. Mr Cowes was saying something to Will, gesticulating agitatedly, and Will appeared to be listening. Her heart sank. Cowes was telling him everything, she was sure—and even though she'd already alerted him to her

secret, she was sure Cowes would portray her in the most unflatter-
ing light possible. Perhaps he'd even claim she was privy to her
father's misdeeds, or that she'd knowingly benefited from his ill-
gotten wealth for years.

And then his words came back: 'I've heard about your services.'
Would he have phrased it like that if he'd started the rumour? Somehow
she didn't think so. And what if he mentioned the rumour to Will?

She stepped away from the window, unable to watch any longer.
She slid down the wall to the floor and raised her knees, burying her
face. Will would ask her to leave now—what other option had he?
And even though just that morning she'd thought that leaving his
house would solve many of her problems, she hadn't been thinking
that debtors' prison might be her destination.

She'd composed herself on the small sofa at the foot of her bed by
the time Will entered her room ten minutes later. He'd never been
inside her bedroom, at least not since it had become hers, and he
gazed round curiously for a few seconds. She wondered how it looked
to him. Untidy, no doubt, which was its normal state, but embarrassing none the less. Two worn velvet cushions were on the floor, joining
the slippers and shawl she'd shed when she'd entered. Papers clut-
tered her writing table—things she didn't want him to see, that would
notify him she'd been looking for a new position. Her plaster bust of
Athena was the room's only decoration; in a whimsical moment,
she'd adorned it with a straw summer bonnet. Will shouldn't be here,
but what point was there in insisting on propriety at a time like this?

'Isabelle?' he said gently, closing the door behind him. 'Are you
all right?'

She blushed, feeling wretched. 'I did not know you'd return today.'

'I came back early,' he said slowly.

She looked away. A good thing he'd returned, too. She pressed her
lips together, trying not to cry. 'I'm so sorry you were involved in that.'

'Why?' He crossed the room and sat down next to her, drawing
her close. 'It wasn't your fault.'

She sniffed, wiped her eyes and brought her stockinged feet up on to the sofa, tucking them beneath her. She knew it wasn't her fault, but what did that matter? She had nothing to say, not even to reprove him for wrapping his arm around her. Not when it felt so nice.

'He won't bother you again. I wish you'd told me.'

She looked up at him, but didn't pull away from his reassuring embrace. 'Tell you?'

'Yes. I don't know why you didn't.'

She sat up. 'That my father was a thief? About the money I owed? What point would there be in telling you?'

'I could have helped you sooner,' he said quietly. 'You should not have had to withstand that man's demands alone.'

She allowed herself to enjoy the warmth created by his words for several seconds, but then their meaning started to permeate her still confused brain. 'Help me sooner? And what do you mean he won't bother me again?'

He sighed and looked at the wall, obviously trying to find the best way to tell her something he knew she wouldn't like. 'I mean he told me what you owed and I've paid him.'

She sat very still, dumbly horrified. She hadn't been expecting that. 'You shouldn't have done that.'

'And you shouldn't be so ungrateful,' he replied curtly.

'*Thank you,*' she said pointedly before repeating her words. 'And you still shouldn't have done it.'

He rose and started pacing. 'What should I have done instead? Allowed him to have you arrested? Do you think I would just let him…let him—'

'I would have been all right,' she said, not wanting him to complete his sentence.

He looked at her incredulously. 'All right? *How* would you have been all right?'

She glared at him stubbornly. 'I have been taking care of myself for three years.'

'And a splendid job you've done, too.'

'I never asked you to help me, my lord.'

He returned to the sofa, looking weary with the argument. 'Don't you think we've moved past that kind of formality? You might use my Christian name.'

The invitation warmed her slightly, but she couldn't do it. 'It wouldn't be proper.'

'*We're* not proper, my dear. You might as well accept it.'

She didn't have the energy to glare at him again, and it really would be churlish of her to do so. As he said, she *should* be grateful, and she was…but her situation wasn't much better now that he'd intervened. All he'd done was transfer her debt from Mr Cowes to himself. And although Will wouldn't threaten her with prison, being in his debt would be far more shaming. She actually cared what he thought about her, and she didn't want to be a drain on his purse. It was bad enough he knew she was the daughter of a thief.

'I didn't want you to know about my father,' she said finally. 'That is why I didn't tell you.'

'Oh, for the love of— It hasn't changed my opinion of you, Isabelle. It doesn't matter.'

She looked away. His words made her want to cry again. They were so kind and also so untrue. Of course he wouldn't understand why it mattered. It wasn't his father.

'I don't mind helping you. It seems as if you've done your best to repay him so far.'

'Help? I don't know how I'll repay you.'

'You don't have to.'

She still couldn't look at him. The problems that had ruined her, solved by him in ten minutes. She couldn't simply accept it.

'I do. I will.'

'Isabelle, it's a lot of money, but not such a crippling sum. To you, maybe, but not to me. You haven't a chance of repaying it, and I don't care if you do.'

'I will.'

'Very well.' He said this to end the argument, not because he expected her to. They sat quietly for a minute. She slumped back in the sofa. Will leaned forwards, his elbows resting on his knees. He appeared deep in thought.

'Your father…' he began slowly.

She completed his sentence. 'Wasn't terribly honest, it seems.'

'But you didn't know about that?'

She shook her head. 'I'd no idea, and if Mr Cowes hadn't told me, I never would have guessed. I don't think my father was dishonest in any other area of his life. It wasn't in his character. He was…not a bad person.'

'Then why do you think he did it?'

'I'm not sure. I…as I said before, the war made travel impossible nearly until his death. For years, everything he sold was shipped to him from Italy sight unseen, and because he was unable to inspect the marbles first…I just don't know.'

'Perhaps he was deceived, too? He must have records of what he spent on the marbles—if he paid a lot, then it seems entirely plausible that he thought he was buying something genuine.'

She knew the records well; he had made a substantial profit on the small sums he paid. 'I like to think so.'

'Everyone makes mistakes,' Will quickly reassured her. He didn't sound entirely convinced. 'It was just to this Cowes chap, then?'

She nodded, not taking her eyes from his. 'I believe so.' Oh, it was one thing to be reticent with the truth, and another thing entirely to tell an outright lie. Even now, in this moment of frankness, she couldn't bear to admit that Cowes was just one of many. She hated herself for being such a coward.

He stroked her hair, noting her distress. 'I can see how that could happen.'

'Do you?' She was desperate to hear him say yes. Even though she knew she wasn't to blame, knowing about her father's deceit and doing nothing to put it right still made her feel complicit.

Her question was followed by a painful silence, and she looked down at her hands.

'Isabelle…' he touched her chin, forcing her to look at him '…I understand. It's not your fault.'

'I know, but that doesn't make me feel much better.'

Will wiped invisible tears from her cheeks, wishing their lives had merged earlier, so that he could have protected her from Sebastian Cowes in the first place—from her father, too, who might have been a perfectly decent chap in some respects, but was still a scoundrel for putting her in this position.

At least her father's dishonesty had brought her to him, but right now Will didn't know if that was a good thing. Here, in her bedroom, with the door closed and her lips looking soft and kissable, his desire to protect her conflicted seriously with his need to push her back on to the sofa and make her forget about everything that had just happened. She was watching his face, her lips slightly parted, and he knew that she wanted him to kiss her, too. That she wanted him to reassure her that he didn't hate her for the trouble she'd caused him. Perhaps she didn't know that he could never hate her.

Kissing seemed like the logical thing to do. Her small hand had somehow found his shoulder, and through his jacket's fabric he could feel indecisive pressure. Then she pulled her hand away, returning it shyly to her lap. Maybe she didn't know what she wanted.

'I missed you, Isabelle.' He didn't expect a response, didn't know why he told her. Her face filled with colour and she bit her lower lip.

He watched her, wishing he were biting it instead. But when he leaned in to kiss her, he didn't head straight for her mouth. He brushed a soft kiss against her forehead. She didn't pull away. She tilted her head up, giving him permission to proceed.

He shouldn't do it. She was upset, overwrought with guilt, and in more clear-headed times she wouldn't permit these liberties. She wouldn't be leaning forwards herself, silently entreating him to kiss her again, to do it properly.

But, damn it, she wasn't clear-headed and neither was he. His voice of reason had grown faint, and he could no more resist kissing her than he could breathing. Once his lips found hers she was immediately kissing him back as if his lips offered some kind of solace. It wasn't a tender kiss, or gentle. It was, in the catalogue of kisses he'd ever given, clumsy, urgent and without finesse. He pushed her back onto the sofa, and she pulled him down on top of her, her hands tugging at his jacket and her legs wrapping around his. His lips trailed down her neck, brushing over the swell of her breasts. Her back arched, and he groaned quietly, wishing he could rip her dress from her to taste her flesh.

He rose to sitting position, dragging her with him, lifting her on to his lap so she straddled his hips. He fumbled with the buttons at the back of her gown, trying futilely to unfasten them without taking his lips from hers. Then he gave up, tugged, and popped three or four loose, just enough to pull her dress down slightly to reveal…her shift, just as frustratingly high-necked as her dress.

Bloody hell. 'I'm going to insist on a new wardrobe.'

'Hmm?'

She hadn't heard him. He didn't repeat himself. Just tugged her dress down even further so her breasts were free of it, separated from his touch by nothing more than soft white linen. They fit his hands perfectly.

Damn. He'd emitted enough mental oaths in the past five minutes to secure his place at Satan's side, if his lecherous actions alone weren't enough. He had to stop, but he felt as if he were going to burst and he wanted nothing more than to thrust inside her. Instead of stopping, he let his hands slide down her back to cup her bottom, pulling her forwards, pressing her against his loins until she moaned. Until her fingers tightened in his hair, bringing his head close for another kiss.

'My lord?'

Some voice, far away but slowly penetrating his febrile brain.

'My lord?' Again. Will went still. Isabelle froze. It was Bartholomew.

God, no, not Bartholomew. The man's timing was horrendous.

He quickly lifted her from his lap and rose from the sofa. He did not want his butler to know where he was. Bartholomew's voice came again, sounding as if he were calling from the second floor, by his bedroom. Unlike the man to make so much noise, but he'd have heard about the incident on the street and had witnessed Isabelle running inside, clearly distressed. He knew that Will had conducted a brief meeting with Mr Cowes, and would have heard their raised voices. Bartholomew knew something was wrong, and he was trying to be discreet by giving them fair warning.

In a few seconds he'd come upstairs, though, and Will did not want to pass him.

'Isabelle—'

'Will you go?' She sounded panicked and angry, and she wouldn't look at him.

'My lord?'

The voice was louder, and he quickly crossed the room. Too quickly, bumping into a flimsy satinwood table as he flung the door open, unbalancing the plaster bust that sat on top of it. He tried to catch it, but the blood that normally serviced his brain was still pumping furiously below the waist, slowing his reflexes. The bust crashed to the floor, breaking into a dozen pieces.

'Blast.' It was unlike him to be so awkward. He bent over to pick up the pieces, but paused to stare. The bust had been hollow, which explained why it had broken so easily. It had also been full of bank notes. Now, a small fortune decorated the floor.

'Isabelle?' He turned around to face her, but she wasn't looking at him. She was trying to tug up her dress to restore her modesty, although she couldn't repair the damage he'd done to her buttons.

Holding it to her chest, she hissed, 'Please go!'

He glanced at the floor again. 'Bloody hell,' he muttered.

'My lord?' Bartholomew now sounded as if he might be standing at the bottom of the stairs. Will paused to look at Isabelle once more as he closed the door behind him. She was sitting up on the sofa, straight and very still. She'd noticed the money.

Chapter Eighteen

Will straightened his cravat as he descended the staircase.

Bartholomew stood on the landing below, wringing his hands as he debated whether he should climb the steps to the third floor. He looked relieved to see Will, pleased not to have to make that decision.

'I was visiting Miss Weston-Burke in the nursery,' Will explained unnecessarily. He knew Bartholomew wouldn't believe him.

The butler nodded vaguely. 'It is Mrs Sandon-Drabbe, my lord. She is in the hall.'

Will certainly wouldn't acquiesce to Henrietta's unreasonable demands right now. Bartholomew's voice had acted like cold water on his desire, but his heart rate had not returned to normal. He wanted to go back to Isabelle's room and carry on where he'd left off. 'Tell her to go away.'

Bartholomew looked increasingly unhappy. 'She says it is urgent, my lord.'

'I don't care,' Will said impatiently. By now, Isabelle would have rearranged her clothes, straightened her hair, primmed herself neatly, unassailably. This had already taken too long. 'She always says it's urgent. Tell her I'll see her tomorrow.'

'William!' Henrietta's voice carried up the stairs.

'Tell her, Bartholomew. Go now.'

The butler turned reluctantly, obviously also in no mood to face her. He was saved from the confrontation, though—Henrietta was already marching up the staircase.

Will frowned at her darkly. 'Henny, I'm rather busy. Come back tomorrow.'

She stopped halfway up to glare at him, looking breathless and annoyed. 'I am not leaving, William! Come downstairs this instant.'

He closed his eyes, searching for patience. 'What, exactly, is the problem?'

Her gaze touched on Bartholomew briefly. 'It is a private matter.'

'Private? Is that why you're making a scene?'

'I will tell you in the drawing room. I have been waiting for your return for days, and I will not leave until we've—'

'Very well,' Will said tersely. The sound of her voice grated on him, and he'd just waste precious time arguing with her any further. It would be some trifling matter. He'd deal with it quickly and send her on her way.

Isabelle sat at the top of the stairs, listening to them arguing on the landing below. The exchange between Will and Bartholomew had been barely audible, but the agitated, high-pitched voice of his cousin had carried clearly. She waited tensely until their voices ceased. They'd almost certainly headed to the drawing room on the first floor and would be there for many minutes. She'd a pretty good idea what had caused the woman's distress. She'd heard the rumour. Unfortunately, at that moment Isabelle was no longer sure it was false. She wasn't Will's mistress, but she'd definitely enjoyed what he'd just done to her. He'd been moments from… Oh, God, and she'd let him do it. She'd been begging for more. How mortifying.

Shaking slightly, she returned to her bedroom. She sat on the floor, next to the broken bust. She shifted the pieces to the side, revealing even more bank notes. Obviously her father had neglected to mention something rather important before his heart had failed. How much was there? Enough to repay Will, she hoped, and perhaps enough to have saved her from being in this situation in the first place.

If only she'd known.

But she hadn't. And now it was too late.

'What in the name of God is this about, Henrietta?' Will demanded once he'd shut the door firmly behind them. His face flushed with anger and frustration, but he tried to remain calm.

Her nostrils flared slightly. '*How* can you not know?'

'Not know what? I've been in the country all week, as you're aware.'

'Yes, but I'm shocked it didn't reach you there, considering *every*one has heard about it. I shrugged it off at first, but everywhere I've been…' She paused, looking at him accusingly. 'Do you know how I learned of your return?'

'I'm sure you'll enlighten me.'

'Mrs Westerham, your neighbour, saw you *strike* a man on the street—just outside. She came to my house and told me at once. She knew I'd been beside myself with anxiety during your absence.'

He wished Henny didn't live so close, and he wished he didn't live next to her gossipy friend, Caroline Westerham. 'Is that what this is about? You raced over here because I hit someone? Does it matter that he deserved it?'

'No, I raced over here because that man, whoever he was, wasn't the only party standing on the pavement, for all to see. Everyone knows that you're carrying on an affair with Miss Weston-Burke's governess, and today you decided to advertise that fact by defending her honour, if she has any, on the street. Are you mad?'

He was silent. He felt like he'd been hit in the stomach, and he was ill prepared to deflect her accusation. Not now. Not after what had just happened in Isabelle's bedroom. 'Actually, Henny, I'm not having an affair with her,' he said tightly.

'I don't believe you.'

He shrugged. 'I don't particularly care.'

'You should care. Your reputation is bad enough already. But it's one thing keeping a mistress, and another thing entirely installing her in your house and setting her up as a young girl's governess. It is…it is depraved. The three of you living together like some sort of…*illegitimate* family. Is that why you agreed to take Mary in? Why you resisted my writing to her aunt? So you could bring that woman—'

'I will repeat myself just once. I am not having an affair with Miss Thomas. She's been living here for two weeks and is employed as a governess. Sorry to disappoint your prurient mind, but there is nothing more to it than that.'

Henrietta crossed her arms. 'What about Miss Lytton? She might not marry you now.'

'I am relieved to hear it, as I had no plans to ask her.'

Henrietta looked more angry than distraught. 'How could you do this to me, Will? I handpicked the girl. It is embarrassing for me. I told her mother that you were keenly interested in her—'

'Then you lied. You should use better judgement next time. The girl is ghastly.'

Henrietta just glowered at him. There was nothing to say since, objectively, he was correct.

In the silence a discreet knock at the door announced the butler's unwelcome return. 'Yes?' Will said unenthusiastically.

Bartholomew entered, looking even more harried. He cleared his throat. 'It is your brother, my lord, and your sister-in-law. Shall I show them in?'

'Why the hell not,' Will muttered. It was turning into a party. He ignored Henrietta's scowl, no doubt brought on by his oath, as James and Eleanor entered. Eleanor, pretty, petite and smiling tentatively, came in first. James followed just a few feet behind.

Uncanny, the way he could come back from the country unexpectedly early, and yet half his family was already in his drawing room, so impatient were they for his return. Will imagined James and Eleanor had come for the same reason as Henrietta. He stared hard at his brother, hoping to detect a clue in his expression. James caught his gaze for just a second before looking guiltily away. Damn.

'You, uh, said you might be home now,' James said, looking at

Henrietta with dismay. They'd never got along well. 'Thought we'd drop by for a chat.'

'I'm sure you didn't,' Will replied. He crossed the room to pour himself a large brandy. 'Drink?' he asked the room at large.

James accepted his offer with a nod. 'Actually, I was hoping to tell you to hie yourself back to the country before Henrietta got to you, but I obviously wasn't quick enough. You've heard the news.'

Will handed him the glass. 'What, that I'm having an affair with my ward's governess? Don't tell me you're reading the scandal sheets now.'

James bristled. 'I don't care *what* you do—'

'We haven't come to pass judgement, Will,' Eleanor said, frowning at her husband. 'But we heard the rumour a few days ago and wanted to prepare you for it. Shall we sit?'

Will obliged, only because he liked Eleanor. 'Fortunately, Henrietta has been filling me in on everything I've missed in my absence.'

'You will behave appropriately, I hope?' Eleanor asked, arranging herself next to her husband on the damask sofa.

Henrietta continued to hover, birdlike, behind them. She vigorously nodded her approval. 'Yes, you must get rid of her.'

Eleanor frowned. 'That's not exactly what I—'

'Getting rid of her won't solve anything,' James said.

Henrietta walked forwards. 'It certainly will. Men are expected to have their peccadilloes. Give her some money, send her away and everyone will forget.'

'I am not sending her away.'

Both James and Eleanor were silent for a heavy second. Carefully, Eleanor suggested, 'Perhaps Henrietta left out a few details.'

Henrietta stared for a minute. 'I've left nothing out.'

'Then perhaps there's something you don't know, Hen,' James said.

'Heavens, there's more?'

Eleanor began, but struggled with the delicate content. 'Well, as you know, some rumours last a few days and then fade, and some…just grow bigger. It's now being said that the girl…uh—'

'Mary,' Will supplied impatiently. 'What's being said?'

'That she's your illegitimate daughter, Will,' James finished. 'With Miss Thomas.'

It was laughable. Laughable and easy to refute if it ever came to that. '*How* could Mary be my daughter?'

'You underestimate society's collective imagination. As I heard it, you had an affair with Miss Thomas long ago,' James explained, 'and now, a dozen years later, she's returned, claiming the child is yours. You've taken them both in.'

'Ridiculous.'

'I agree. I first heard the expanded version yesterday afternoon at the club. But when I tried to deny it, Charles Prestwick volunteered that he'd seen the three of you at the British Museum together. I can't think of anything more out of character. What in God's name were you doing at a museum with a child and a governess?'

'She's Arthur's blasted daughter. I saw his wife when she was heavy with child. I saw the girl soon after she was born. I can tell you categorically she is not mine.'

'*I* know she's not yours, Will. You needn't convince me. But Arthur wasn't one of the shining lights of the London social scene. After his brief career at Eton and Oxford, he pretty much disappeared. His wife was even more obscure. *You* might claim that they're Mary's parents, but for most concerned, you could very well be making them up.'

It took a while for it to sink in. 'Miss Thomas would have to have been fourteen when she conceived. Does that even sound plausible?'

'Well, it's not as if her age has been widely advertised. No one knows anything about her…except…do they look rather alike?'

'No.'

'Not at all? Didn't note much resemblance myself, but I wasn't looking for one, either. Prestwick, on the other hand, thought the girl was the image of the governess.'

She wasn't. Not really. Isabelle was exceptionally beautiful, in her quirky way, and Mary was…just quirky. But then, well, there *were* certain similarities. 'They've both got red hair. They're tall. That's about it.'

James's expression said that was clearly enough.

'What are you going to do?' asked Eleanor, always practical.

'Vanessa might still marry you,' Henrietta supplied. 'Her family's greedy enough. I suggest you ask her quickly, and it might just cover up this scandal.'

Will sighed. 'No, Henny, I'll go on as normal. I've done nothing wrong. Miss Thomas is not my mistress and Mary's not my child.'

Eleanor shrugged. 'Yes, and I'm sure you'll survive. But if you don't care about your own reputation, you must care about the girl's future. Everyone will think she's your natural child. It will ruin her prospects.'

Will knew that was probably true. Eventually the rumour would fade, but she would always be followed by the shadow of doubt.

'Who could have started these rumours?' Henrietta demanded.

Will was quiet for a moment. Sebastian Cowes came immediately to mind, but he didn't think it was him. He suspected the rumour originated with someone far more treacherous. 'Vanessa Lytton or her mother, perhaps.'

'Impossible. Why should they have even known anything about the governess?' Henrietta asked.

'It doesn't matter why, although the fact that you invited them to come to my house on my behalf might have something to do with it. They're spiteful and jealous, and Miss Thomas is very pretty. I wouldn't be at all surprised if they were behind this.'

'What will you do?' Eleanor asked again.

'As I said before, I'll just repeat the truth. Mary is not my child, and Miss Thomas is not my mistress.'

'She's your betrothed, then, is she?' James asked sarcastically.

'No, of course not,' Will answered sharply.

'You can't pretend you didn't plan for her to be your mistress all along.'

Will didn't answer. He couldn't deny his brother's words, and he didn't have a solution. He wouldn't care about the rumour if others weren't involved, but…

What *would* he do? Go to the country, maybe, and wait for the scandal to subside. He'd take Isabelle with him, of course. He wouldn't let her go.

Luckily, Henrietta stepped into the silence before he had to think of something to say. 'What was that?' she asked, staring hard at the door. 'I heard something.'

Chapter Nineteen

Isabelle backed away from the drawing room when she heard the woman's shrill question, muffled only slightly by the closed door. Until then, she'd been frozen, wishing she could be in the room to defend herself. Will hadn't done much of a job of it, and his words still raged in her mind:

'...Miss Thomas is not my mistress.'

'She's your betrothed, then, is she?'

'No, of course not.'

'You can't pretend you didn't plan for her to be your mistress all along.'

And then he'd said nothing. His words made her angry, but the ensuing silence made her livid. He wouldn't even try to deny it, and his actions in her bedroom that afternoon—and on so many other occasions—only supported the accusation. She felt ten times a fool. She'd truly thought he was trying to help her, but he was little better than Mr Cowes. At least Cowes was honest in his intentions.

She gripped her leather bag tighter in her hand and started walking briskly to the staircase. She'd packed quickly, stuffing in what clothes she'd need for the next few days and leaving the rest. She had money, too, both the money she'd earned and the money that was, without warning, to be her unscrupulous inheritance, at least until someone else came along to take it away from her. She'd left enough on her dresser to reimburse Will, though, so he would have no reason to seek her out. She still refused to be a thief.

She'd descended only a few steps when she heard the drawing-room door open behind her.

'You're not leaving.'

Will's words hit her in the back, stealing her breath and forcing her to stop. She turned slowly. He stood at the top of the staircase, looking annoyed; his brother and two ladies stared at her curiously from a few paces behind him. How humiliating.

Running would do no good, since he would catch her easily. She'd probably just trip on the steps and make herself look even more foolish. Isabelle raised her chin, but since she stood at a disadvantage, a quarter of the way down the staircase, the gesture was of little significance.

She wanted to cry, but she tried to sound strong. 'I am.'

He started walking towards her. 'Where are you going, then?'

She said nothing, but stood her ground. Just six steps separated them.

One woman began to speak. '*She* could have started this scandal, William.'

'Do be quiet, Henrietta,' he said, not bothering to look at her. 'Isabelle?' He was in front of her now, his voice low. 'Don't cry.'

'I'm not.' She wasn't, either, but denying it made the urge to do so even greater. She bit her lip, trying very hard.

'I hope you didn't hear anything that would have upset you.'

'Perhaps we should go.' The pretty brown-haired lady spoke now, sounding more sympathetic than Cousin Henrietta.

'That's a very good idea,' Will replied, still looking at Isabelle.

'*I* don't think we should go,' said Henrietta.

'Ignore her.' Will spoke quietly enough for only Isabelle to hear. 'And come talk to me. I won't let you leave.' He took her hand and tugged gently. 'My study. We'll be alone.'

She glanced uncertainly up the staircase. His brother and the brown-haired lady—presumably his wife—looked considerately away, although his cousin was less tactful. She withdrew her hand, but answered, 'Very well.'

* * *

'An eventful day,' Will said as he closed the door behind them. 'I'm sorry about Henrietta. I did warn you.'

'She thinks I'm your mistress,' she said quietly, facing one of the tall windows that lined the room. It was still only afternoon, but she felt like so much time had passed since she'd gone out that morning.

'You know what we were talking about, then.'

She nodded.

'Was that the first you heard of these rumours?'

Should she tell him that she'd heard while looking for a new position? Why not, now that they were being honest. 'Like you, I learned today. I went to an interview for another position this morning. The woman blanched when she saw I worked for you. I meant to tell you—'

'You were distracted by other events.'

She turned to face him. 'Mr Cowes implied that he'd heard it, too. I had worried that he would say something to you.' She fell silent. 'He might have started the rumour.'

His lack of surprise suggested he'd already considered this possibility. 'I doubt it—how would he hope to benefit?'

'Maybe he thought the rumour would force you to make me leave.'

He shook his head, walking closer. 'I won't let you leave.'

She looked away. His words thrilled her, and she wished they didn't. 'If he's responsible, I'm very sorry.'

'Don't be sorry.'

'I have to be, because your reputation has suffered. Mary's, too, and it's quite possible it's entirely my fault.'

'I don't care what anyone thinks, Isabelle. Ignore my cousin. She's just annoyed because she wanted me to marry Miss Lytton and this has ruined her plans.'

If one thing good came out of it... 'You have to marry someone.'

'Not her. In my opinion, the Lyttons are most likely behind this talk. I didn't part on good terms with them, and I'd expect them to do something like invent pernicious gossip. It's a retaliation more suited to women than men, you must admit.'

He had a point, but the fact remained that even if the Lyttons had concocted the rumour, they wouldn't have done so if not for her presence in his house.

'But you must marry someone else, then. Eventually. You've told me so more than once.'

He didn't deny it, didn't say anything. The room was silent except for the tick of the clock. She couldn't bear it. It hurt too much to think about him marrying anyone, which could only mean she'd stupidly allowed herself to love him.

She knew then that, no matter how difficult it would be, she couldn't stay.

'I'll leave. That will be for the best.'

'The best for whom?' he asked angrily. 'You have nowhere to go. You won't find another position. You've no money, no family—'

'The best for both of us. And I can find somewhere.'

'How? Dr Collins?'

She closed her eyes briefly, then spoke slowly. 'I did not invite him to visit, Will, nor did I encourage his attentions in any way. I merely meant that I have a bit of money now. I…I don't quite understand it, but—'

He snorted. 'Unless it's as false as everything else your father touched.'

That hurt, but she went on. 'Obviously my presence here has caused problems.'

'Imagined problems, Isabelle, conjured up by jealous women.'

'Not entirely imagined.'

He flushed at the reminder of how close they'd come, less than an hour earlier, to making the rumour true. 'Very well then. Where will you live?'

'I've enough money to take rooms again. That would suit me well enough for the present.'

'I'm not letting you set off blindly, having made no arrangements—'

'Do you think I want to leave like this? I haven't a choice, though.'

'You've plenty of choices. Choose to stay.'

'I can't stay! Do you think I want to be thought of as your mistress? Should I remain here to cast further doubt on Mary's parentage?'

'Isabelle—'

She was too upset to stop. 'And do you propose to find your suitable wife with me still living in this house? Your mother might not have minded that your father married her while having designs on another woman, but I doubt most will be so accommodating.'

'Perhaps he should have married the other woman to begin with.'

'What do you mean?'

'I mean if I'm going to marry anyone, then I'll marry you.'

Will hadn't planned on those words coming out. He hadn't even been thinking them. They came from nowhere, and he hoped he didn't look as shocked as Isabelle did. The colour had drained from her face, except for a bright spot on each cheek.

'How can you say that?' she asked slowly, angrily.

He paused for several seconds before answering. Having said it, he didn't feel too bad. He could think of a dozen reasons not to marry her, but actually…

There was no one he'd rather marry, and he very much doubted there ever would be. So why not?

'I should have asked.'

'Asked what?'

'Will you marry me, Isabelle?'

Her lips thinned and her face darkened. She turned on her heel and walked quickly to the door. It wasn't the response he'd expected.

He followed close behind her.

James, Eleanor and Henrietta were descending the staircase as the study door burst open. James and Eleanor were no doubt preparing to leave, but Will knew Henrietta would stay until forcefully ejected.

'What are you going to do, William?' she demanded.

He didn't answer at first. He didn't want to tell her his decision, didn't want her trying to talk him out of it. But she was watching him, waiting for him to say something. Defiance, as much as anything else, made him speak.

'I've asked Miss Thomas to marry me.'

That was the wrong thing to say, for both Henrietta and Isabelle. Isabelle stared at him, furious and aghast.

'How can you?' she asked very quietly.

'Have you lost your mind?' Henrietta's voice grew louder and higher in pitch.

'No,' he said tightly, 'I have not.'

'I don't want to marry you.'

The words hurt. Why the hell was she being so difficult? He didn't bother looking at Isabelle properly, just glanced at her dismissively. 'Don't be a fool.'

'She's being perfectly sensible. It's one thing to have an affair with a governess, but you can't seriously propose to marry her.'

'Yes, I can.'

'Please stop. I don't want to marry you,' Isabelle pleaded.

'There. She doesn't even want to marry you. I can hardly imagine a less suitable match.'

Isabelle glared at Henrietta and opened her mouth to retort. Thinking better of it, she bit her tongue. Will wasn't so polite.

'I think you should leave.'

Henrietta flushed. 'What?'

'Leave, Henny. When you can be civil you can return.'

Henrietta pursed her lips before marching to the door. She slammed it behind her, making the pictures on the walls shake.

Will returned his attention to Isabelle. He'd never seen anyone look so miserable, and he wished he'd handled himself better. It wasn't her fault she been thrust into this situation, but she was the one who'd been humiliated.

As for Eleanor and James…they just looked at each other uncomfortably. 'Perhaps we should leave, too,' James said.

Seemed like a good idea to Will. 'Come round tomorrow.'

But they didn't turn to leave. Just stood there and glanced at each other again.

'Well?' he asked.

'Perhaps Miss Thomas should come with us.'

He frowned at his sister-in-law. 'Why?'

'She can't stay here, Will. It's bad enough already. I…I don't know what you should do, but for now—' She stopped, addressing her next words to Isabelle. 'Have you anywhere else to go?'

Isabelle wanted to lie and say yes, he knew it, but at the last minute she shook her head instead.

'Then come with us tonight, Miss Thomas. You can decide what to do in the morning, but it's getting rather late to find new accommodation.'

'I want to come with her.' Everyone turned at the sound of the new voice. Clear and young. Mary stood at the top of the landing, looking down nervously. Nervous but not ready to back down.

Will stared up at her, accepting that there was some superficial resemblance between her and Isabelle. They possessed completely different features, though. How could anybody suspect…?

But it was enough. He could admit that much. 'Go back to your room, Mary.'

She stood her ground, and he realised that arguing with her would be pointless. Like him, she cared for Isabelle. If she'd overheard even half of what Henrietta had said, he couldn't blame her for feeling protective.

'If it's all right, Will, why doesn't she come?' Eleanor asked.

He had no reason to object, other than the house would seem empty without them. He felt rather as if he were being abandoned by a makeshift, adopted family. Adopted, but his.

He nodded. 'Yes. Yes, of course.'

Ten minutes later, they'd all left. Will retired to his bedroom, where he was least likely to be disturbed. He stretched out on his bed and thought about Isabelle, as he'd done many times since he'd met her. His thoughts were different today, though. Had he made a mistake? He'd just proposed to do something that went against long-held views, and he felt instinctively that he should be panicking.

He wondered why he wasn't.

All that really worried him was that she hadn't accepted him yet.

Chapter Twenty

Isabelle awoke the next morning to a light knocking on her bedroom door. She'd slept badly and had spent much of the night tossing and turning in the strange bed, trying to get comfortable.

At least the room was nice. She'd assumed they'd put her in the servants' quarters somewhere, but instead she'd been given a proper bedroom with a four-poster bed—the sort normally bestowed upon esteemed guests and elderly aunts. Will's brother and his wife hadn't spoken much during the ride back to their house, but they seemed kind enough. Isabelle was grateful for their restraint; she didn't want to be there and would have refused their offer if she'd anywhere else to go. She felt certain they didn't really want her there, either. By the end of the day, she hoped to have secured new lodgings.

'Isabelle?' It was Mary, whispering through the door. She reluctantly rose to open it.

Half an hour later they were in the park, walking slowly. Mary had suggested the outing—apparently she, too, had suffered a restless night. Isabelle needed the distraction, and she didn't want to remain in the house, where she'd have to make polite conversation with people who probably were embarrassed by her. On the other hand, she didn't want to speak to Mary, either. She didn't know how much the girl had overheard last night, but much of what had been discussed was unsuitable for twelve-year-old ears. She no doubt had a score of embarrassing questions to ask.

Her feet felt heavy, and she had to force each step. It was hard to imagine how her once dull life had become so…so horribly unpredictable. And what was she going to do now? Eleanor had told her she could decide what to do in the morning, but it was now the morning and she'd still no idea. She certainly wouldn't marry him, not that he'd actually meant it.

'Miss Thomas?'

She glanced at Mary. They'd spoken very little so far, and the girl looked anxious.

'Yes?'

'That story I told you—about why I cut off Amelia Fitzgerald's hair…'

Why bring it up now? She waited patiently for her to continue.

'It wasn't true.'

'You didn't do it?'

'No, I did.' Mary sighed. 'But not for the reason I told you.'

'What other reason could you have, then?'

'I disliked her completely. She was the most unpleasant girl at school.'

Isabelle frowned, but in fact, she was relieved to have something to think about other than herself. 'Disliking her is no reason to cut her hair off.'

'I only cut off a little. I meant to do more, but I couldn't—'

'But why do it at all?'

Mary looked at the path. 'Celia suggested it. I kept telling her that I wanted to be sent away, and she said I'd have to do something really dreadful, since Miss Hume was being paid to keep me. I'd only met Lord Lennox a few times, but he seemed nice enough, and not too strict, and I knew he'd been my father's friend. Cutting Amelia's hair was the worst thing I could think of, and I thought her parents would insist I was sent away.'

'It worked.'

'Yes, but once I got to my godfather's house I realised he planned to send me away, too. I didn't want to like him any more. Or you.'

That was why she'd been so unfriendly. 'Then why lie about it? Why invent that ridiculous story about the girl trying to curl her hair?'

'Because by then I'd decided that you weren't so bad. I lied because I knew how awful the truth sounded, and I didn't want you to dislike me.'

Isabelle put her hand on Mary's shoulder. She didn't shrug it off. 'I do like you. Lord Lennox likes you, too. And you don't know for certain that he still plans to send you away. I know for a fact he's made no provisions for such an event.'

'Maybe not, but he probably will now. I heard what was being said about me.'

Isabelle understood Mary's fear. The girl's situation was no less precarious than her own. Presumably Will still planned to find a wife to produce his dratted heir—and she didn't think for one minute that he truly hoped she'd fill the position. But what future Lady Lennox wouldn't refuse to cross his threshold as long as his bastard daughter remained inside?

And yet she knew he'd never send Mary away against her wishes, no matter what anyone thought. He would never be that cruel.

'I don't think you need to worry.'

'Celia's mother will never let her visit now,' Mary continued.

That was no doubt true, although Isabelle opened her mouth to reassure her otherwise. But she didn't get the chance.

'Oh, no.'

'What?' Mary asked. She followed Isabelle's nervous gaze. 'Oh, no.'

'Yes, Mary, exactly. Try to ignore her.'

It seemed hardly possible that Miss Lytton should be walking up the path in the opposite direction. It was too late to turn back, and it was also too late to hope that she would just ignore them. Two friends accompanied her, and the chance to show off in front of them wasn't one to be missed. A tight smile broke across her pretty face.

'How do you do, Miss Thomas.'

Isabelle debated not responding, but then she'd look like the rude one. 'Miss Lytton.'

And then in a louder voice, Vanessa explained to her friends, 'You might have heard of Miss Thomas. My mother and I happened upon Lord Lennox and her a week ago. It was…most embarrassing.'

'That is completely false!'

Vanessa shrugged. 'No need to scold me. If your behaviour has caused censure, then that is *your* fault, not mine.'

Isabelle struggled for calm. 'I have done nothing wrong, Miss Lytton. You concocted this rumour out of spite.'

'Concocted this rumour? Mama and I merely decided it was time to spread the truth about Lord Lennox's character. Everyone knows he wanted to marry me. He even asked me—begged me to forgive this lapse—but I had to turn him down. He was devastated.'

'You're lying.' Mary's eyes sparkled angrily. 'He didn't ask you to marry him. He doesn't even like you.'

'How would you know?' Then, loudly again for her friends, 'And this is Miss Thomas's natural daughter. You can see the resemblance, I'm certain.'

Isabelle put a hand on Mary's shoulder, but the girl wouldn't be calmed. 'She is not my mother! My mother died when I was two.'

Vanessa smirked. 'Yes, well, I'm sure that's what you've been told, and you're gullible enough to believe it. She must be your mother, with that vulgar red hair.'

'She is not! But I wish she were. And I'd rather have red hair than a brain the size of a pea.'

Vanessa's tiny, perfect nostrils flared, but it seemed for a fraction of a second that she might control her temper. She didn't, though; she raised her hand and slapped Mary across the cheek. The girl's head turned slightly with the force.

And Isabelle, propelled by anger, slapped her back in just the same fashion.

Mary stared at her. Vanessa's friends stared at her. Vanessa stared, too, and Isabelle thought, for a moment, that she would return the favor. All the prettiness left her face, and she just looked mean. 'I don't believe you did that,' she said.

Isabelle couldn't believe she'd done it, either, and she fought desperately to keep the shock and fear from her expression. She'd never struck anyone. She didn't even like killing spiders.

In a daze, she took Mary's hand, turned, and walked back down the path in the direction they had come, her spine rigid with humiliation. She could hear outraged murmurs behind her back and knew they were speaking about her. She also knew that she'd added fuel to the rumour by losing her temper. But how could she have done nothing? Personally, she could take the insults—she could even have taken the blow. But she couldn't let someone treat Mary that way.

They walked numbly through the park back to the road, and then they wandered silently through Mayfair for well over an hour. Isabelle couldn't face returning to Will's brother's house.

'My feet hurt,' Mary said finally.

'Do you want to sit?'

'I want to go home.'

She nodded unenthusiastically. They had to eventually.

'I'm sorry that happened,' Isabelle said as they started back in the right direction. 'You shouldn't have been involved.'

'It's not your fault. Miss Lytton already didn't like me.' Mary paused, looking ahead into the distance. 'Why don't you want to marry Lord Lennox?'

It was the last subject she wanted to talk about. 'He does not wish to marry me. He just offered because he thought it was the proper thing to do.'

Mary shrugged, looking unconvinced. 'Maybe not. I overheard one of the maids at his house saying that he's a rake. But then he wouldn't ask you to marry him just because he thought it was honourable to do so. Not if he's such a rake, I mean.'

'He's an honourable rake, then.'

'*I'd* like you to marry him.'

Isabelle glanced at her. 'You shall be disappointed, then.'

'I think he loves you.'

She snorted, but Mary's words actually hurt. She knew that he liked her, or at least used to, but love? There wasn't a chance. 'And I think you read far too many novels.'

'Probably,' Mary said reluctantly. 'Do you—'

'No, I do not. I don't want to discuss it.'

They reached the house fifteen minutes later. Isabelle planned to hide in her room for as long as she could, but Will's carriage was parked on the street by the front door. She wanted to keep walking, head back to the park, go even farther, she didn't know where. In the time that she'd been wandering around, he might have learned what had happened.

Henrietta greeted them at the door of the drawing room. Isabelle was disappointed, but not surprised to see her. The woman was apparently ubiquitous.

'Where have you been?' she demanded. 'We've heard what you did.'

Ubiquitous and annoyingly *au fait*. Isabelle apologised right away. Owning up to crimes immediately was always wise. 'I'm so sorry.'

'Don't know why you're apologizing to me. You didn't hit *me*.'

Time to abandon diplomacy. 'She struck Mary,' Isabelle said, crossing her arms defiantly over her chest.

Henrietta looked like she wanted to utter some cutting remark, but creativity failed her. 'Oh, she *is* dreadful. I am sorry to have introduced her, but honestly, did you have to strike her back?'

Isabelle didn't answer. She took a deep breath, marshalling her thoughts, but in the end she had no defence. She walked quickly from the room before she started to cry.

Several minutes later, Will knocked on her bedroom door. He opened it quietly without waiting for permission. Isabelle was sitting on a small, striped sofa, and she looked up as he entered. He closed the door and leaned against it.

'I missed you downstairs. Hoped to catch you before Henrietta did, but I was having a word with my brother.'

'Your cousin seems to be everywhere.'

'Unfortunately, yes. Miss Lytton arrived at her house hysterical after she left you. Henny then came to find me, and Bartholomew told her I was here… I'm so sorry. This is awful for you.'

She shrugged, trying to appear as if she didn't care. 'I have survived awful things before. It will be far worse for Mary.'

'I've just been to see her. Strangely enough, she seemed in quite good spirits. I think you impressed her.'

He crossed the room and sat on the mahogany window seat, just a few feet from her. She glanced away, knowing that she looked very tired.

'I've caused you an inordinate amount of trouble,' she said slowly. 'You must hate me.'

'Because you hit Miss Lytton? There you're wrong. Nothing could make me prouder.'

'I accused her of starting the rumour. She all but admitted it.'

'I thought as much. By the by, whose poor image did I break last night?'

He was looking at the bust, broken in a box on the floor at the foot of her bed. She'd gathered up the pieces while she'd been waiting for Mary's bag to be packed. 'Athena. She was made of plaster, so you didn't break anything valuable. Worth nothing to anyone but me.'

'Worth more broken than intact, it would seem.'

She blushed. 'My father gave her to me for my twenty-third birthday. He would have, anyway, except he died three days too soon. I couldn't bear to open the gift for a month. When I finally did, there she was.'

'Goddess of war, right? Rather apposite given this morning's activities.'

'And wisdom, which is less so. Sprang from her father's head fully formed.'

'That would be Zeus, would it? I did pay *some* attention at school, Isabelle.'

She smiled at his teasing. 'She was the favourite of his many children.'

'You don't talk about your father much.'

'No, well, it's been rather awkward. There wasn't much I wanted to tell. He did love me, for all his faults.'

'You say that as if it wouldn't be evident.'

'I don't know that it ever was. I never felt terribly confident of his affection. He cared a great deal about my education, but otherwise took little heed of me. I've often wondered…if I'd shown no aptitude for languages and history, would he even have known what to say to me?'

'What do you mean?'

She glanced at the bust, feeling suddenly cross. 'Well, if I hadn't adapted my own interests to suit his, then I don't think he would have been interested in me. If I'd cared instead about…say, fashion, or—'

'It's rather refreshing, Isabelle, that you have a mind as lovely as your face.'

She blushed at the compliment. 'Well, I…I'm grateful to be educated, but perhaps I'd rather have…gone to parties on occasion and at least learned to dance. Do you know I've never had one fashionable dress?'

'In that case I very much look forward to corrupting you.'

She made a face at him, but she couldn't quite hide her smile. 'You've done enough of that already, thank you.'

'Have you thought about my offer?'

At first she'd no idea what he was referring to. It took her several seconds to answer. 'You didn't mean it.'

'No, I hadn't planned to say it. Hadn't even thought of it. But I did mean it, Isabelle.'

'No, you didn't. You don't want to marry me.'

'I don't know what I want, except that I don't want to lose you. You wouldn't consent to being my mistress, would you?' Before she could retort, he added, 'Might I point out that I've already asked the honourable question, and you've turned me down?'

They were both quiet for a minute. He crossed the room and sat next to her on the sofa.

'I cannot simply let you leave without any consideration for what will happen to you. Henrietta has suggested I give you money, so you can live quietly in the country for as long as it takes for this scandal to fade.'

'I will not accept it.'

'Yes, I know—and you don't need it any more, either. Won't have to rely on me again, it seems.' He paused. 'Thank you, while we're on the subject, for repaying me. You didn't need to. I'll insist on returning it.'

'I don't want to be in your debt.'

'Then consider yourself free.'

She glanced out of the window, watching small, fleecy clouds sail across the blue sky. She didn't feel free at all. 'I wondered where my father's money went. It never made any sense that he could have spent all of it and left me destitute. How…?' She paused, uncomfortable asking such a direct question. 'How long do you think it will last me?'

He shrugged. 'I haven't counted it. A long time, I'd imagine, but not for ever. You'd have to curb your taste for expensive racehorses.'

She almost smiled at his jest, but she felt too worried to manage it. The money might last an even shorter time than he'd guess, at least if anyone else learned what Sebastian Cowes had.

'A question, Isabelle.'

She looked at him, waiting.

'Why would your father have been hiding it inside the bust in the first place? Why not just give it to you?'

'I don't think he was hiding it, exactly. He'd no idea that anyone would discover his deception when he gave it to me—Mr Cowes didn't learn of it until after his death. I suppose he meant to surprise me one day. It was just an elaborate and fanciful gift.'

'Was there no note?'

'No. Perhaps he meant to write one.'

'He obviously was successful to have made such a sum.'

She knew that she would have to tell him the truth. 'I lied to you yesterday.'

'Oh?'

'When you asked if Mr Cowes was the only person my father deceived. He wasn't. As I told you, he made an arrangement with an Italian dealer to have marbles shipped to him from Rome without first inspecting them.'

His expression registered no surprise, and it occurred to her that he might've suspected she'd lied all along. Still, he offered her father the benefit of the doubt. 'And therefore his mistake is understandable.'

'Except I don't think it *was* a mistake. From what I can tell, he must have felt that his business was threatened by the war—'

'Because he couldn't travel to the Continent to find new artefacts to sell himself?'

'Nor could any such things easily reach England. I imagine supplies must have thinned and he became desperate, which is perhaps why he resorted to other means. I've seen his records. I inspected them immediately when Cowes first approached me. Compared to what he paid for similar but genuine marbles in earlier years, he paid far less.'

'But still sold them on for the same amount.'

She nodded. 'The profit, in the end, was significantly greater.'

He considered that, returning his gaze to the broken plaster bust. 'It seems possible he knew someone would discover his secret eventually. If he'd still been alive when that day had come, he perhaps preferred playing bankrupt and serving his debt in prison, all the while keeping the money safely hidden for you.'

'I assure you my father would not have enjoyed prison.'

'He probably assumed it wouldn't come to that. It seemed a risk worth taking. Obviously he just wanted to provide for you.'

'It miscarried greatly, if that was the plan.'

'Does anyone else know?'

'No. Only Cowes. And as far as I know, he thinks he was the only one to be so deceived.'

Will nodded, but she saw doubt in his eyes. 'He might start to wonder, though. He might investigate—he'd love to have something else to hold over your head. I threatened him never to bother you again, but it would be fairly difficult to prevent him. Particularly if you're on your own.'

Silence again. She was well aware of the danger she faced.

'How many others, Isabelle? Do you know their names?'

She rose and fished the heavy ledger from one of her bags. 'They're at the back. Starting in 1803, all sent by Signor Ricci—that's how Mr Cowes found out, you see. He went to the man's shop in Rome and realised what was happening. There are ten more buyers, not including Mr Cowes.'

'Ten doesn't sound a lot,' he said, perusing the names. 'What do the figures in the right column signify? Not how much they spent, surely.'

She cringed. 'I'm afraid so. This one…' She paused, scanning for the name. 'He spent three times what Mr Cowes did.'

Will met her gaze briefly, and then looked back at the list. 'I know him.'

'You do?'

'I know most of these men, actually. Ned Tilman—I went to school with his brother. Freddie Lathrope-Hughes—I see him about once a week at my club. What if they find out, Isabelle?'

It was even worse than she'd feared. 'They haven't found out yet.'

'They might. You'll have to tell them the truth.'

'The truth?' She hadn't even contemplated it, and wouldn't.

'It's the honourable thing to do—rather than wait to be discovered.'

'*Why* is it more honourable?'

'Because the truth just is.'

'Then I'll leave honour to those who can afford it.' She paused, wishing so much it hurt that she possessed the funds to repay everyone. 'And what if it's never discovered?'

'Do you think you can live with that uncertainty?'

'It looks as if I haven't much choice.'

They sat silently. He now knew everything. She glanced at him, wondering how he would take it. He'd asked her to marry him, but now that he knew she'd indirectly stolen thousands of pounds from his friends and acquaintances she didn't expect the offer again. The best she could hope for was that he didn't hate her.

'You won't tell anyone, will you?' she asked quietly.

He shook his head. 'If you should ever want to, I could help you. But, no, I won't. It would ruin you, and I don't think that would be honourable at all.'

'Thank you.'

'Will you stay here?' he asked.

'What do you mean?'

'I mean now that you're an heiress and you could go anywhere. Just for a few more days. I can help you find somewhere to live, if you like. But I'll need a bit of time.'

'I don't want to impose on your brother and his wife.'

'I have already spoken to them this morning, before you returned. They don't mind—does them no harm since no one knows you're here. It would be wise if you didn't go out in public again, though, just in order to keep it that way. Can you manage?'

'Yes, of course.' It would be easy. She didn't even plan on leaving her room if she could avoid it. Did she have enough books to entertain her? What about food? The thought of having to venture to the kitchen or dining room...

She watched him rise with a growing sense of apprehension. 'You're leaving?'

'I've a lot to do—a few people I might ask about accommodation for you. Will you be—?'

'I'll be all right.'

After he'd left, she continued to sit for several minutes, wishing he hadn't gone. How reassuring it was, though, to know that he was helping her find a home. How inappropriate, too, and how like the behaviour of a gentleman to his mistress.

She should have insisted on taking control of her own future. Taking care of herself, as she claimed to be so good at.

Only it *was* nice to have someone take care of her for a change.

Chapter Twenty-One

Isabelle's stomach growled late the next morning. It was nearly eleven, and she'd been awake and dressed for hours, but she hadn't yet found the nerve to go downstairs to seek food. A maid had brought both her lunch and her supper to her room yesterday, and she'd been able to eat in private, off a tray. She'd thought it very considerate of someone to sense her unease and make the arrangement. Today, though, no such tray had arrived and she couldn't wait any longer; she would find Mary and send her down to collect something.

She opened the door slowly, having already acquainted herself with its tendency to creak. Mary resided just a few rooms down.

'Hello.'

Drat. Isabelle turned around guiltily. Will's sister-in-law, Eleanor, was walking down the corridor from the other direction, her footsteps muffled by the thick carpet.

'Have you had breakfast, Miss Thomas?' she asked, sounding friendly enough.

'No. I…I was afraid I'd missed it. I will wait for lunch.'

'Don't be silly. I was hoping to see you, in case you decided to go out.'

'Lord Lennox suggested I not appear public.'

'Yes, well, a wise suggestion. Would you like to come to the garden with me? I can have refreshments sent there.'

Isabelle's stomach rumbled again, forcing her to nod. She didn't want to be rude, and she was certain Eleanor only asked for the same reason. No doubt she couldn't wait for Isabelle to leave.

'What did you wish to speak to me about?' she asked as they descended the stairs.

'Oh, just to tell you that my modiste is coming this afternoon. Mary will need a new wardrobe. And if there's anything you would like—'

'No. No, thank you,' Isabelle answered quickly.

'Will is coming for dinner tonight. You'll join us, I hope.'

She didn't want to. It was painful, how polite her hostess was being. 'If you wish.'

'Yes, of course. I don't think he'd be coming if you weren't here.'

That made her blush. 'I'm sorry I'm here.'

'Oh? Is it that awful?'

'No, no, it's lovely—what I meant—'

Eleanor smiled. 'You needn't explain. You needn't apologise, either. Will spoke to us yesterday, and it's obviously what's best.'

She wondered what he'd told them. Presumably he'd made it clear that she'd never been his mistress—otherwise, they wouldn't tolerate her presence in their house for more than one night.

She hoped so.

'Diana should be outside with Miss Baxter,' Eleanor said as she opened the back door. 'You must like children a great deal, to be a governess. That or have tremendous reserves of patience.'

'I've spent little time with children as young as your daughter,' Isabelle answered, looking suspiciously at the two-year-old girl sitting on the lawn, her white cotton dress spread out around her. Miss Baxter, her governess, was a pleasant-faced, slightly plump woman of middle years. She waved merrily at Eleanor.

Isabelle couldn't help but remark, 'Miss Baxter would be appalled if she knew what people were saying about me.'

Eleanor snorted prettily. 'She might know, and I doubt it. She'd think you were an inspiration to governesses everywhere.'

They started down a shady path bordered on one side by unruly perennials and on the other by well-tended lawn. Isabelle began to worry about thinking of something to say, but Eleanor spoke first.

'I should not be so free, but…do you wish to marry my brother-in-law?'

She realised then that, for all her charm, Eleanor was probably as determined as Henrietta that she would not. 'No.'

They walked in silence, stopping when they reached a creeping rosebush. Eleanor removed a small pair of shears from her pocket. Frowning in concentration at a particularly lush, pink bloom, she said, 'You needn't worry that he doesn't wish to marry you.'

'He feels he has to.'

Eleanor looked up. 'No, he's never done anything simply because he felt as if he had to.'

Why, oh, why had she agreed to come outside? Where was the food she'd been promised? 'He wants to marry someone else. He's told me several times.'

'Really? Who?'

'Someone not like me.'

Eleanor returned her gaze to the rosebush and carefully clipped a stem. She dropped it on the ground. 'Strange, then, that you're the only one he's ever asked.'

'He's never been in this situation before.'

'I suppose not, although he didn't have to offer to marry you. Most gentlemen would not have.'

'He won't ask again.'

'That's not what he told us yesterday.'

'I assure you, he will not,' Isabelle said firmly. 'Undoubtedly he just wanted to ensure you'd let me stay here for a few more days until I can find other lodgings.'

Eleanor clipped another stem, looking doubtful. 'My brother-in-law is a contradictory character.'

'How do you mean?'

'Well, he seems to be a charming rogue who doesn't take anything seriously, and yet he takes his responsibilities more seriously than anyone I know. He…' She paused. 'It's an unhappy history, the one my husband and his brother share.'

'It is?'

'Do you know they had an older brother?'

Isabelle nodded, wondering where this was headed.

'Richard was a thorough reprobate. Prone to intemperance and cruelty. Will never suffered directly, in part because he'd been sent away to school, but mostly because he was Richard's heir and full brother. Richard hated James, though.'

'Why?'

'Because he disapproved of his stepmother—'

'Your husband's real mother?'

'Yes. He taunted him and, as years passed, his taunts escalated into physical cruelty. James's parents weren't alive to protect him, and Will knew nothing of it, since he was at school. By the time he finally did learn, James could no longer bear Richard's abuse. He ran away before Will could intervene—didn't come back for twelve years. Will has never forgiven himself for not stopping it earlier.'

'But he didn't know.'

'No, and he was very young. Richard was seven years older than Will, who wasn't yet eighteen when my husband ran away. Perhaps it's the result of that experience, perhaps it's just his nature, but Will is the sort of person who rather likes protecting others—'

'And also the sort of person who knows the importance of marrying someone from his own background,' Isabelle said, more sharply than she intended.

'Of course it's important, but it's not the *most* important thing. He's tenacious. It's a most annoying family trait. If he really wants to marry you—and my guess is that he does—then he won't give up easily.' Eleanor paused, giving her roses one last, critical glance. 'You don't seem to be a fool, Miss Thomas.'

'I hope not.'

'I think you would be if you refused him.'

* * *

Isabelle thumbed the blue silk nervously. She didn't know how she'd allowed herself to be talked into it, but she had a new dress. New to her, anyway, and even more novel for its stylish, low neckline. Eleanor had borrowed it—unbidden—from a sister who was apparently nearly as tall as Isabelle. The modiste who'd come to outfit Mary had only needed to make a few adjustments. Isabelle planned to insist that it was returned at the end of the night, but for now…she desperately needed the dress, even if it did make her feel quite naked. Without it, she would have felt even more out of place, and as it was she still felt completely unworthy of her seat at the elegant dining table.

Will's expression when he'd first seen her, however, had more than made up for any discomfort caused by her exposed flesh. He stepped out of his brother's study just as she was coming down the staircase, and his eyes had warmed perceptibly, turning that peculiar shade of green that always made her heart beat faster. He made no bones about staring at her, to the point that James, coming out of the room behind him, had had to clear his throat. She'd never felt so beautiful—never so embarrassed, either, but no matter.

She said very little over dinner. She'd no desire to talk about herself, and no one asked personal questions. Instead she mainly listened, enjoying the friendly banter between the two brothers. Luckily, James suggested a game of speculation as the plates were being cleared away. She was actually quite good at card games, and she hoped it would facilitate conversation.

They all retired to the drawing room, but somehow the cards were missing, and both Eleanor and James disappeared to go and find them. Isabelle and Will were suddenly alone. She'd been alone with him many times before, but now it felt different. She glanced at the closed mahogany door, wondering if the cards had been intentionally misplaced.

'You look beautiful,' he said over his shoulder while pouring glasses of wine for both of them.

'Your sister-in-law lent me the dress.'

He turned around. 'I told her you were lamenting your lack of fashionable clothes.'

'You didn't,' she said with dismay.

'I certainly did—'

'But it's humiliating.'

He crossed the room, handing Isabelle her glass when he reached her side. His gaze wandered slowly down her neck. 'I don't care. Never seen this much of you before and I'm rather enjoying it.'

Dear God, and now all that pale, freckled skin was turning pink. 'I...I still feel I'm imposing enough already without their charity.'

'You're not imposing at all. You'll be pleased to hear, though, that I've found a cottage you might rent. It's just outside London, on some land that belongs to a friend. Quite rural, really—would you mind?'

She shook her head, bemused. Events had moved so quickly.

'I'll take you tomorrow, and if you like it you can move in immediately. It would be within your means, provided your luck holds.'

She wished he hadn't reminded her about her tenuous position. She sank down on to the damask sofa, suddenly depleted. 'You think it's wrong, don't you? That I should propose to live on funds that were gained dishonestly.'

He sat next to her. 'You've nothing else to live on, Isabelle. I understand that. A sensible girl would just marry me, but as we've discussed wisdom isn't your strong suit.'

She couldn't believe he'd brought it up again. 'Marry you? After you saw that list? You want to marry your social equal, not...not someone with such a burden. What if any of those men should discover my secret? How would you explain to your acquaintances that you'd wed the girl whose father had cheated them?'

He didn't answer immediately, and she held her breath, waiting. Finally, he said, 'I can't deny it's problematical. But I'm not going to waste time worrying about something I can't control.'

'You don't want to marry at all.'

He looked like he was starting to lose patience with her. 'I don't know any man who wants to be married. One or two, maybe. I think we all need to feel as if we're being forced.'

'I'm not forcing you.'

'For the love of God, Isabelle, then let me pretend you are. If my option is to marry you or leave you to the wolves, then I don't have to think about it. Maybe you shouldn't think too much about it, either.'

His words made her go quiet. Perhaps she *was* thinking too much. But she just couldn't believe that he would be happy with her. Not in a year. Not even in six months. And if he ever rejected her, or started to despise her for who she really was, it would be too painful for her to bear.

'I'm not suitable, and you know it.'

'But you *are* interesting. One would never be bored.'

'So much so that one would pine for boredom,' she retorted.

'Not so. Arguing with you these past weeks has much improved my mental agility.'

'You want a stubborn, argumentative wife? I thought you wanted *dull*.'

'Henrietta wanted dull. I want you.'

She couldn't be clever when he looked at her like that. When his voice grew husky. She ached with wanting to accept his proposal, so much that the pain forced her to look away. Quietly, she said, 'Yesterday you told me I should do the honourable thing. I cannot marry you.'

'Then be my mistress, Isabelle. Just don't tell me I'll never see you again.'

His words…so tempting, and so saddening, too, because that was the best she could hope for. The last thing she wanted was never to see him. She wanted a life with him, not some lonely existence in a cottage with only chickens for company. More immediately, she wanted his wide chest to press her into the sofa, for his lips to find hers. His eyes had grown dark, and he leaned forwards.

Voices in the hall, unnaturally loud to give fair warning. Will's gaze trailed down to her mouth. Isabelle felt frozen, unable to look away even though she knew she had to. He sat up slowly.

When James and Eleanor entered the drawing room a minute later, Will had removed himself to an armchair. Isabelle sat uncomfortably in the centre of the sofa, trying to force from her mind the dull, throbbing frustration of not having kissed him. Her heart still beat like a small bird's wings, but her mind had slowed to a crawl with the apprehension that she might not mind being his mistress. It was that or be nothing at all.

What would tomorrow bring?

Chapter Twenty-Two

William collected Isabelle at noon to take her to inspect the cottage. She brought along all her belongings since she'd no intention of rejecting it—the cottage would have to be downright uninhabitable for her to consider returning to London to accept any more of his brother's hospitality. Will had packed a bag as well; he planned to travel on to Wentwich Castle provided she found everything satisfactory.

She glanced at him covertly from across the carriage. In her former life, she would have protested at riding alone with him, but her resolve had worn very thin. She was precariously close to abandoning common sense and letting her heart take over. What if he tried to kiss her? She didn't think she'd push him away. She thought she'd be disappointed if he didn't. Since he'd been annoyingly well behaved during the journey today—rather quiet, perhaps preoccupied—she was starting to get a bit worried. Why wasn't he trying to seduce her?

No, no, she mustn't think like that. If she let her heart make decisions, it would only get broken. Mistresses were disposable, unlike wives. If she became his mistress, he'd lose interest in her quickly enough. And when he did eventually marry—someone else—she'd be devastated.

She looked outside, trying to concentrate on something other than the handsome gentleman on the seat across from her. She'd said goodbye to Mary before she'd left, and she assumed she might not see her again. She hated being yet another person to abandon her. Perhaps the girl could come for a visit…but, no, that just wasn't feasible. Not now, while the gossip was still so fresh. Soon, though, she hoped.

They'd been driving for just over an hour and had said little. Although their destination was only a few miles outside London, the scenery had changed quite markedly, growing hillier and leafier the further they went. In the distance, she could see the silver river winding along beside them, specked with boats on such a pleasant day.

The carriage turned down a rutted drive and a minute later stopped. 'I think we're there.'

She turned her head to glance curiously out of the opposite window. From her position she could see a slate roof and a limed brick wall partially covered with ivy. Just a suggestion of a rather nice cottage, the whole picture framed by an auspiciously blue sky.

Will opened the door, stepped out, and then turned to help her. As she exited, she took in the rest of the house, allowing his hand to clasp hers longer than was strictly necessary. The warm pressure reassured her, for at that moment she couldn't quite believe her luck. It was a small house, really, rather than a cottage. Generously sized windows, freshly painted white, were evenly spaced along the brick façade; during the day, the interior would flood with light. Flowers scented the air, suggesting a large garden behind. Bordering the front of the house, white and yellow hollyhocks swayed in the breeze.

'This is it?' she asked. Since uncertainty had plagued the last three years of her life, she couldn't imagine living somewhere so charming.

'I think so. Never seen it before. Only learned about it yesterday afternoon from my friend, Christopher Hawkings. I hope it's not too small for you. Do you like it?'

Small by his standards, perhaps, but not hers. 'I'm sure I can't afford it.'

His hand slipped up her arm to support her elbow. 'Kit offered it at a good price, although if we weren't friends perhaps you'd be right. It's been empty for a month and he's keen to let it. Shall we go in?'

Her palms sweated inside her gloves. She nodded and allowed him to lead her to the door.

'There should be a key…' He trailed off as he reached above the window to the right of the door. 'Ah. Here it is.'

He opened the door, and she entered cautiously, letting her eyes adjust to the dimmer light of the vestibule. Pegs lined the wall, waiting for hats and coats; she untied her bonnet and hung it up.

Will followed her into the generous sitting room, made bright by south-facing windows. Her gaze travelled round it, looking for faults but finding none. It had been furnished comfortably and sensibly with a sofa, several side chairs and a stool, the latter pulled close to the fireplace. A mahogany drum table sat in front of the bow window, surrounded by a quartet of caned beech chairs, painted black and highlighted with gilt anthemia.

'What do you think?' he asked.

'I…it's more than I could have hoped for. I should never want to leave.'

'A housekeeper will come in twice a week to replenish supplies and cook. The kitchen should have been stocked yesterday.'

'A housekeeper is too extravagant.'

'Don't be silly.'

She blushed. To him, a housekeeper would be essential, so he wouldn't exactly understand her protest.

She walked over to the bow window and gazed out. A wide lawn sprawled out to the side of the house, and in the distance she thought she could still see the river, judging by the occasional sparkle of reflected sunlight. It really was perfect, and she'd no qualms about accepting it. But what would he do now? Leave for Norfolk immediately?

No. Not yet.

She turned around, feeling panic take hold. 'You'll stay for tea?'

His gaze searched her face. 'Shall we inspect the kitchen?'

She nodded nervously and wandered to the back of the house, pulling off her sticky gloves as they walked. They passed another sitting room, a bright breakfast room and a worn staircase, leading to the first floor. Finally, the kitchen—cheerful and clean, like everything else. More importantly, it appeared to be well stocked. An oak table dominated its centre, surmounted by several loaves of bread, a bowl of strawberries and another of eggs. An oak dresser to match it displayed prettily enamelled blue-and-white plates, cups and saucers.

'You must be hungry,' she said, pausing in the doorway and turning to look up at him. He shook his head slowly, and she wished she had the nerve and the experience to tell him what she wanted—wished she knew herself what it was. All she felt certain of was that she didn't want him to leave. She wanted to wrap her arms around him, to stand on tiptoe and find his lips. He was close enough. 'Thank you for helping me. It's perfect.'

He reached out to tuck an errant curl behind her ear. 'I enjoy helping you.'

She didn't pull away. 'You do too much.'

'I want to do more.'

'No. I couldn't wish for more.'

They were both quiet for a long moment. Isabelle, feeling awkward, walked over to the large window, pretending interest in the potted herbs that grew on its sill. Outside, she saw what seemed to be a vigorous kitchen garden. Lettuce, peas, an orchard in the distance...

She should ask him if he'd like to go out to look at the plants. That was one way to stall for time.

'Will, would you—?' She turned around as she spoke, but he had moved closer while she wasn't looking. Only a few paces now separated them.

'Yes?'

'Would you like to see the garden?' she asked quietly, moving back to the table.

'Not just now.'

It didn't help, how unforthcoming he was being. 'What...what are you thinking?'

'That perhaps I should compromise you thoroughly.'

She hadn't been expecting that response. A wave of pleasure and anticipation swept over her. Apprehension, too, since this time there was no butler to save her. She gripped the table as if it would protect her, then took a step backwards.

'You've already done so, I think.'

He was warming to the subject. His eyes glowed wickedly. 'No, not thoroughly. If I made love to you, for example, you'd have no choice but to marry me.'

She stared at him, but didn't move. 'What?'

He took a leisurely step forwards. 'No. Because if I made love to you, then you might carry my child. My real child, and not just the one the gossips have made up.'

Will watched her. She'd gone very still at his words. Understandably, given the subject. He hadn't really planned on putting it like that. He'd phrased it too much as a challenge, and he'd always found challenges difficult to resist.

She didn't move, other than to part her lips slightly, probably without even knowing it. His own mouth felt dry, his throat thick. Sitting in the carriage with her for so long had been akin to torture, albeit the most enjoyable kind. He stroked her cheek, and she stood like a statue, letting him, meeting his gaze shyly before looking away. Her skin was soft, flushed. She moistened her lips with the tip of her pink tongue.

Her tongue was his undoing. His hand moved round to cup the back of her head, bringing her forwards to meet his lips—gently, though. Not too quickly. He'd tried and failed to kiss her properly before; each kiss had been too urgent, like that of a youth to his first love. Ridiculous, considering his experience. He schooled himself to go slowly this time, and it was the hardest thing he'd ever done. Kissing instead of ravishing, gently tugging at her lower lip with his teeth when he wanted to devour her. One hand buried in her hair, dislodging pins and releasing copper curls. The other hand trailed down her spine to cup her bottom. She stood on tip-toe to accommodate him, instinctively fitting herself more snugly against his body.

That was a bit much for him to bear. He couldn't be expected to go slowly when she did things like that. He groaned, deep in his throat.

'Slow down, darling.'

His words made her stop, suddenly worried. 'Have I done something wrong?'

God, no, but he hadn't the mental capacity to explain at that moment. 'You're getting rather good at kissing.'

'Should I stop?'

He shook his head, answering her by gripping her bottom tighter, pulling her close and rocking her against him. A gentle rhythm, slow at first, then faster until she moaned, her cry muffled by his mouth. Her head fell back, and his lips travelled down her throat, pausing at the quickly beating pulse at its base.

God, he wanted her. More than he'd wanted anyone before. More by a vast degree. Again, he found himself fighting for the self-control that usually came naturally. If he obeyed his base instincts, it would all be over within a few minutes, and he wanted to make love to her for the rest of the afternoon.

In which case lifting her on to the dresser and fitting his hips between her knees wasn't the cleverest way to prolong things. But it felt so good, especially when he pulled her forwards, so his hardness pressed between her legs. He leaned her back, supporting her with one arm while raising her skirts to her thighs with the other. She wrapped her legs around his hips, pulling him tight. His fingers worked expertly down her back, unfastening her gown as they went.

God, no, he shouldn't do this. Not in the kitchen. What if someone came by, looked in the window...?

'Isabelle?'

'Hmm?'

No, never mind, it didn't matter. Not when he'd just managed to loosen her gown enough to tug it down to her waist. He kissed her breasts through her linen shift, grazing each nipple with his teeth until she called out.

It was the most wonderful sound he'd ever heard, but bloody hell, he *couldn't* take her virginity in a kitchen. But stopping long enough to locate a bedroom might take too long. She might change her mind. He didn't want her to think about what was about to happen— didn't want her to think at all. Not now.

'Isabelle?' His lips brushed against hers.

She opened her eyes. Dark blue, unfocused. Her pale skin flushed with pleasure. So beautiful he held his breath.

'Should we go upstairs?' he asked quietly.

She didn't answer immediately. Just straightened slightly. He could see the outline of her breasts beneath her shift, and he swallowed hard. Slowly, without taking her gaze from his, she nodded her head.

He hadn't realised how anxious he'd been until that moment that she might actually refuse. He felt a powerful surge of relief, and of blood below the waist. He kissed her again, not gently this time. It wasn't even clear who was kissing whom. Without taking his lips from hers, he lifted her from the dresser as if she weighed no more than a leaf. He let her down to the floor slowly, savouring the feel of her in his arms.

'Go upstairs, then. I'll lock the door and be up soon.'

Will didn't rush through his task. He needed time to collect himself, or else he'd be giving her a brief and bad introduction to lovemaking. He spoke to his driver, directing him to spend the night at an inn; he locked the front door and checked the back. He finally found her five minutes later, seated nervously on the bed in the largest bedroom. A nice room, he noted abstractedly, although he'd rather be making love to her in his own bed. That would come, with luck.

She rose anxiously when he opened the door.

He closed it behind him, leaning back against it. Just watched her for several seconds. She'd loosened her hair the rest of the way, so it floated softly around her shoulders and down her back. 'Come here.'

At first she didn't move. She felt glued to the spot. In his absence, she'd had time to regain her self-control. She knew what he wanted from her, and she knew she was foolish and wicked to want it, too. But she did. She loved him, needed him, and asking him to leave now…she could no more turn him away than she could food and drink.

She walked towards him slowly, stopping when only a few steps away. She met his gaze, then looked down shyly.

'Turn around.'

She did so, grateful to avoid his unnerving green eyes. She hadn't managed to refasten her gown, had just tugged it up into a more respectable position. He made quick work with the rest of her buttons so the gown slid easily to her waist. With just a tug it fell the rest of the way to the floor to pool at her feet. She closed her eyes, feeling the hot, pink blush that stained the back of her neck, just above the careless bow at the top of her shift. He gave that a tug as well, to loosen it. She drew her breath sharply.

He nearly stopped breathing at the sight of the smooth skin of her back, revealed by her parted shift. Gently, he lowered it, revealing graceful shoulder blades, a few scattered freckles that begged to be kissed. He pushed the shift down over her arms until it stopped at her hips.

She turned around slowly, covering her breasts with her hands, suddenly self-conscious.

His mouth was so dry he didn't know how he managed to speak. 'Don't. You look beautiful.'

With the greatest will-power, she lowered her hands. Then she stepped from her slippers, pushing them to the side with her foot. He couldn't help staring. She was even lovelier than he could have imagined. Breasts full for someone with such a slim frame, her nipples small and pink. He might be the experienced one, but God, in that moment she'd conquered him completely. He reached out to touch her, but she shyly caught his hand and returned it to his side. Then, with her own small hands, she pushed his jacket from his shoulders. It joined her gown on the floor.

She frowned slightly, as if debating what to do next. He didn't know how long he could go on allowing her to undress him, but for the moment it was the most exquisite torment. Her slender fingers found the buttons of his waistcoat and carefully, rather timidly, began to unbutton them. It was taking too long.

He grabbed her hand, stopping her. She glanced up at him quickly, and he caught her lips in his while he finished the job himself. Without taking his mouth from hers, he shrugged off his waistcoat and then, with one decisive yank, he pulled her shift the rest of the way from her hips.

She gasped, but before she had time to step away he pulled her closer, settling her pale, lithe limbs against his broad body. Hands running down her naked back, squeezing her perfect bottom, pressing her against his hardness once more. She tugged at his linen shirt, and he broke their kiss just long enough to pull it over his head. Her hands spread over his back, down to his waist, one bold finger finding its way to the top of his breeches and then down...

He grabbed her hand and relocated it to his shoulder. The bed was thankfully near. He eased on to it, taking her with him, covering her with his body. He found her breasts once more, rolling one nipple around his tongue while his fingers teased the other. She held his head, hands tangling in thick, golden hair, lost in the moment. With his mouth still on her breast, one hand moved down her stomach, finding the soft junction of her thighs. Teasing her until she bucked beneath him. Her long legs, still clothed in white silk stockings, wrapped around his hips, pulling him close, pleading for something she probably didn't fully understand.

She called out his name, and it was more than he could take. He sat up, unfastening his breeches, stripping them off. She sat up, too, pulling the quilt with her, covering her breasts. But before she had too long to feel exposed, he'd found her lips again. His hand slipped below her stocking, tugging down. First one off, and then the other. He pressed her to the bed, settled in between her legs. Kissed a trail down her stomach.

He found her again, his hand teasing, tormenting. Making her back arch and her fingers dig into the bedclothes. Then, with one swift movement, he'd entered her. His whole body throbbed with the need to find his release, but he held very still, holding his breath. He'd felt her stiffen and wished it didn't have to hurt.

'Darling?' He kissed her nose, her cheek.

'Is that it?'

He shook his head and moved slightly.

'Oh.' It was a nice 'oh'—surprised and rather pleased.

'It won't hurt again.'

'It doesn't any more,' she said. She moved against him, experimenting.

He closed his eyes with a groan, willing away the wave of sensation that threatened to overpower him. Then he slowly began to move. Rhythmic thrusts, building steadily. So good he wanted it to last for ever, so good it couldn't possibly. Her legs wrapped around him. Her hands gripped him tightly. Head back, mouth open, calling out as pleasure racked her body. With a cry of his own, Will followed her over the brink.

For many minutes they lay there, allowing their breathing to return to normal, allowing the sweat to dry. The evening was early, but soon both had fallen into the deepest sleep.

Waking up next to a man was a completely novel experience, so Isabelle lay very still for several minutes, just thinking and watching the early morning sky gradually brighten. It was a pleasant room, now that she had a moment to take it in. She'd been too nervous the night before. Quite big, and well furnished with a mahogany dressing table and a chest of drawers. The walls were painted a pale green; floral-patterned curtains matched a comfortable-looking wingback armchair. She could be happy here, she thought, as long as he was with her.

She felt happy at that very moment. Mostly, anyway. She'd known she'd enjoy making love to Will, but she'd no idea how nice it would be. *Nice* wasn't the word at all. *Earth-shattering* was more like it. So nice she felt like a different person, and she supposed she was.

She didn't regret making love to him; it had been inevitable, so there wasn't much point in worrying about what she should have done differently.

But her happiness *was* tinged with sorrow. Just a little bit. This situation wasn't perfect. Her life had just changed permanently, and although she felt good enough now, she might feel differently with the passing of time. What if she became with child? It could happen; he'd mentioned the possibility himself. How would she feel if— more likely when—he married someone else? He might not want to, but his need to produce an heir, and a legitimate one, wouldn't vanish. If that happened she'd regret not accepting his proposal, even if she knew deep down that refusing him was the right thing to do.

She certainly wouldn't be happy if he left her.

But then again, perhaps he wouldn't leave her to marry someone else. Duty hadn't yet compelled him to find a wife, and some men kept their mistresses for decades, even after they'd married. That's what his father had done. And maybe she'd never swell with child. Such was the fate of some women.

She didn't want to examine why the thought made her so sad.

'Isabelle?'

She rolled her head on her pillow to look at him, unwilling to let dark thoughts cloud her morning. The sun was beginning to part her bedroom curtains, slicing through the room with determined cheeriness. Will had propped himself up on an elbow, and was smiling down at her face. She glanced at his bare chest, no less thrilled by his handsomeness than she had been the very first time she saw him. Muscles. Good heavens. It really was remarkable that someone who led a life of leisure could have a chest like that.

She loved him so much that it scared her.

'Good morning,' she said.

He kissed her on the nose and, before she had time to prepare for it, he'd rolled over, taking her with him so she lay on top of him.

'Good morning to you,' he said, brushing her hair away from her face and tucking it behind her neck.

She looked down at him, worry now adding to her sense of ambivalence. Was it just the strangeness of waking up naked with a similarly naked man that troubled her? No—the problem was she still didn't know what was going to happen. Would he leave for Norfolk today? She didn't want him to, but he couldn't stay for ever. What about, for instance—

'But what about your driver? He hasn't been outside all night, has he?'

'After you went upstairs I told him to pass the night at an inn. There's one just a few miles away. He'll come back today and I can give him instructions.'

He still hadn't answered the question of how long he planned to stay with her.

'You will be going to Wentwich Castle today?' she asked.

He shook his head and began nibbling on the soft flesh of her neck. She closed her eyes briefly as warm sensations danced across her shoulders.

'But you said that was what you intended to do.'

'Are you trying to get rid of me?'

'No, I—'

He interrupted her by rolling over again, this time so that he ended up on top. 'I was hoping to stay here with you for a while, actually.'

She narrowed her eyes suspiciously. 'Were you ever intending to go?'

He looked charmingly sheepish. 'Would you be terribly angry if I told you I was not?'

'Then why did you say so?'

'I rather hoped you'd invite me to stay here with you a while. I needed an excuse to bring along several changes of clothes.'

She wasn't angry at all. Thrilled, in fact. His open-ended 'a while' wasn't as precise as she might like, but it meant that for a short time she could pretend he'd be there indefinitely.

Like playing house when she was a child, but better. Because now she had someone to play with.

'Darling, you look as if you're thinking too much again.'

She realised she'd become lost in thought, and she forced her expression into a cheeky grin. Not difficult because her worries had temporarily vanished. 'It's better than talking too much, surely.'

'I'd rather you were doing neither.' He sighed. 'I suppose I shall have to do something about it.'

So she let him.

Will put his hands in his pockets. The day was hot and humid, and he wished he could remove his dark woollen jacket. They'd taken to wandering along the towpath that meandered behind the cottage every morning or afternoon, depending on how long they stayed abed. It had rained heavily during the night, causing the river to flood slightly. The fishermen had come out in number, taking advantage of the swarming midges who made the fish rise to the surface.

He glanced at Isabelle's profile, so beautiful in its odd way. The sun had brought out more freckles and lightened her hair. He'd spent four days there with her, four of the happiest days of his memory. But he would have to leave soon—he couldn't simply ignore his responsibilities by pretending the real world didn't exist.

She noticed he was watching her and smiled shyly.

'I'll have to return tomorrow,' he said, wishing it weren't the case. 'I've a few things to attend to in London, but I shouldn't be away long.'

He couldn't read her expression. He wanted her to try to persuade him not to go, but she just looked out over the swollen river. 'You'll send Mary my regards?'

'Yes, of course, if she hasn't burned my brother's house to the ground. She'll miss you.'

'I…I hope you will explain.'

'Yes, of course—as much as I can, anyway. When I return, I can bring her along for a visit, if you'd like.'

'You would not be able to spend the night.'

'A good point. Probably why I haven't proposed it earlier.'

'And then I should miss you.'

He squeezed her hand. They walked along for several minutes, dodging mud puddles and nodding silent greetings at the hunched forms of patient fisherman. 'You could come back to London,' Will said eventually. He'd been waiting for her to suggest it. 'Perhaps you'll get bored of the country.'

'I won't, and where would I stay in London? I can't stay with you, and I don't think your brother would be delighted to have me again.'

'I could find you a house.'

'I cannot afford two homes, Will.'

He didn't offer to pay for her, even though he'd be happy to do so. She'd never accept his money, and she didn't know that he was already heavily subsidising her rent. It was true what he'd said about his friend offering the cottage at a reasonable price, but even so she could never afford it on her own. Not for more than a few years, anyway—not without any other income. But he'd no qualms about being underhanded if it kept her comfortable and safe.

'I should assure you that James and Eleanor liked you tremendously, but I suppose having one's brother's...uh—'

'Mistress will do.'

He knew she didn't like the word, even though she herself had chosen the position. 'Yes, well, having you to stay wouldn't exactly be the done thing, but other than that they'd be delighted to have you. They wouldn't have invited you to dinner if they disapproved of you.' Will knew that to be true. He'd told them both how he felt about Isabelle, and knowing the depth of his affection for her, they would never make her feel unwelcome. Actually, they were the only ones who knew he loved her, since Will hadn't yet told her. He didn't know if he was ready to, not while she kept turning him down.

He changed the subject. 'If the country does begin to bore you, I can think up any number of rural activities to entertain us.'

'Rolling in haystacks, perhaps?' she asked, grinning cheekily.

'You obviously know how my mind works, but no. Delightful as that sounds, I think we're—correction, *I'm*—far too old.' He regarded a pair of boys sitting on the riverbank, each holding a fishing pole over the turgid water. It reminded him of himself and James when they'd been that age, before everything had gone wrong.

'What about fishing?' he asked. 'I used to do quite a lot of it.'

'Never done it at all. We might try. I think there are poles at the cottage.'

Will wondered if they'd ever have children. He supposed they would, as long as they kept making love—and he certainly had no intention to stop. He wanted children with her. Eight sounded like a good number. Enough so that they could protect each other if for any reason he wasn't around to do so.

First, he'd have to convince her that he'd still want to marry her even if her father had had horns and a tail, let alone an unpleasant secret.

'Shall I tell you a secret?' he asked rather suddenly.

She turned her head to look at him, smiling. 'I like secrets.'

He didn't think she'd like this one. It was worse than hers—bad enough that he'd never told anyone. Sharing it with her had been a sudden impulse, but he hoped it might help. It was now too late to stop.

'You know I had another brother.'

She nodded slowly, but her smile faltered. She looked away guiltily. 'Eleanor told me about him. I hope you don't mind. He sounds awful.'

Will usually tried not to think about him. 'He was, I'm afraid. He was so much older than James and me that he never even seemed like a brother. Did Eleanor tell you how he died?'

'No.'

'Richard was shot. In his London house—where I now live—by an intruder. That's what everyone believes, anyway.'

She looked paler, but perhaps it was just the light. 'I don't understand. Was the man not apprehended?'

'No, because there was no intruder.'

She stopped walking, her eyes searching his face for clues. 'Who killed him, then?'

Several years had passed, and he could hardly remember the sequence of events. He didn't know where to begin.

'It happened four years ago. I'd just had a row with Richard. We weren't actually on speaking terms, and hadn't been for more than a dozen years, since, well—'

'Eleanor explained. You don't need to.'

He put his hands in his pockets. 'He'd always possessed a violent streak, but he'd grown worse over the years. Drinking more, too.'

'What could you row about if you hadn't spoken in so long?'

'A relationship he was having with a girl. She was the daughter of his butler—'

'Bartholomew?'

He started walking again as it all came back. 'No, we'd a different one back then, a widower with three grown children. Rawlings. This daughter had just moved to London to work as a lady's maid, or some such thing. I wouldn't normally care who Richard carried on with, but her father had worked for my family for years—I'd known him my entire life. He came to me in distress, telling me he thought Richard had designs on the girl, and if he'd seduced her she'd have been…well, you can imagine she'd have a difficult time keeping her position or finding a respectable husband.'

'Yes, of course. What…what did you do?'

'I approached Richard about it, and he confirmed his actions, but didn't seem inclined to stop. I told Rawlings that his concern was justified and said I'd keep an eye on my brother. A day or two later, I saw Richard in St James's with the girl. They didn't see me, and I followed them home.'

'You saved her?' Isabelle asked hopefully, her face worried.

'I wish I had. Richard was…more than unkind. He took pleasure in hurting others, and the girl was young and naïve—I think she thought he might care for her, that he might give her supper and praise her eyebrows. It wasn't like that—by the time I arrived just a few minutes behind them…well—'

'I understand,' she assured him quickly.

'The front door had been locked behind him, and I was delayed, trying to get in through a back window—'

'Richard would take her to his house when her father was the butler?'

'It was late. Rawlings would have retired. He must have heard something, though, because he came running up the stairs right behind me, carrying the shotgun that was kept in his room in case of intruders. As we reached the bedroom, we heard the sound of a struggle, and then a thud, like someone falling to the floor.'

'He hurt her.'

'He tried to. But the noise we'd heard…it wasn't her falling, Isabelle. It was him. She'd hit him on the head with a mantel clock. Bronze. Very heavy.'

Isabelle stared for a minute. 'You mean *she* killed him?'

'Very possibly. It would be just if she had, but I can't be sure. He didn't move—I shan't labour the details, but he appeared to be dead. Then Rawlings shot him anyway.'

She frowned. 'I don't understand—for good measure?'

'Yes, and also I imagine so he'd be blamed rather than his daughter. There wasn't much time for him to consider his actions.'

'But you didn't tell anyone what happened.'

'No, which was wrong, I suppose, at least in a legal sense. Instead I stayed up late with Rawlings, devising a plausible story.'

'He was defending his daughter.'

'And he would have been all right, I think. Usually the law deals harshly with members of the lower classes who harm their superiors, but I would have testified for him. Who can say how it would have turned out, though? My testimony might only have hurt him. It was well known that I detested Richard, and I also benefited directly from his death. My motives would have been questioned.'

'That would have been—'

'It would have been a huge scandal, and Rawlings would have been tainted, too, along with his silly daughter. I've never regretted lying.'

'And you really never told anyone?'

The cottage appeared around the bend, looking welcoming and homely. He wished he could stay with her another day. His own austere house was far too big for him alone. 'Just you. Can't tell anyone now because it would seem I'd been concealing something. I've wondered sometimes if I should tell James, but bringing it up would only resurrect bad memories. Much better for him to think that Richard's death was some act of God, mysterious, unexplainable and right.'

'Where is Rawlings now?'

'It was time for him to retire anyway, so I found him a comfortable home in the country. As far as I know, he spends his time tending his roses. His daughter married soon after the incident.'

'Then that's a happy ending of sorts.'

'Of sorts. At any rate, I dare say my secret is worse than yours.' He put his arm around her waist, drawing her near. 'Shall we go inside?'

She nodded. They walked without speaking until they reached the garden gate. She tilted her head up and kissed his cheek. 'Thank you for telling me. I'm sorry it happened to you.'

He felt better for having told her. It was an enviable position, having somebody to confide in. 'The worst happened to other people, not me.'

'Must you really leave tomorrow?'

'In the morning. I've quite a lot to do in London.'

'My cottage will feel positively massive without you. I don't think I shall be able to sleep for fear of the dark.'

'In my experience, all noises one hears in the middle of the night can be attributed to foxes and mice. You've nothing to worry about.'

'You'll come back soon?'

'As soon as possible.'

He didn't return as soon as she would have liked. She counted the days. On the first day, she nearly set the kitchen alight while making toast. On the third, strange noises kept her awake all night, a candlestick poised at the ready beside her bed—nothing more than a nest of squirrels in the loft, she'd discovered in the morning. On the fifth, she tackled the garden, tying up unruly vegetables and uprooting dandelions. Her efforts had blackened her nails and scratched the fair skin on her hands, but without Will around she didn't care how she looked. After ten days, she'd begun tidying the cottage in anticipation of his return, putting flowers in vases and plumping pillows.

On the fourteenth day, though, bad news arrived by post. Something awful had happened.

On the sixteenth day, Will joined the bad news. It was sitting silently on the kitchen table, waiting for his arrival next to a loaf of bread. Isabelle was in the garden when she heard his carriage roll down the drive, but she didn't stop what she was doing. Just continued clipping long sprigs of lavender from a well-tended bed.

They would look nice on the kitchen table as well, she thought.

She heard the front door close; one had to yank quite hard to manage it. She imagined him walking through the house wondering why she hadn't leapt to greet him. He'd be in the kitchen now, and it—a marble head of a classical maiden, about one foot high— would be watching him with silent accusation.

The kitchen door opened. Footsteps on the gravel path.

'Hello.'

She snipped one more sprig and added it to her basket. Then she rose and returned to the house. She placed her basket on the table.

'You're ignoring me.'

She hadn't looked at Will until then, but now she turned. Despite her anger, he still remained the most handsome man she'd ever seen. He looked tired, his eyes slightly drawn and his hair tousled, but still he made her breath catch in her throat.

She suppressed any tender emotions. 'No, I *was* ignoring you.'

'Pleased to hear you've changed your mind.'

'I shouldn't be pleased too quickly if I were you. What is this?' She indicated the marble head. She knew the answer. Her father had sold it. It was an out-and-out forgery, almost identical to one that Sebastian Cowes had showed her. What she really wanted to know was why it had been delivered to her cottage in a wooden box two days earlier.

He didn't answer her question. His eyes wandered slowly over her face. 'I've missed you, Isabelle.'

She could have stamped her foot in fury, but she coutned to five and tried to remain calm. 'You said you wouldn't tell anyone.'

'And I didn't.'

'Then why—*how*—is this here?'

He followed her gaze, finally looking at the object in question. 'You don't like it.'

'No, I don't like it.'

'A pity, since I bought it. There's no giving it back now.'

'But why did you?'

He was getting annoyed. 'There's no rule that says I can't buy anything I please.'

'Not written down, but yes, there is!'

'I bought it because you would have, if you could have. But you can't, so you should stop being so stubborn and accept it graciously.'

'Oh?'

'Yes.' He said the word with finality, hoping to end the debate. His expression, though, a few seconds later, said that he hadn't yet revealed the worst. His words confirmed it. 'The rest should arrive in the next few days. Thought it might raise eyebrows if I had them all sent to my London address.'

The rest...? She covered her ears. 'Oh, you shouldn't have.'

'Why not?'

'Because you did it for me.'

'Not just for you,' he said quietly.

She sat, putting her head in her hands, feeling utterly bemused. She looked up. 'You bought them all? Did you even buy the right ones?'

'God, I hope so. Dashed expensive if I got them wrong. But the invoices in your ledger were quite specific. I transcribed them while I was here.'

Her hand grazed cool marble. The statue really was rather pretty. Why did it have to be so wrong? 'None of this changes the fact that you promised not to tell.'

He sat on the chair next to hers. 'I didn't have to tell anyone. You'd provided me with the names—I merely used that list to locate everything. I even knew how much everything had cost, so I knew what sums to offer.'

'You just…arrived on those men's doorsteps?'

'Well…yes, pretty much. Wasn't that difficult, since I know many of them, and the others would have known me by repute.'

It couldn't have been that easy. 'But how did you explain yourself?'

'Simple. I professed a sudden interest in antiquities.'

'People will wonder, surely.'

'It's a well-known fact that madness runs in my family.' He glanced at the statue again. 'I think I could grow to like most of them. The gallery at Wentwich is rather bare, and I imagine it could accommodate the lot.'

She didn't say anything right away. Sunlight streamed in through the window, warming the room. She idly traced the grain of the oak table with her index finger. He'd done this. For her. He'd lifted a great burden from her shoulders, but she didn't know if she felt buoyed by its absence. She'd never wanted to shift the load on to him. 'This was your important business in London?' she asked hesitantly.

He took her hand. 'I wouldn't have left you for anything less.'

'How much?' She couldn't quite meet his gaze.

'Well, I didn't have to pay much more than the original price for most. Ned Tilman had grown attached, though, and took some persuading.'

'A fortune, you mean.' Now she looked at him. She wished she hadn't, though. Eyes like emeralds. Like the devil's, she'd thought so many weeks ago. She'd been quite wrong.

'You're worth a hundred fortunes,' he said, not looking away.

She stood unsteadily and walked to the window. She stared out over her garden. 'How will I repay you?'

'Perhaps some handsome aristocrat will ask you to marry him.'

'Don't tease me.'

He rose to stand by her and put his arm around her tense shoulders. 'Darling, I've never been more serious.'

'You can't protect everyone all the time.'

'Yes, I can.'

'You can't. Not everyone. Not if it means sacrificing yourself.'

'I hate to disillusion you, darling, but I'm not that good. Marrying you would be no sacrifice.'

She kissed him then, on the chin. A spontaneous action brought on by the sudden swell of happiness his words caused.

'What was that for?' he asked.

One more time, on the lips. She didn't have it in her to fight anymore. 'You're terribly good. I won't hear differently.'

'I had an entirely selfish motive. You refused to marry me because someone might have discovered your secret. Now no one can discover a thing because we own all the evidence.'

And so they did.

He leaned back against the table, looking terribly pleased with himself. 'You've no more excuses, Miss Thomas. Admit defeat.'

'You really want to marry me?'

'That's what I keep telling you. I love you, Isabelle.'

Those three short words had the power to knock the wind out of her. She took a deep breath. 'You said you wouldn't marry for love.'

'I said it was unwise to marry for love. I'm asking you to marry me because I can't spend the rest of my life driving back and forth to London. Because I'll go to Wentwich soon and I don't think I can go without you. It is a matter of purest practicality.' He went quiet, then asked, 'Do you love me? Because if you don't we'll have to end it here. I've survived more than three decades without having my heart broken and I don't fancy changing that now.'

'I couldn't break your heart.'

'Yes, I'm afraid you could.'

Could she? What a thrilling thought that she—a slight, red-headed no one—could in any way affect him. She certainly did love him, and had known it for nearly as long as she'd known him. At the moment, her wit had dried up, and she'd nothing to say but the truth. 'I love you. Of course I love you. You must know that.'

'Then marry me.'

Could she really do it? She'd spent so much time telling herself that it wasn't possible, but he'd defeated all her arguments. Or nearly all…

She grinned. 'But about this madness—'

'Skips a generation. My grandfather was the last to be truly mad.'

'You'll start howling at the moon any day now, will you?'

'Perhaps. I can offer you no guarantees.'

'But our children should be all right?'

'More than all right.'

'Then I suppose I must say yes.'

'You suppose?' He took a step forwards, his eyes dark and teasing. It was a look she'd seen many times before and which never failed to excite her.

She continued to grin, holding her ground. 'Well, yes. You've presented a logical case, and I've always been sensible. It's a good offer, even if I was holding out for a duke—'

She didn't finish. She didn't have time. He'd closed the gap. And his lips found hers. Soon she didn't even remember what she'd been saying, just knew that it didn't matter. Not with his mouth working its way down her neck, not with his warm, strong hands cupping her head. She closed her eyes and bid goodbye to being sensible.

She bid goodbye to her shoes as he carried her upstairs.

Epilogue

Happily ever after? The tiny but realistic voice in Isabelle's head insisted that happily ever afters didn't exist. Cinderella might have married her prince, but did anyone forget she'd once worn rags?

Even though no one would learn Isabelle's darkest secret, *everyone* knew she'd been a governess. She feared that, like Will's stepmother, she'd struggle to make friends in society. Her transgression was great; not only had she had an affair with her employer, but she'd then had the nerve to marry him, too. What gently bred lady would forgive such audacity?

And yet strangely everything was all right. Just three weeks after her wedding she found herself besieged with invitations. For morning rides, for afternoon teas, for dinner. Thankfully, she could decline most since they were leaving for Wentwich Castle in three days' time.

She lifted her gaze slightly to regard her husband. They were in the drawing room; sun filtered in, making his hair and skin golden. Since she'd long ago resigned herself to spinsterhood, it seemed nothing short of miraculous that she should end up with a husband like him. But less than a month had passed; perhaps she'd eventually grow used to the idea.

She smiled at the thought. Grow used to it? It seemed unlikely that marriage to him would ever be less than novel and exciting. Not when looking at him now, doing nothing more than frowning at his newspaper, made her heart expand.

'Bad news?' she asked.

He looked up from the paper, and his frown melted away. 'No, good. Vanessa Lytton is to be married.'

'Oh?'

'To a Mr John Brookshaw. The heir to a vast hinge fortune.'

Now Isabelle frowned. 'Hinge? As in hinges on a door?'

'Hmm.' He nodded. 'Apparently a lot of money to be made in hinges.'

'Would it be unkind to say I hope he'll take her far away from London?'

'Not at all. And as luck would have it, she'll be moving to Birmingham by the end of the month.'

'Marriage might be good for her. Perhaps children will keep her occupied enough to stay out of trouble.'

He closed his paper. 'Well, Mr Brookshaw *could* be her grandfather.'

'Then perhaps she will not have children.'

'A great favour to the world.'

A knock on the door announced the arrival of Martha, the downstairs maid. She struggled with a large tea tray while their new footman held the door. He'd been hired to fill the gap created when Rogers left; Mrs Graham, too, had been dismissed. Household chitchat, delivered to Will by a blushing Bartholomew, revealed that they'd provided the Lyttons' footman with ample gossip to fuel a scandal. Uncharitable though it might have been, Isabelle was pleased to see them out on their ears without references.

Martha left their post on a table and discreetly eased from the room. Isabelle rose to examine it. One letter for Will, from his steward at Wentwich. The remaining five were for her. Thick white paper and curlicue script. Without opening them, she knew they were invitations. She'd had so many recently that she recognised the signs.

Feeling a little bewildered, she crossed the room, stopping in front of the sofa. Will pulled her into his lap; she kicked off her shoes and pulled up her legs.

'What have we got?'

She handed him his letter. 'This is for you.'

He groaned. 'Mortimer knows we're leaving in three days. Don't know why this can't wait till we get there. What about those?'

'Some invitations.'

'You've become very popular.'

'I suppose. I don't quite know how it happened and I'm not sure it will last. I must thank your cousin.'

'Why? Don't thank her for anything if you can avoid it. That's my advice.'

'But I wouldn't have been invited anywhere if not for her.'

'If not for *you*, darling. Everyone's heard how you charmed Lady Trim.'

Isabelle wasn't convinced that her charm had anything to do with it. It was just that for once perverse Fate had done her a good turn.

The cousin in question was Venetia, Henrietta's better half. She'd returned from the country a week before the wedding. Isabelle had been staying with James and Eleanor again, an arrangement deemed more appropriate for a soon-to-be countess. She'd dreaded meeting her, and indeed Venetia was every bit as meddlesome as her sister. But *in extremis*—and Isabelle certainly had been facing social death—Venetia's brash confidence proved just the thing.

Venetia had merely regarded Isabelle critically before announcing that the next day they'd visit her dear friend, Lady Trim.

Eleanor, in the sitting room to help Isabelle examine her wedding gown, looked up nervously. 'But Lady Trim is rather—'

'Darling,' Venetia cut in, 'we cannot pretend it didn't happen. We can only pretend we don't care.'

It, Isabelle understood, meant her, and so the next day, the trio visited the Marchioness of Trim, London's unofficial arbiter of taste and manners. The good lady was obviously curious about her scandalous guest, but otherwise seemed displeased to see them. As they entered the tense drawing room, Isabelle felt as if they'd entered a civil war. Lady Trim's husband, a small man with a prominent brow, had obviously annoyed her. She kept shooting him malevolent looks as he wandered benignly around the back of the room, talking to himself softly whilst tenderly passing a dust cloth over his collection of ancient Greek vases.

'I despise him.' That was Lady Trim, speaking quietly, but as if she really meant it.

'Oh?' Isabelle asked uncomfortably. She meant to be friendly, but Lady Trim's expression suggested she'd not yet earned the right to speak.

The marchioness continued, directing her comments at Venetia. 'Just look at him. Ridiculous man. Won't let anyone else touch those hideous pots. Spends all day dusting them like some distracted parlourmaid.'

'Gentlemen *will* have their follies,' Eleanor said diplomatically.

Lady Trim snorted. 'Yes, and if he spent his money on women and horses like a decent chap, then I shouldn't care. But I *cannot* endure his taste for broken pots. He spent a fortune just last week buying that one by the window—and Letty's to have her coming out next year! All her friends' fathers are supplying them with new gowns and jewels, but my husband…' she sniffed disdainfully '…my husband will squander everything on clay pots without pausing to think of his family.'

Lord Trim had by this point realised he was the center of attention. He crossed the room to join them, his eyes sparkling with the prospect of further combat.

'Lady Trim has been telling us about your latest purchase,' Venetia remarked, obviously keen to witness the exchange of fire.

'Do *not* encourage him, Venetia.'

'No, no, *do*,' Lord Trim said. 'But to which purchase do you refer?'

'For shame, Lord Trim. There's more than one?'

Isabelle decided to try again, hoping the grinning marquess was less offended by the sound of her voice. 'The amphora by the window. It *is* lovely.'

Lady Trim scowled at her darkly, and Isabelle despaired once more of ever making friends. But Lord Trim glowed as if she'd just complimented his favourite child. 'You've an excellent eye, Miss Thomas. Bought it from a chap in Regent Street.'

'Oh? From Mr Taylor?'

He was impressed. 'Clever girl. Would you like to see my other purchase?'

'No,' Lady Trim interjected, 'we would not.'

'I'm speaking to Miss Thomas.'

'I, well…' Isabelle glanced from husband to wife, feeling as if she was walking a diplomatic tightrope. 'I should be delighted.'

The four women followed him reluctantly across the room. He talked the whole time. 'Bought her in Rome last year, but she only just arrived. From a Signor Ricci.'

Isabelle followed his loving gaze towards a life-sized head of Medusa, her mind too numb to answer. Hesitantly, she asked a question of her own. 'It is…old?'

'Yes, yes, of course. Cost a packet, but worth it, don't you think, for something this fine? I plan to buy another one next summer.'

Still not thinking properly…but could it be? She stared at the bust, her mind working over the facts. Signor Ricci hadn't known her father fobbed off his brilliant forgeries as the real thing until Cowes had told him. But now it appeared he'd taken a leaf from her father's book.

'She rather reminds me of m'wife.'

Isabelle's mind cleared slowly. 'Yes? I mean, no, she looks nothing like Lady Trim. I was just thinking of…oh, you *mustn't* buy any more.'

'Why on earth not?'

Lady Trim's hard expression softened slightly. 'Do *not* argue with my visitor, husband. I think it's perfectly sensible advice.'

Hope flickered uncertainly in Isabelle's chest. She needed to make friends—not with ageing gentlemen, but with ladies. She didn't want to repeat Will's stepmother's experience—for her husband's sake, for the sake of their children, and for herself.

'It is a fake,' she said with bald conviction. How wonderful it felt to be honest.

Lady Trim looked ready to crow. 'Doesn't surprise me in the least. Horatio, you *are* a fool.'

He reddened. 'Did my wife tell you to make that claim?'

'No, sir, your wife is far too kind. I know because my father was Sir Walter Thomas—'

'Not the famous antiquary?'

'The very one. And he knew perfectly well that Ricci dealt in fraudulent goods. I recommend that you not only halt all future purchases, but that you return this one and insist the man refund your money. He must be stopped.'

She held her breath, thinking she'd gone too far. But after several seconds, he spoke.

'I'm appalled by this knowledge.'

'I am sorry to bear bad news.'

He sighed. 'No, you needn't be. I feel a bit of a dupe, but at least you've saved me a great deal of money. What shall I spend it on, then?'

She couldn't have hoped for a more advantageous question. 'Well, Lord Trim, I hear you have a beautiful daughter…and her début next year won't be free of charge…'

And that had been that. When Isabelle had left the house twenty minutes later, Lady Trim had pressed her hand with gratitude. She'd been approved.

Will warily opened one of her invitations. 'Oh, bother. I was rather hoping to abstain from balls for the near future.'

'That's not because I persist in stepping on your toes, is it?'

'No, darling…you haven't stepped on my toes in at least two days. But surely avoiding balls is one of my rewards as a married man?'

She had to smile at his obvious aversion. 'One of *many* rewards, surely.'

'Of course.' He kissed her neck. A pleasant shiver ran up her back. 'Do let's refuse them all.'

'Well…since we're leaving for Norfolk so soon, I suppose we must.'

'That's a wonderful thought. I hope you like it there.' He perused his own letter. 'But, oh, Mortimer writes that the roof is leaking. Into our bedroom. On to the bed itself, in fact.'

'You did warn me.'

He read further. 'And Tobias, my cat—the other one, I mean—'

'The Second.'

'The Second, yes. A bird flew into the drawing room and he clawed his way to the top of the Aubusson tapestry trying to catch it—whole thing crashed to the floor, taking m'grandfather's collection of teapots with it. Rather valuable, some of them.'

'Well…there shall be less to dust.'

'Yes—you'd think my housekeeper'd appreciate that. But, no, she wants to get rid of him. To make things worse, he's taken a wife—'

'The cat?'

'Yes, and Mrs Tobias the Second had kittens in the nursery.'

'Mary will enjoy looking after them.'

'A good point. Don't tell her—let it be a surprise.'

Isabelle smiled again. She smiled a lot these days. Difficult not to, when she was so happy. Mary was happy, too. She'd been able to see Celia Bligh after all. The girl had come to London for her sister's wedding, and they'd spent several days wandering around the house, lazing about the garden and speaking in confidential whispers. Mary had even consented to a visit from the dressmaker, and now boasted an impressive pile of clothes to take with her to Norfolk. So, too, did Isabelle.

'What are you thinking about?' he asked.

'Just how fortunate I am. Every bit of bad luck I've had in the past few months has been good luck in disguise.'

'Like what?'

'Well, if that boy hadn't tried to rob me when I was walking to the pawnbroker's, then you would never have rescued me. I probably would never have met you.'

'I'd have found another excuse to talk to you. I'd seen you from my carriage.'

'If Mary hadn't put a newt in her French tutor's teacup, then you would never have been driving there in the first place.'

'True. I'll thank her.'

'And if she hadn't cut off Amelia Fitzgerald's hair, then you wouldn't have needed a governess. You'd have had no reason to keep me after I returned your watch.'

'I'd have thought of something.'

His lips returned to her neck, starting just below her ear and working their way down to the pulse at the base of her throat. She closed her eyes with a sigh. She was happy, and intended to be so for a very long time. For ever after, in fact, just as the fairy tale went.

HISTORICAL

Novels coming in October 2009

COMPROMISED MISS
Anne O'Brien

Despite being unconscious at the time, Lucius has been accused of compromising a lady! Now he must marry Miss Harriette Lydyard. The Earl of Venmore is lethally attractive, and Harriette knows she should refuse him. But her reputation is in tatters – she must make a pact with this disreputable, dangerous devil of a man!

THE WAYWARD GOVERNESS
Joanna Fulford

Claire Davenport flees to Yorkshire, where enigmatic Marcus, Viscount Destermere, employs her as a governess. Revenge has all but consumed Marcus until Claire enters his life. She is irresistible – but forbidden fruit. Then their secrets threaten them both and Marcus realises he cannot let happiness slip through his fingers again…

RUNAWAY LADY, CONQUERING LORD
Carol Townend

Lady Emma of Fulford is a fallen woman and desperate to escape the brutish father of her son. She begs honourable Sir Richard of Asculf for help – and offers the only thing she has…herself. Sir Richard is only human, and Lady Emma tempts him. Can this conquering knight tame his runaway lady and stop her running for good?

HISTORICAL

Another exciting novel available this month is:

DEVILISH LORD, MYSTERIOUS MISS

Annie Burrows

Is she his lost love?

With his dark, haunted eyes and forbidding expression, the menacing Lord Matthison has the reputation of the devil. Living on the fringes of polite society, he has still to get over the death of his one true love seven years ago. But Cora Montague's body has never been found…

So when he encounters a fragile-looking woman, the image of his betrothed, working in a London dressmakers, Matthison is convinced Cora is still alive. But what should he do to claim her…?